How to Fall in Love
A novel

For beautiful Karen
and Pete,
who know a thing
or two about
falling in love!

♡

Dal & Rich

How to Fall in Love
A novel

by Dalma Heyn
and Richard Marek

THE
ST●RY
PLANT

The Story Plant
Studio Digital CT, LLC
P.O. Box 4331
Stamford, CT 06907

Story Plant hardcover ISBN-13: 978-1-61188-262-9
Fiction Studio Books E-book ISBN: 978-1-945839-25-2

Visit our website at www.TheStoryPlant.com

First Story Plant Printing: February 2019

Printed in the United States of America

0 9 8 7 6 5 4 3 2 1

For Adam, Nicholas, Emily and Matthew

"I'M DOWNSIZING THE HEAVENS!"

Jove's stunning announcement, reported just like that at his weekly briefing, spread fear across the pantheon faster than any news since the declaration that Diana had been turned into a tree.

The "downsizing" meant me, as the summons from Jove moments after the briefing ended confirmed.

I entered his office. He sat behind his massive desk, scowling, helmet on his head, lightning bolt in hand. Somewhere on Earth, I knew, a tornado raged. His eagle, perched on the back of his throne, refused to meet my eyes. Not a good sign.

"I'm phasing you out," Jove said without preamble, confirming my worst fear.

"No!" I shouted. "Too soon. I've only had ten thousand years."

"Afraid I have to, my boy." He had the grace to look uncomfortable. After all, it was I—his son—who fixed him up with Leda.

"People no longer need your ministrations," he boomed. "It's not your fault, but they're all wired, every one of them. They conduct their romances on the net, woo by sexting, make virtual love." No news to me! Where had he been?

He went on orating, a habit of his. "They require full dossiers on each other before they'll agree to meet for a cup of coffee!"

7

"Sir," I said, trying to regain composure, "is this your way of announcing the appointment of some new upstart, a god of the wires—a cyberspace Cupid? Because everything else you've been telling me I know and grapple with daily."

"What do we need any love god for?" he shouted. "How can the ping of even a perfectly placed arrow be felt by a woman babbling into a headset? What can a man racing to work poking at his smart watch know about the delicacy of stardust, the subtlety of a purple flower's nectar, or other demonstrations of your art?"

Precisely my complaints. Plus, there are billions more people now than when I began untold centuries ago. Of late, I've had far less time for individual instruction, less opportunity for teaching the gentle art of persuasion so crucial to helping people awaken to their innermost desires. My work has become too frenetic, forcing me to speed from one continent to the other, mending this broken heart, inspiring that shy suitor—then rushing off on a new assignment before being sure of the results.

It used to be that my touch was longed for. Today it often engenders suspicion, wariness. Desensitized by too much static interference, humans can't feel the subtlety, the inventiveness of my delicate ministrations, the languor of lovely infatuation.

My wings ache.

But a leap from that to dismissal? To relegate me to eons of inactivity? To subject me to an eternity without matchmaking? Why, it would render me impotent! There could be no crueler fate for me, Eros!

"By phasing me out, you're phasing out love itself," I began, stalling for time. I had to think quickly. He couldn't resist a good gamble, this god who was crowned Lord of the Sky by drawing lots with his brothers and winning.

"What if I prove that love still matters?" I asked, desperate.

"How? You'd need special people: a Romeo and Juliet, a Tristan and Isolde, a Duke and Duchess of Windsor. Those were great lovers, and great lovers don't exist anymore."

"Sir," I said, "I'll wager I can find you an ordinary man and woman who build just as great a love as theirs!"

I could see the wheels turning under his helmet.

"Great as Burton and Taylor?" He laid his lightning bolt down on his desk, his interest piqued. He had a thing about movie stars.

"As great or greater."

"As Beatrice and Benedick?"

And a passion for Shakespeare.

"Yes," I said. Great *real* people, though. Not movie stars or tabloid celebrities, but ordinary people as remarkably transformed by love as any king, queen, or celebrity and as magnificent as anyone Shakespeare could dream up." I shot him a glance. "Equal even to any god," I gulped. "That's what makes them remarkable."

"You jest." He picked up the bolt. "Two mere mortals, chosen at random, can love as I love?" He waited for me to laugh along with him at this absurdity.

You? I thought. *The most narcissistic of all narcissists in the universe? Just ask Hera, who left you! Don't go there, you fool,* I told myself. *Concede.* "No, of course not," I lied. "You're...unique."

Flattery goes far with the god of gods.

"Father, ask the soldiers and farmers, the bus conductors and nannies, writers, architects, peddlers, even the hedge-fund managers I've put together. In their hearts, they've thanked me for being transformed by love—that they've become more than they were before they fell in love."

Jove actually said nothing.

It's true. I can bring human beings—what Jove calls "mere mortals"—to titanic love, though it can take some doing. This time, I have to choose very carefully. Great love requires a great deal, and I'll have to bring all my centuries of fine-tuned intuition to this one.

"Give me a chance to prove it," I said recklessly.

His eagle, Lulu, usually on my side (she's had a little crush on me for centuries), squalled something that sounded like "Beware!"

Jove sighed loudly, his brief attention span kaput. "You've got six months."

"Sir! Six measly months? For great love to be planted, nourished, nurtured, sown? Couples take their time these days! They're overly protective of themselves. At least a year."

"Seven months, then."

"Ten. Can't do it in less."

"Seven," he shouted. "Negotiation over!" Lulu let out a blistering screech.

I dared look at Jove straight on. I wasn't about to risk my reputation for nothing. "If I do it, you must swear on Apollo's head that my job will be secure forever."

He took eons to enunciate his answer. "On two conditions."

Oh Hades.

"First: no magic, no potions, no tricks. You may pick your candidate at random and do whatever you do in the way of subtle manipulation...but once he or she chooses someone, you must honor the choice. Even if you don't approve.

"Sir, I have to do this my way."

With a wave of his lightning bolt, all of Olympus turned a ghostly white.

"Agreed!" I coughed.

"And second…"

I held my breath.

"You get one chance to intervene when things start going wrong." He smirked. "And they always do."

Ah, fatherly love. Seven months? No magic? One intervention? I'd never been so handicapped.

"Done," I said sullenly. "My candidate's name will be on your desk by five."

He pulled out his mammoth universal calendar, found Earth, and circled the following June in celestial blue ink to remind himself. "You can do it, my boy," he said. The eagle flapped about Jove's desk happily then flew over, perched on my shoulder, and kissed me. "Or you're history."

1.

EVAN CAMERON IS SITTING IN ROW E at the David H. Koch Theater at Lincoln Center watching the New York City Ballet's *Romeo and Juliet* the night before Thanksgiving. That's a promising start, although it is obvious the man is miserable, cramped, bored, and no doubt wondering how he got stuck doing precisely what he likes to do least: watching other people move while he sits still.

He's wearing jeans, a white shirt, a black fleece jacket. He is a book editor—well-known for his carefully selected anthologies of writers' works. On his lap is a manila envelope he is rarely without, notes scrawled all over the front and back. His tie, a boring red paisley, looks like a leftover business gift from years before, but in truth he bought it that afternoon at a tiny British haberdashery on Madison Avenue just for this occasion. He looks like dozens of other modern men who make the transition from day to evening without changing clothes. A closer look reveals a speck of black under one fingernail, residue of grease from his beloved vintage Porsche under which he was tinkering just a few days ago. He notices the grease and, removing his handkerchief from his pocket, works at it surreptitiously for several moments until his nails are clean as a marine's. He tucks his handkerchief back in his pocket, behind a copy of *Outside* magazine.

The invitation to the ballet came from Claire Barrett, who now sits next to him and, unlike him, is enraptured by the dancers onstage. Claire is the best friend of Ruth, Evan's former girlfriend, who broke up with him a year ago. Claire is also one of the few mortals capable of sympathizing with both members of a doomed affair and remaining close to each. Perhaps she'll be another of my subjects someday—if I survive—for she is unmarried still and, on quick evaluation, capable of deep love. But not now. I've got to succeed with Evan first, for his is the name that went into Jove's in-box, and I'm getting nervous.

→

Evan is worlds away from the dancing. Usually when he's bored he reflects on his beloved car engine, its power and precision, but at the moment, he's thinking about the power and precision of words. As an editor, he is enamored of them. But he's one of those men who, as expressive as the next man in everyday interactions, cannot find words when they're needed most. In matters of the heart, he is as articulate as a steering wheel. So it's strange that his head is now teeming with words—passionate words foreign to him but abounding in that great treasure trove he has been assigned to work on: the love letters of the poets, novelists, statesmen, and monarchs whose outpourings of ardor have been preserved through the centuries.

He's worried about a future for letter writers. The early part of the century produced a rich lode of such letters, but in the last decade or so they've dried up.

Cast into cyberspace. Emails and tweets, he believes, are dangerous not merely because of their obvious availability, nor because of the dirty tricks they can play, but because the feelings expressed are so haphazard, hastily written, and temporary. A permanent record of fleeting moods. It's as though people today feel that their rages and outbursts have no consequences. He prefers a letter to be a thoughtful record of abiding, not just momentary, emotions—a considered expression that the writer won't regret having dumped on the recipient later. That would be...a letter.

Evan writes his own letters, business and personal, in a neat longhand with one of his beloved Watermans, on the eggshell-colored, deckle-edged stationery he received as a gift from Ruth years ago. His mother, an English teacher, taught him that a few handwritten words carried more weight than any tome printed out. She would have been mortified to see any deep feeling emailed, texted, or, God help us, sexted.

He's pleased to find himself steeped in these early, heroic letters. Just two weeks ago, after his usual breakfast of grapefruit, cereal, and coffee, and his customary daily run back and forth—from his ground-floor San Francisco apartment on Chestnut and Leavenworth to Fisherman's Wharf—he found, deposited at his door, a huge Federal Express box from his boss. He unearthed a messy, sprawling file dotted with pink Post-it notes, lavender margin notes, and colorful paper clips. Underneath was a sixteen-hundred-page manuscript entitled *Be My Good Angel: The Greatest Love Letters of All Time*, edited by Lorelei Layton.

The obvious delivery error amused him. He scooped up the sloppy bundle, put it back in the FedEx box, and called his publisher in New York to find out where to reroute it. "Wrong guy, John. How did I get these mash notes?" he said when he got him on the phone.

"Do you have a minute to talk?" his boss whispered.

"Sure."

"Lorelei Layton *died* yesterday."

"Oh, I'm sorry." Evan knew the famous anthologist by reputation but had never met her.

"That unpublishable mess you see there? That morass only she could have comprehended? It's her new book, and it's already way overdue." At that, John Scroopman sighed. "'*Eminent Author, eighty-six, Suffers Fatal Heart Attack,*'" he recited with a deep moan, as though he himself were about to suffer a similar fate. "So says the obit from the *Times.*"

"That's too bad, but what's it got to do with me?"

"Just listen," his boss barked. "'*The celebrated octogenarian love-letter anthologist was the immensely popular and famously eccentric mainstay of W.W. Norton and Company, bringing in substantial profits to the company with her books, according to Norton's publisher, John Scroopman. Ms. Layton, whose own love affairs were well publicized internationally, was perfectly healthy, her daughter alleges, until just weeks ago, when her lover, half her age at forty-three, left her.*'"

"Sounds like she died of a broken heart," Evan said.

"Not as heartbroken as I'll be if we don't get this book onto the presses by New Year's," John groaned. "I know you're going to say it's not right for you..."

"It's not right for me."

"But that you'll do it anyway."

"Me? Do *what*?"

"You know what. The running notes. The remaining permissions. The cover design. Fix her preface. Write an introduction. *Get the book out*, that's what."

"Out of the question. May I remind you that I have a contract to do my vintage car book—you're its publisher, remember?"

"How could I forget?"

"I've already gone through the first part of my advance, and I need to get it in for more money. You remember that, don't you, John? Authors get paid? Anyway, as you well know, I do anthologies about concrete *things*. Baseball. Antiques. Flags. *Love letters?* I couldn't even tell my sainted *mother* I loved her! Besides, what do I know about permissions?"

More emotional expression than he'd uttered in months. Years, maybe.

Scroopman spoke calmly. "The entire research department is at your disposal. You'll be given an office here, a hotel to stay in. Look, I'll be frank. We went down our list of anthologists and you're the only one who knows how to write."

"Good to know," Evan said.

"This introduction has to be more than just a preface. It has to sum up Layton's whole career—explore her life, her appeal, her unique point of view." His subdued tone became agitated. "You're perfect, Evan: an anthologist is an anthologist no matter what the anthology. Come to New York next week for four or five days..."

"What in my 'no' do you not understand? I want to do my car book. After which I plan to climb a very tall mountain somewhere far away."

Scroopman was pleading now. "We'll give you first-class plane tickets—for this book *and* for wherever the hell you go when you do the damn car book."

Evan hesitated just long enough to consider the food in first class. Overseas? He was thinking of his trip to Germany for the Porsche chapter.

"And a top-notch hotel." Scroopman's voice became a rasp. "And a sizable bonus."

Evan accepted.

→

Waiting now for the act to end, Evan clutches his manila envelope, filled with Lorelei Layton's correspondence, and recalls the precise moment this project went from a nightmarish time-waster into consuming passion. It was eleven days ago. He'd been reading the correspondence between Layton and the estate of Elizabeth Barrett Browning. The estate had finally consented to allow the publisher to use the poet's words. "*I'm grateful to you for allowing me to publish these important letters,*" Ms. Layton had written back by hand, no doubt in the rose-colored ink that had become her trademark (the file held only the copy). Then she'd launched into her usual spirited diatribe.

> What a difference between the precise, intimate, sealed, handwritten letter from a lover, and the impulsive email written by an exhibitionist opening his emotions to an internet chat room.

A switch flipped on in Evan when he read her words. He began to feel a deep kinship with the lady of pink ink. He got it, her outrage over matchmaking by computer. ("*Relationships are not mergers!*" she'd written and then underlined twice.) From that moment on, Evan took to the project with unexpected pleasure, as if his soul were thirsting for the experience, hungering as she had for loving words written in longhand. Then, when he read what Nathaniel Hawthorne wrote to the young, sickly Sophia Peabody, the woman who would become his wife, he thought, *Could any other means of communication have possibly conveyed...* Well, just read it:

> Dearest,
>
> I wish I had the gift of making rhymes, for methinks there is poetry in my head and heart since I have been in love with you. You are a Poem. Of what sort, then? Epic? Mercy on me, no! A sonnet? No; for that is too labored and artificial. You are a sort of sweet, simple, gay, pathetic ballad, which Nature is singing, sometimes with tears, sometimes with smiles, and sometimes with intermingled smiles and tears.

And he was awed by Keats's heartfelt reassurance to his beloved Fanny Brawne:

> Sweetest Fanny,
>
> You fear, sometimes, I do not love you so much as you wish? My dear Girl. I love you ever and ever and without reserve. The more I have known you the more have I lov'd. In every way—even my jealousies have been agonies of Love, in the hottest fit I ever had I would have died for you...

The task before him now has become more a privilege than a burden. The introduction will be the most challenging part, he knows, since not a word of it has yet been written—nor even conceived. It will be difficult to get into her head, to discern the deceased author's intentions and then articulate them. He wishes Ms. Layton were available for consultation. Still, he finds himself hoping these astonishing letters will be an inspiration and a reproach to his skittish contemporaries—and to himself. Maybe they'll come to realize, as he has, how great a tool letters can be for introspection as well as expression. Maybe they'll understand that words set down on paper are not ephemeral but eternal, meant to resonate forever in the souls of both the receiver and the sender. Maybe they'll understand what Plato meant when he said that a man without love is like a creature without limbs.

Plato aside, he himself has forsworn his chances of great love, transcendent love, suspecting he hasn't the capacity for it or is just unlucky. Evan is somewhat of a loner, and he accepts this self-definition as his destiny, since it is the pleasure of doing things by himself that takes him higher than love ever has. He looks back on his doomed relationship with Ruth Gottman and wonders how it lasted as long as it did, given her anger at the end. He'd told her upfront about his suspected deficiencies, even his hunch that he might never marry. She seemed to ignore this and to adore him and, perhaps taking his words as a challenge, pushed, cajoled, and persuaded him that he was otherwise—until, convinced, he finally let her move in with him. He loved her as much for loving him as for her determination to turn him around.

And to that end, she seemed inexhaustible. "You're becoming more relational," she'd say occasionally, beaming like a proud mom.

She worked on herself as well. She gave him his freedom, she told him often, to fuss with his cars, go through his silences, smoke his weed, watch his sports, go on his hikes. "I want you to be yourself," she'd said, and so he was, albeit with some guilt. But he felt he was there when she needed him, and all she had to do to get his attention was ask.

The latitude she provided turned out to be a kind of control, though. In retrospect, he'd felt queasy enjoying his freedoms, feeling her moral, observing eyes upon him even when camped alone deep in the Sierras with meals prepared by her. It turned out that she was all along steaming over his taking her at her word. He saw that his guilt was at least partially a product of her feigned generosity, and her heralded acceptance of his nature a form of subtle emotional blackmail.

Then one day, Ruth burst, turning on him with a rage he'd never witnessed in her or in anyone else.

"You're not just remote," she shouted, hurling her clothes into suitcases and boxes lined up on the bed. "You're terminally detached. Inarticulate? Don't flatter yourself. That's the least of it. You're unavailable. Once in a while, when it dawned on you that I might have needs, you found a way not to attend to them. I watched you do it time after time. And I'm...*done*."

Each word hit Evan like a poisoned dart.

"Done?" he asked earnestly. "What do you mean?" But as his childlike questions made their way from the fog of his brain—Needs? Done?—into the toxic air around them, Ruth batted them away. She'd long felt abandoned, she began again. "And it was willful, intentional!" Once more he tried to transform his panic into a semblance of a sentence. No luck: she was infuriated anew by his seeming paralysis.

"Look at you. Even now feigning surprise."

If ever he was without words, it was then, stunned by the venom with which she leveled him, over-

whelmed by his itemized deficiencies and the unjust-
ness of her accusations.

Ruth snapped her cases shut and carried them out
to her shiny red Volkswagen, black hair tucked into her
signature red beret. "And another thing," she said, her
face red now, too. "You feel more passion for your car
than you ever did for me."

"Where are you going?" he managed.

"I'm leaving you."

And she peeled out onto the street as ferociously as
she'd entered his life three years before.

For weeks after she left, even as the resonance of
her hurtful departing words festered, he'd conjured
up his initial image of her in that beret. She reminded him of those toy-sized dogs, no bigger than a
man's foot, barking their minuscule heads off at Lab
retrievers twenty times their size. She was always
bravely hurling herself at him, talking a mile a minute, insisting he love her. And he had needed that
prodding, depended on it, never thinking of the cost
to her of such relentless effort. He actually thought
it had brought her pleasure, this endless persuad-
ing, cajoling, begging—her Herculean effort to move
him. But she wasn't Hercules, it turned out. More
like Sisyphus, pushing him only to find herself at
the bottom of the hill again.

Evan tried to hold on to his own anger, but it paled
next to his guilt, his shame. He had not only let her down,
he'd done it so blithely, unconsciously, believing it was all
okay with her. He talked to his friends about men accused
of similar emotional crimes by women—those egotists
women talk about, those narcissists, men he never identified with. And when they were left, he discovered that
these too claimed not to have had a clue.

But Evan hadn't felt clueless. He believed he'd been devoted to her, knew that he loved her in return. His genuine encouragement in everything she wanted to do, his acceptance of her eagerness, her pluck—wasn't that evidence of his love?

Nice enough, he was learning, but intimacy it wasn't.

An interior designer, Ruth had redecorated everything—first his home, in the bright primary colors she loved, then by putting leather bindings on his favorite books and fine silver fountain pens in lovely cases on his office desk, till his already organized work life took on the patina of comfortable finality. But her aesthetic vision, fine as it might be, was not his own.

Time only proved how right Ruth was to leave. His relief over the fact that she'd made no effort to return embarrassed him a little, but he knew now he had never felt close to experiencing what they both needed him to feel—what, for example, Robert Browning had expressed when he courted Elizabeth. "*Real warm Spring, dear Miss Barrett,*" the poet desultorily began one of his letters in early 1845, "*and the birds know it; and in Spring I shall see you, surely see you—for when did I once fail to get whatever I had set my heart upon?*" Now there was a man who knew what he wanted, risked all by saying so—and got it! No, Evan felt he himself would always remain on love's sidelines. *Those who can't*, he thought wryly, *anthologize.*

→

Evan is taken out of his reverie as act one ends, by Claire's hand on his arm and her whispered, "Isn't it glorious?"

Glorious? Not bloody likely. He feels trapped, and with still two acts to go, he fights a panicky desire to bolt. Maybe he could catch a plane back home to Northern California tonight and be biking tomorrow in the shade of the redwood forests along the Pacific Coast Highway—Santa Cruz, maybe, or Point Reyes— or running along an isolated patch of warm sand at Big Sur. It would be easier to work in California, too, three thousand miles away from his publisher. He's already sick of Scroopman's mantra: "The introduction, remember?"

But Claire is his loyal friend. So he decides to flee only as far as the lobby during intermission and asks her to join him. Mercifully, she declines. Relieved, he pops up out of his seat, mumbles something about stretching his legs, and makes his way up the crowded aisle, nearly trampling a bejeweled blonde woman in his urge to escape.

"Sorry," he says, scanning her for visible damage. He gets a furious glare from icy blue eyes and turns away, but not before he's noticed the voluptuousness of her figure and the Renoir glow of her cheeks. Why, she could be from California.

You SEE? It doesn't take much to get things started. The inherited manuscript as initial dart, Claire's "decision" to stay in her seat—delicate touches, gentle probes, nothing heavy-handed. It's the best I can do for Evan now. I chose him for his potential, something I'm gifted at seeing, but I'll get nervous watching over him too closely.

So I will divert my attention with other business, with lovers elsewhere who need me. A certain gorgeous young prince in Belgravia is looking for a suitable princess; an oil-rich sultan in a remote part of India craves a sultana. I like working with royalty, dodgy as they are. Harry and Meghan were pure pleasure.

There are seven unattached women in the lobby, candidates all, equally lovely. I hope one of them is destined for Evan. Regretfully, by Jove's rules, I won't make that decision. Evan will.

2.

A WOMAN WAS CRYING IN THE LOBBY, silently, unobtrusively. Even across the enormous space of the David H. Koch Theater, she appeared sharply defined and as luminous as if only inches away from Evan. He removed his glasses, rubbed his eyes. Still he saw her clearly, exclusively, as if no one else were in the theater. Words rushed into his head: "*I will imagine you Venus tonight, and pray, pray, pray to your star like a Heathen.*" More of John Keats's words to Fanny Brawne.

The woman was tallish, perhaps five six or seven. Fine auburn hair fell freely in waves around her neck. As he approached, he saw that her eyes were copper-brown behind the tears, and her lashes were thick; her freckled face, unmade up, was completely adorable to him. She was slim, dressed in body-hugging pants, a loose-fitting white sweater and a big silky green shawl. Her legs—ah, her legs!—were long and finely tapered. She wore flats—which emphasized the elongated curve of her calves and the delicacy of her ankles. He guessed her to be in her thirties or forties, but he never could tell women's ages.

Her hands trembled. Delicate hands, the bones as long and fine as the veins in a leaf. She raised the left one to her face in a gentle gesture that touched him.

He was surprised to find himself imagining the two of them holding hands as they walked among the redwoods.

She seemed to be in trouble. He would help her.

Evan rushed to her. "You're crying," he said to the beautiful stranger.

"You okay? Can I help?"

The woman, startled, smiled up at him—laughed, really—as she shook her head no.

Evan laughed too. "If only I cheered up everyone in my life so quickly."

"And I'm not even in your life." She sniffled as she took a tissue from her bag.

If only, he thought.

"Sorry to accost you," he said, not knowing what to do next. "Only you looked so unhappy, I thought I might help."

"You did. I always cry at this ballet. Don't you?"

"Actually, this is my first ballet." He put his hand out. "Evan," he said. "Evan Cameron. Sure I can't get you something? A Coke? A glass of water? Champagne?"

"Not a thing. I'm Eve." She returned his formal handshake just as soberly and then looked at him warmly. "Really, I'm fine."

As if his life depended on getting some sentence out of his mouth other than another beverage offer, he spit out, "How can you feel so overcome when nobody onstage has said a word?"

"Oh," she said, shaking her head slowly, "you're one of those."

"Those?"

"Who think artists have to speak to convey something important."

"They could maybe sing?"

"Well, let's see. Does a flower by Georgia O'Keeffe not speak? A face by Gauguin? Does Bach say nothing to you?"

"I'm afraid," he said, lifting up his manila envelope as evidence, "I'm pretty much a word guy."

She threw up her hands with a dramatic inhale. "Ah!" she said. "Me, I feel people's emotions, their motives, most when they move. Show, don't tell, right?"

"You can feel them?"

"I can."

He squinted. "But if you don't hear them say or sing anything, how..."

Without pause, she corrected him gently. "No one narrates a ballet, no one sings it, no chorus reveals any warnings...but when the young lovers move together, you feel what they feel." She looked up at him hopefully. "And isn't that the highest form of art?"

He smiled. "You're not crying anymore, and I feel good about that."

"You didn't answer my question," she said sweetly.

"I don't remember it."

"Art. The highest form. Okay, I'll ask it a different way. When two people breathe together, they become more than partners; they become..."

He awaited the answer, not having one himself.

She looked into his eyes. "Conspirators. From *conspirare*, 'to breathe together.'"

He breathed deeply, shoved his hands in his fleece jacket pockets. "So...you're an athlete, then?"

"A dancer. Was. My husband was a choreographer. He's the one who taught me that thing about conspirators."

Evan felt himself wince and looked at her ring finger, hoping she didn't notice. "You're married," he said flatly.

"A widow. But whenever I come back to Lincoln Center, I'm pretty much as overcome as I am now."

He noticed she'd changed the subject deftly. And was she looking at the manila envelope in his right hand, or was she checking out his left hand? Evan thought the latter but was interrupted by the bell signaling the end of intermission. Just then, three women who had been observing them both—Evan presumed they'd been as worried about the weeping stranger as he had been—moved toward them. The oldest one stepped up to Eve and gushed in Spanish, "*A salute! A salute!*" and kissed her cheek.

Eve smiled back at her and her companions, then glanced warmly at Evan and said to them all, "I've got to get down to my row quickly. I'm sorry. *Gracias.*"

Still trying to figure out the exchange, Evan called after her, "Wait! Have dinner with me. You can't just—"

"I'm so sorry, Evan!" she called back. "I can't. I'm busy. But I loved meeting you. Enjoy the rest of the ballet!" She turned back to him. "Don't forget, feel them breathing together!"

Eve vanished into the sea of strangers rushing down the aisles to their seats. Evan chased after her, surprising himself and her. She wheeled around, seeming frightened, when he touched her shoulder.

"Please, Eve. This is too important. Where do you live?"

She pulled away carefully from him. "Vermont," she said. "And"—he saw a hint of regret cross her face as she slid past the couple on the aisle to her seat and removed her shawl. "I really must see this. The curtain is about to go up."

Before she could sit down, though, a distinguished-looking man with a black bow tie behind her in row B caught her eye and, clapping softly in a gesture meant for her alone, whispered, "*Brava!*" The fat man ensconced in the seat on her left and the woman with a pillbox hat to her right noticed and turned to see whom they were next to. When they saw, they too clapped gently. Eve nodded to each one graciously just as the curtain rose.

3.

Evan slid back into his row as the conductor returned to the pit. Who was Eve that she was so recog-
nizable, that she received such reverence?

"I thought I'd lost you to some woman," Claire
whispered.

In truth, he knew that would be the last thing she'd
think. Although his days after Ruth had slowly filled
with women—a succession of smart, athletic, eager
young beauties—Claire now clearly worried about him.
She let him know that she feared that Ruth's departure
had so traumatized him that he'd reinstate his habit of
brief affairs and not risk loving again. She seemed to
believe, as other friends did, that he hadn't gotten over
Ruth—and that her ruthless exit had left him alone to
sail through life without a rudder.

Perhaps this was why Claire chose the three-min-
ute scenery change to update Evan about her.

"Ruth hasn't been well, you know," she said softly.

Still puzzling out the mystery of the beautiful ballerina, Evan mumbled a distracted "I'm sorry to hear
that" and leafed through his program.

"She's going for some sophisticated tests with a
famous specialist in San Francisco," Claire persisted.
"She's out there right now. Do you want to see her?"

He dropped his program.

See Ruth? Seriously? The answer was yes and no. Yes, because in one way he regretted not having her with him—her intensity, her competence, her body, her permanence, even her moodiness. No, because, well, enough of all that. Yes, because he'd loved being cared for. No, because she'd devastated him. No. No.

Did Claire imagine that Ruth's illness, diagnosed long after she left him, altered the terms of their break-up? Was she suggesting he had an obligation to her, even now? Sure, Ruth had brought him, yanked him, toward maturity. But so what?

"Give her my best, but there's no reason for us to meet," he was about to say as irritably as he felt it, but he fell mute.

The theater had quieted to an occasional cough, and now Evan didn't have to speak.

Instead he stewed about Eve. Did she think he'd approached her because he recognized her? Did she take umbrage that he'd pretty much grabbed her shoulder twice? And who was she, anyway? Should he have recognized her?

Stop obsessing, he thought. *Watch the dancing. If you can't tell her at the next intermission that you've felt something, after she seemed to care deeply that you do so, what then?* He longed for something illuminating to say that would prove to her that his appreciation of her beloved art had been heightened during this second act because of her. And more important, that he was someone worthy of conspiring with.

Then it struck him: plotting to find words to say exactly what she expressly told him she didn't want to hear was pig-headed. She wanted him to *feel* something, not deliver a treatise about feelings.

So this was his first aha moment—that phrase he loathed. He'd have to grapple with his terrifying inability to *express* his feelings. But his excitement to be once more in front of Eve's freckled, fine face, and the gentle, mocking smile that seemed to take him in completely was spellbinding. *What's going on here?* He was in a state unfamiliar to him, a state the poets he knew so well and whose words they romanticized seemed to cherish. But it was something that felt to him now like motion sickness.

Was this what Eve was feeling? Can one person feel such a thing without the other? Was this what Eve meant by conspiring?

He cursed himself for having left her with no real impression of him. He felt her joy in her world yet conveyed to her no sense of the pleasure he took in his own—polishing his ancient Porsche; paddling his kayak; hiking in the Arches. She could be watching the ballet now, absorbed, any thoughts of him long evaporated because he'd been so unmemorable.

The second intermission finally came. Evan felt as if he'd been immersed in an anxiety dream, a kid awakening from a nightmare about flunking an exam. Just then, Claire announced that she was off to the ladies' room and would meet him back at their seats at the end of intermission.

Evan raced to the lobby. He hadn't figured out what to say to Eve, or what not to say—there it was again!— he just wanted to find her. He bought two glasses of Chardonnay at the bar and waited, the words of Keats and Shelley swirling about in his head. Ever since he'd begun work on the love anthology, the moment Evan felt any emotion—fear, anger, outrage, joy—along came the great poets, to implant their words in his brain.

Proof enough that he had none of his own to come up with. *It's irrelevant*, he told himself. He wished only that Eve would show up.

She didn't. With a steely, slow rhythm, as if he were pacing the stacks of a library in search of an out-of-print volume, he jettisoned the wine and made his way down the side aisle to look for Eve in her seat. Perhaps she had stayed behind to read the program or make a call. Or she might be crying again but hiding this time, not wanting to let this strange man pierce her joy. He got to the first row and looked over to the center seat. She wasn't there.

Had she gone to the ladies' room? Did she get waylaid by more fans? Did she *leave*? No, she wouldn't have left before the death of Romeo or Juliet—of that Evan was certain.

When the intermission bell jingled, he went back to his seat, still in a panic.

Claire noticed his agitation. "You okay?" she asked. "You look a little funny."

Evan fiddled with his glasses, willing his eyes to see Eve. There! Eve's auburn hair shining in the footlights. She was taking her seat.

"I'm fine," Evan replied, giving Claire an impromptu squeeze of her hand. He laid the manila envelope on his lap and settled in to watch the unfortunate fate of the famous lovers.

Ah, inspiration! He would write Eve a note from a pad in his envelope. It was his only hope. Otherwise, she would go back to her part of the world and he to his. And this thrilling thing, whatever it was, would vanish as surely as Romeo and Juliet's happiness.

What words could he write? *Here we go again*, he thought. But hell, he couldn't say, "*Meet me tomorrow night or I will die."* No. But he couldn't let muteness, his old bugaboo, stand in his way, not now. He'd rather have her reject him than let fear of rejection stop him. So he would borrow from the poets, who had the right words for the occasion. *"How can I see you?"* he wrote. *"Must it be that you will leave without my seeing you? When will it be convenient to present myself?"*

There. Simple, eloquent, urgent, but not excessively. They happened to have been Stendhal's words. But hey, if the French novelist had used them to get a woman to meet with him, why change the script?

He scribbled down the words verbatim, then added *"Lincoln Center, 7:30, tomorrow night."* He folded the paper, tucked it in his pocket, and waited till the ovation had begun. Leaning over to Claire, he said, "Meet you in the lobby at the front doors," then hurried into the aisle and raced down to the first row, before Eve could have begun to put on her coat. She saw him, pushing past the departing audience to get to her, and her eyes widened happily. She returned his insistent gaze with equal intensity and smiled. He pressed the note into her hand, and she accepted it as though she'd been awaiting it. Still holding her gaze and her hand, he said, "Read this." Then, with the slightest of smiles, he added, "Please." He turned and walked away.

4.

SHE CAUGHT ONLY A GLIMPSE OF HIM before the note landed. She read it quickly, realized that Evan had not heard her say she lived in Vermont, and tried in vain to stop him. She read it again after dinner in her hotel room.

> *Must it be that you will leave without my seeing you?*

In fact, no, she thought, *maybe not*. She could possibly extend her stay for another day. The small-farm business convention she had come for was over, and many of the attendees and several colleagues from Vermont—maple sugar farmers like herself—were staying to "do" New York. She was sure her hotel would give her, as it had them, the same convention rates for an extra night. And that she could catch a ride back with one of them.

There was nothing urgent at home in late November. The trees had made their sugar—the brilliant orange leaves signaling that they were locking in nutrients for the winter. Sapping didn't begin till mid-February, when, with days at about forty-five degrees and nights down to twenty, she worked like crazy for six to eight weeks collecting running sap, then boiled it down and began processing. They were approaching another busy time, when the syrup from last year would be bottled and jarred, and the sugar formed into stars, snowflakes, maple leaves, and sleigh bells for Christmas—nobody around was more artistic, more imaginative than she, and Eve took pride in her new art. But she could spare a day. For now it was simply a matter of managing the small retail shop set up to sell maple syrup and candies at the entrance to her farm. Her assistant, Kitty, or Mark, the caretaker, could do that easily.

So why not simply call the reservations desk and make the arrangements?

> *When will it be convenient for me to present myself?*

What a peculiar way to ask for a date, particularly since he'd named the time and place! It was like a movie, a rom-com with a nutty, brainy hero. Technically it would be *she* presenting herself to *him*, since he would be waiting for her at Lincoln Center when she arrived. But she wanted to go easy on this lovely, shy man with the rugged face and earnest eyes, even in her thoughts. She'd teased him enough already.

Should she do it? Why not? She'd been so elusive with him, first weeping in the lobby then bowing to fans; he easily could have written her off. Something about the sweetness of his goofy persistence, though, his essential gallantry sailing high in that sea of distracted balletomanes moved her. No, thrilled her.

She didn't know where he lived, where he worked, how to contact him. They hadn't exchanged phone numbers, even, which was really odd for anyone living in this century. So whatever her decision, stay or not, she didn't want to leave him stranded, just waiting in vain at the fountains, never to hear from her again.

She fell asleep thinking about the look on his face when he thought she was married. And the pleasure she felt when she saw no ring on his finger. All she really knew about Evan Cameron was that he knew nothing about ballet. "Hardly a promising start to an evening with a prima ballerina," she said aloud before dropping off.

5.

SHE WOKE WITH A START AT 4 A.M. and pieced together
the night before, shocked by what she'd planned. It was
a bad hour for enthusiasm about anything, let alone an
expensive layover for an adventure that now felt as exciting as a blind date set up online.

Except that she had met the date and been willing the night before to go to great lengths to ditch her
plans for today in order to see him again. This was not
her style. She conjured up what she could of him. His
voice: low, a little gravelly, muffled by shyness. His face:
blue eyes, a slight cleft in his chin, and a shaving nick
under his jawline, which she spotted when he lunged
at her to deliver his note. Thick brown hair tinged with
gray, wavy and unselfconsciously tousled. Forties, she
guessed, give or take, with that ageless, boyish aura
some men keep all their lives. Not a New Yorker; the
clothes were too casual, the look too healthy and open.

It was his body that got her—this she had an eye
for after years of partnering with dozens of wonderful bodies. Even through the wintry clothing she could
tell. And she liked the way he walked—surprisingly
fluid for someone with a big build, with a slightly sloping posture she would correct in a dancer but, in him,
wouldn't want to change.

Was it just too impulsive, though, too much trouble? She'd have to skip her yoga class's annual open house, which she had offered to her six staff members as a treat (and even paid Kitty, who was certified, to teach a class), scheduled to be held in her own dance studio tonight with dinner afterward. The students were all deeply committed to the class, grateful for it, and hated to miss it—and they couldn't wait for this dinner. It was the ideal excuse, and Evan would understand—if in fact she could tell him. But she couldn't, which at this wee hour made her angry. It was meet him at seven thirty or never see him again. Why hadn't they exchanged numbers so she could text her way out of this and not feel so pressured?

But also she felt something that wasn't anger, something deeper and scarier, a queer void in her chest, as though her heart had stopped just to await her decision. It was a physical pressure, an irritant somewhat like stage fright, and because the sensation was old and somewhat familiar, she welcomed it without actually comprehending its power.

She turned the shower on hot and stepped in. She'd kept herself too long from men, she knew. Her late husband, the most famous choreographer in the land, had been her revered teacher, her father—her mother, even—and her inspiration. He had drawn from her all the artistic power in her body—perhaps breathed it into her limbs. Sometimes in their partnership it was hard to tell who left off where. "God and Princess," they were called. "Pygmalion and Galatea" was how some described them, which always made Laddie beam.

The grief counselor to whom the ballet kindly sent her after his death wasn't so enthralled by the comparison. She pointed out that the fabled Galatea, fortunate as she may have been at the beginning, had wound up deeply dissatisfied with the terms of her transformation. "When one person has ultimate control," the counselor offered gently after hearing Eve's story, "the other may appreciate it for a while. But then there's the alienation, the resentment…" Eve hadn't dared investigate her own alienation and resentment—not at the time.

Vladmir Golyakovsky was just too compelling, too famous, too brilliant for a young girl to question. He was, for anyone associated with the ballet, God. And as for control, his was total. He had convinced her that their art was all-consuming, must be her reason for being, and that she was his chosen one—therefore above the world of ordinary "trivial" relationships. He kept her from such trivia. She became his muse, and together they created beauty hidden to all but the privileged few.

When the grief counselor urged Eve to understand that there was a term for their relationship: they had been *enmeshed*—"an arrangement that doesn't allow much room for *breathing*," she said—a light went on. The use of that word was an awakening. "Your life was not your own; it was inseparable from his," the kindly woman ventured. "And of the two lives, I'm afraid yours was the less important one."

It was then that the reckoning occurred. Eve slowly began to understand the complexity of this idealized love they had shared, a love Laddie had assured her was the only meaningful kind, the only one that could last. It couldn't sour because, he said confidently, it reached beyond itself. Maybe so, she realized. But her life had been subsumed into his.

Once, briefly, when she was still barely out of her teens and on the brink of becoming a prima ballerina, just before Laddie claimed her as his own, she had known the kind of love he disdained—a prosaic love: messy, sexy, complicated, filled with laughter and late-night phone calls. In the name of art, and a fear of Laddie, she gave it up. Now for the first time, feeling the hot water flow over her neck and back, she felt its desolate absence in her bones. As a reward for her discipline, and for forswearing the everyday world, Laddie every year had given her a Christmas tree ornament from the original production of *The Nutcracker*, each one a Victorian masterpiece. Whenever she'd needed reassurance that the parts of herself she'd sacrificed were worth giving up, she looked at them—all lined up in her bedroom, ready to perform.

Remembering them now, still standing at attention back on the mantel in her Vermont home with nary a scratch or chip to mar their shiny glaze, all she felt was a hollow ache in her diaphragm. And each one of those forfeited parts of her, duped into hiding, begged for attention as insistent as phantom limbs.

She dressed slowly. She considered Evan's cobalt eyes—it was all coming back to her—the pulsing vein in his neck; the scar on his chin; the tan, muscled forearm that had slid out when he had reached for her the second time; the slight stoop. Everyone, she tried to remind herself, had eyes, veins, muscles, forearms! Still, she admitted she had found their configuration in him magnificent—manly, scary, sexy. Recalling him in the lobby, brooding and tall and hovering over her like some modern-day Heathcliff, she began to pace the room the way she used to before going onstage, concentrating on him as she'd once concentrated on her roles. Okay. Spend the evening with him, go back to Vermont tomorrow.

The concierge was happy to reserve her room for an additional night, and with that decided, her heart resumed its steady beat. The truth was she couldn't wait to see him again. She'd kill the day at the Metropolitan Museum, cruise through Saks Fifth Avenue, watch the skaters at Rockefeller Center, and get her nails done.

OH, MOST PROMISING, MOST PROMISING INDEED! The light in Evan's eyes when he met Eve reminded me of me when I first spied my wife, Psyche, at the top of the mountain! "Your gaze lit up the Milky Way," said my mother, Venus, who was watching intently, of course. And it's no secret that the stars in the galaxy have remained bright from that day forward.

Evan's a mere mortal, though, and thus incapable of spawning such heavenly fireworks. His tongue-tied attempts at self-expression—all he really had to do was conspire with Eve—don't help my cause, but they do betray a level of potential feeling that's gone unnoticed by him. Hidden beneath his burnished exterior lies a hillside where the wild thyme grows (Jove would approve of the Shakespearean reference), and I believe I can lead him to it. He's a tricky subject, so closed yet seemingly so open, but this venture wouldn't be challenging if he were a simple sort. I have to trust my instinct about a person's character. And he has definitely ignited a glow in Eve. I like her. I just do.

It's an auspicious enough start to allow me to relax for a moment and spend more time with Psyche. I've neglected my lovely, mercurial bride of late, and she resents it. The mercilessness of immortals is infamous, as you know, but a converted mortal like her can make life as miserable for a god as any goddess could. Even as she acknowledges how hard my job has become now

that hooking up and hanging out have replaced the lan-
guorous, luxurious courtships for which I'm famous;
even as she desperately wants me to beat Jove at his
downsizing game; and even as she's proud of my success over the centuries—she nevertheless can't stand
the amount of time I'm forced to put in these days just
to save my job.

"If you were just starting out, that would be one
thing," she has said. "But you're a legend. You should
stay home more."

What's more, she has no patience for my anxiety.
Nor does our daughter, Pleasure, whose stormy adoles-
cence has required both Psyche's and my constant attention, and who has gotten used to having me around
to dish about her boyfriends.

So you see my problem. "Prove that you're needed,"
says my father. "Pay attention to me!" says my wife.
"Hang with me!" says my daughter.

As I watch over our earthly lovers, I pray that these
high-maintenance creatures don't wreck everything.

6.

A LIGHT SNOW FELL ON LINCOLN CENTER. He had said he would meet her but had not specified where, precisely, in the complex of buildings around the fountains.

That figure standing under the overhang at the entrance to the ballet—surely it was Evan. Yes! She felt a sudden rush. Even at this distance she could sense his solid shoulders and those warm, big hands. She remembered his firm handshake. Now he walked toward her in a steel-gray overcoat with a red scarf tossed around his neck. And boots. She was glad she had dressed up. What she'd packed for the trip wasn't elegant but dressy enough.

He was carrying flowers. Yellow roses. Whatever for?

He had spotted her. She saw him take one giant step forward, stop, then come toward her at a fast, steady pace, his eyes as blue as she remembered, his shy smile vaguely ironic. Now he was beside her, panting like a sprinter, his exhales creating smokelike puffs in the frigid air, holding his arms out as if welcoming her to fall into them, then pulling one arm back and, with the other, thrusting the flowers at her like a schoolboy.

"But I've no place to put them," she said, accepting them and holding them like a newborn in her arms.

"I'm at a hotel, going back home tomorrow. And I don't want to carry—"

"Oh, they're not for keeping; they're a talisman. For me, really. To make sure you'd come. They've served their purpose. We can throw them away." He added: "Home? Where do you live? Come, let's walk. Tell me everything."

She had a sense memory: bouquets of roses thrown to her onstage after she played Juliet the first time. The stage had quickly become nothing short of a botanical garden that night.

"Vermont," she said, then, lowering her head, "Sorry. I wasn't listening."

"That's a world's record. People often stop listening to me, but generally they give it at least ten seconds."

A snowflake seemed to sizzle on her nose. "It's just a bit strange," she said. "You and the flowers and…"

He had the same look in his eyes she remembered from the first night. "And what?"

"I'm surprised—I don't know exactly why I'm here."

"To finish last night's discussion. To breathe in this snowy night together. To get to know each other."

Eve shivered. "Do you think we could get to know each other someplace out of the cold?" *Come, gentle night, come, loving, black-brow'd night, give me my Romeo.* She was thinking of words she didn't know she knew.

He took her arm. "That's just what I was suggesting when you tuned me out. I thought we could go to the Russian Tea Room, a few blocks down from here. I've heard it's where dancers go. But then you know that."

"Well, yes, but it's been years."

He increased the pressure on her arm, and they were off, walking quickly across Sixty-Fifth Street to the east side of Broadway.

She let herself be led, a mountain climber roped to a more experienced guide. So different from a dancer being led by her partner: there was danger in this expedition—this powerful, erotic attraction could start an avalanche. She shivered again.

Not looking up she said, "So, what, are you a florist?"

"An anthologist. I'm here in New York to complete a book on the world's greatest love letters. Yes, really. It isn't my project. I inherited it from another anthologist, who recently died. I'm nervous because it's due in a month. And the hardest part is this introduction I have to write, which could take God knows how much longer."

"Have you done other books?"

"One on American antique furniture, another on 1930s movies, the most recent on the Civil War. I was about to do one on cars—vintage cars—but then was called into action on the letters."

"You like this new one?"

"Yeah, I do. More than I expected. I can't get over how passionate, open, unprotected people can be with each other—on paper. As Dr. Johnson put it, '*In a man's letters, madam, his soul lies naked.*'"

"Ah, words again!" Eve said, laughing.

He looked at her. "I like other things besides words."

"Tell me."

"The outdoors. Hiking, kayaking. And cars. Porsches, really. Going to the racetrack. Last year I went to Laguna Seca to celebrate with other pals from the Three-fifty-six Registry."

"Three fifty-six what?"

"Sorry, my car. A 1950 356 Cabriolet. A rare, redone rig. A registry is a bunch of people who have the same car. We meet from time to time and schmooze. It's called a holiday."

She envisioned her own dented and rusted-out Ford F-250 pickup, probably snowed under, its battery surely dead. A Porsche! To own a Porsche in Glover, Vermont, and at this time of year would be ridiculous; it wouldn't get out of anyone's driveway if you could even find it under the heaps of snow. To see one on the road would be tantamount to a UFO sighting.

Evan squeezed her arm, bringing her back to New York City, to this first date in years and in one of her old haunts to boot—and to the fact that she could still get a thrill from a squeeze, even atop layers of clothing. She remembered the words of her best friend, Luann, whose commentaries on dating—about which she seemed to know more than she wanted to—delighted Eve. "I'm forty, have been with dozens of men, but *have never been asked out on a real date*," Luann recently confided. They'd both grinned at the revelation. But neither, in fact, had Eve.

She tucked her arm in Evan's, noticing yet again the patrician profile and deep, weathered lines around his eyes, etching their way down to his cheeks. Snow wet her lips.

At the corner of Sixty-Second Street and Broadway, he took the flowers from her hand and one by one tossed them into a trash bin. She watched them, transfixed. Yellow roses, like lighted candles falling through the snow. They landed on old newspapers, crumpled brown bags, someone's unwanted letters, and made them all beautiful.

7.

THE MINUTE SHE STEPPED INSIDE THE DOOR OF THE
RUSSIAN TEA ROOM, renovated to czar-like luxury,
Eve recalled a party there in her honor the night of her
twentieth birthday. Laddie had insisted on this spot,
his favorite restaurant in the city, to celebrate what
he announced was her "maturity" as a dancer and as
a woman. She remembered less of the substance of
that evening than the red walls, the waiters in their
high-collared red coats and belts, her own gorgeous
new pale blue satin dress—fitted on her like a couture
gown by Olga, the City Ballet's extraordinary seam-
stress—the sophistication and festivity and excitement. And the guests! Laddie had chosen the guest list
carefully: ballet critics, impresarios, Lincoln Kirstein
and other heavy hitters, and a smattering of his favorite principal dancers.

But for all her celebrated coming-of-age, she was allowed no more than a sip of one of the exquisite vodkas
lining the rich mahogany bar, and not a drop of fes-
tive Champagne from the icy flutes floating around on
waiters' trays. *That's impossible*, she thought now. *Was I
that impressionable? Did I not yet do as I pleased?* Just one
year shy of legal drinking age yet a featured dancer in
a production at the great State Theater the next night,
she was treated by her husband-to-be like a child.

"Fun is for later," Laddie had told her, his thick Russian accent adding to the severity of another of his many severe life lessons. She had not had the nerve to ask him, "*When?*"

The room now was jammed. By the time Evan took her coat and left it in the tiny cloakroom, Eve recalled still more of that evening. Champagne flowed. Her friends protested the liquor ban imposed on Eve, exhorting Laddie to let her drink (they, too, were dancing the next day), but he refused. So they called her into the ladies' room repeatedly all evening, saying "Here! Drink fast!" behind the maestro's back. She found herself, long after the party was over, sewing the ribbons on her toe shoes so off-center they were unwearable at rehearsal the next morning.

Evan had reserved a table in the back. Two couples seated to their left were helping themselves to a heaping platter of blintzes; an older couple to the right were guzzling glasses of icy Stoli straight-up, washing down what appeared to be plates of beef Stroganoff.

"I'm so happy not to be a dancer anymore," Eve said. "I was always on some sort of regimen. Always eyeing food wistfully."

"Do you have footage of yourself dancing?"

"Mmm." A waiter brought menus, and she opened hers avidly. "I was always hungry," she repeated distractedly.

"I plan to fatten you up. Care for caviar?"

He was taken aback by her look of gratitude—or was it pleasure?

"These drinks are right up your alley," he said. "Here's one called the Balanchine Sizzle. Want one?"

"Anything but a Golyakovsky Guzzle."

"You're kidding. They named a drink after your husband?"

"Yup."

"I'll have Stoli straight-up," he told the waiter. "Ice and olives on the side."

"Me, too," Eve said. "And I'm going to the ladies' room. Be right back."

Evan took out his pen and scribbled a note on his manila envelope: *Library, AM*, to remind himself to look once more at the love letters of Robert Browning and Elizabeth Barrett. *"You were made perfectly to be loved,"* the poet had written to her husband, *"and surely I have loved you, in the idea of you, my whole life long."* Was it actually "made perfectly" to be loved, or "perfectly made" to be loved? And why was Evan thinking about this detail *now*? Why was he thinking about anything other than this magical night? Even he could sense his old routine of trying to shield tender feelings through obsessive thoughts about work. But why defend against these wanted feelings, so welcome and so promising?

Something was happening here. He wanted to know everything about Eve, and yet even knowing nothing, he felt deeply connected to her not an hour into their first date. Osmosis? A love potion? It was weird.

"You don't love me enough," Ruth had told him, yet he thought he did love her, "and never will." He'd heard that theme not only from her, but from other women. He had begun to feel himself missing some essential love gene. "You can't be intimate," they'd said, even after making love, as if briefed by one another at a secret global meeting. This particular vocabulary—all those words forming irritating phrases like *emotional availability* and *capacity for closeness*— had to have been decided upon in advance at this summit. He knew the women must be expressing their true feelings. But he knew now, as surely as he knew anything, that they, and his own self-diagnosis, had been wrong.

Eve returned. Electrified again by the sight of her—she was a rainbow!—he stood to greet her, then leaned in to pull out her chair. The waiter placed their vodkas, in frosty glasses big as birdbaths, on the table. "I'll be drunk," she said, happily encircling her goblet with both hands. "You'll have to pour me home."

He glanced at her quickly. Was this an invitation? Just as quickly, he decided it wasn't and raised his glass.

"*Skol!*" They clinked glasses and drank.

Eve coughed. "I can't tell you how much I need this! There's not a lot of time for slacking off at my farm."

"Tell me about your farm."

"No, first, you tell me about you. Please. About editing. Writing. Anthologizing."

"I'll tell you everything. But you first, just even a brief outline."

She laughed. "Okay. I'll be quick. My grandmother ran the farm until she died. I was brought up by my grandparents—my mother died when I was three, and my father remarried and moved to Wyoming. We haven't been in contact since."

"More." He poured a little of his own vodka into her glass and gave her three olives on a toothpick.

She wiped her brow. *The heat of the vodka or the memory?* he wondered.

"I knew it was a tough life but didn't realize how tough. They knew early on I could be—would be—a dancer. I made my debut at eleven in *The Nutcracker* in Boston. Laddie was there, scouting for young dancers. He was...impressed. So he came to the farm and asked my grandparents if they would let me train with him. I was—we were—over the moon."

"Now you," Eve ordered. She ate the last olive.

"Soon enough. Finish." He leaned in to be closer to her.

She imitated his movement. "So my grandfather died, leaving my grandmother alone to run the farm, a hardship so severe she never did pay off the mortgage. I offered to go back to help, but she wouldn't hear of it. Her name was Eve, too. The townsfolk called her Big Eve. Laddie tried to give her money to pay off the mortgage, but she always refused. She died, left me the farm, mortgage unpaid. There! I did it! Done!"

"You run it all alone?" Evan asked.

"Oh, no, there are seven of us, including three part-timers, who work only during sapping. Making syrup is hard work. Ever seen it done?"

"Nope."

They held each other's hands now across the table. "Takes forty-three gallons of sap to make a gallon of syrup—it goes into this diatomaceous earth filter at about sixty gallons a minute." Eve was clearly excited. "We get rid of about seventy-five percent of the sap's water before we start boiling. Our best crop was in 2013…Evan, *I'm talking too much.* And I haven't even begun to tell you what the warm winters are doing to us."

She had pulled her hands away from his and was highlighting her story with hand gestures, painting graceful word pictures of melting forests, burning leaves, boiling sugars.

Evan wondered what it would be like to use his own hands when speaking. Would it help him pull his words out? "Let's order, then," he said.

They ordered pelmeni, chicken Kiev, and salad. They talked about the state of the world.

Over coffee later, Eve looked pensive. "You live alone?" she asked. She reached over the table for his hands again.

"Yes. I did live with a woman not long ago. We weren't married. We broke up a year ago."

"She still in your life?"

"Not really. She's back in Connecticut, where she's from. Quite frail—I just heard. Hasn't been well."

"You keep in touch."

"Only through Claire, the woman I was with at the ballet last night. She's a friend of both of ours, and she keeps me posted."

"I'll finish my endless story so we can get to you, finally," she said. Her words were an elixir for Evan, who couldn't get enough of them, of her.

"The finale is that I love my farm and Christmas Eve Candies—my company—with my whole heart. And I've recently paid off that wretched mortgage!"

He considered this for a moment. "Love your company name." *And I love you,* he thought but didn't say. *What is going on here?*

"I'd never done anything on my own before. From the age of ten, my financial affairs were handled for me. I was typical of young dancers, handing over my life that way. Even when I became, well, a star, Laddie handled *every* aspect of my life, from what I ate and wore and *smelled* like—he even chose my perfume—to what I earned. I suspected I had no skills whatsoever if I couldn't dance. Paying that mortgage—I used the money Laddie left me—was, well, at last I was in complete control of my life."

Evan smiled. "From toe shoes to snow shoes."

She laughed and pulled one hand from his to look at her watch. "It's almost midnight! I talked all night!"

Four hours had indeed disappeared, as had all other diners. "To be continued," he said. "Come, I'll drop you at your hotel."

"I'm at the Sheraton."

Snow was falling heavily. Evan hailed a cab and they slid in. To his horror he found himself not just anxious over their pending separation but speechless. He had the urge to sweep her up, feel her skin against his, tell her she was the first person he could remember he'd wanted to open up to—ever! That he'd felt something important shift inside him tonight—no, in fact, the moment he met her—but more so tonight. It blew him away. But he sat, looking straight ahead, mute as the cabbie's medallion. The idea of sleeping with her that night...well, he simply didn't have the courage or ease to go there. He'd have to get his voice back first.

They looked at each other and smiled awkwardly. Eve told him, suddenly, that she liked his chipped front tooth, his weathered skin, the off-center cleft in his chin.

The cab stopped in front of the Sheraton.

"Oh, Evan, thank you for this wonderful dinner." She held up her left hand to touch his right cheek, in a gesture of warmth as intimate as a kiss. "And for making me too fat to get out of the taxi."

He looked at her shining, expectant eyes but managed nothing but a peck on her cheek. *Oh, brilliant, brilliant!* he thought. *You fool. Say something! Do something!*

She waved brightly as she walked away, her russet hair alive as autumn roses as she glided inside the great hotel's revolving doors.

Evan watched her, seeing her as clearly as he had the night they'd met.

"Where to now?" the cabbie asked.

Evan thought for a moment. "Nowhere," he said, clapping a twenty-dollar bill into the driver's hand while the car door was still open. "Thanks."

He raced after her into the hotel and scanned the lobby. After seeing she wasn't at the front desk, he ran toward the bank of elevators and looked inside each one. Eve was standing, alone, in the center of the fourth one, pulling off a glove.

"Eve!"

"Wow. Evan. Hi!" She fumbled to find the Door Open button. "What's the matter?"

"Stay with me." He reconsidered. "At least have breakfast with me. Please." He was still standing outside the elevator. He looked different. Disheveled.

"Now? Nah, I'm too full." Anything, apparently even a bad joke, to calm the man down.

"In the morning. I'll pick you up. We'll have coffee. I'll even have a chance to tell you about myself. I'll tell you everything you want to know."

"You know I'll just interrupt you." Her smile was that of a concerned nurse for a mental patient.

He knew he looked as damp and haggard as an old blues singer.

"Did something happen to you in the last five minutes?" she asked sweetly. "You look awful."

"Nothing, no. Will you? Have breakfast with me?"

She hesitated. "As long as I get on the three-thirty flight to Burlington."

"You will. I'll take you to the airport. Eight o'clock tomorrow morning then, right here?"

"All right, but listen to me." She spoke sweetly, slowly. "Get some sleep. Okay?" She pressed the Door Close button. "Don't read tonight, Evan. Stretch. If you have some valerian, take a few drops. And *breathe*."

"Valerian?" Was it a steroid? A prescription?

"At the health food store—an herb, a root. Helps you relax."

The doors shut and he wondered idly if there was a health food store nearby. He breathed in deeply and exhaled a long, plaintive sigh that seemed to come from somewhere within his solar plexus, where he'd never felt breath before. He couldn't wait for morning. His only hope for rest of any kind tonight was to read *Motor World* and pray for sleep.

Suddenly, the doors opened and the two of them stared at each other yet again. In a gesture that could only come from years of dance training, Eve plucked him by the front of his overcoat and, as though rescuing a tourist from a falling flower pot, drew him into the elevator. Once they were nose to nose, she released him, placed both hands around his neck, and, in yet another sinuous motion, stood on her toes to press her lips to his. It was a long, slow, deep kiss. Then, completing her impromptu choreography, she gazed into his eyes, kissed him again not so deeply, and gently pushed him backward, out of the elevator. As the elevator doors moved to meet each other, she waved goodbye.

8.

HOURS AFTER SHE'D GRABBED EVAN, inexplicably, uncontrollably, and planted a kiss, she was lying in bed still recounting the whole scene. The elevator. His bluesy, heartsick, crumpled face and clothes. But it wasn't like her to obsess like this the whole night. Her way of coping with feelings good and bad was physical. She worked them out literally—on the dance floor, sapping trees (oh yeah, and this time, grabbing a guy in an elevator and planting a kiss on his lips). The grief counselor she'd seen after Laddie's death had told her, "It's healthy, your way. It's a good thing."

And where was it now, this good thing? What was this new inability to transfer what she felt within to without? What had changed in her makeup that she neither wanted to dismiss thoughts of Evan through *doing* anything, *creating* anything, nor could she if she tried. She liked it just the way it was, going around in her head. Under a spell.

Still in bed long after she usually got up, she located this extraordinary new sensation. It was as though someone had downloaded a glorious new other person into her, amplifying her real self, not diminishing it. She laughed aloud recalling the movie *All of Me* in which a ghost—Lily Tomlin—had come back and entered the actor Steve Martin, to his horror. *Yes, it's like that*, she thought, only unlike in the movie, she *welcomed* this intruder. Evan had gotten her, found his way into her soul. She wasn't taken over by him, she wasn't subsumed by him; he just blended in, filling her up from marrow to skin. Would Evan appreciate her computer imagery, she wondered; would he get the notion of a soul's software? *He seemed more attached to his manila envelope than any device*, she thought, pushing away the covers to begin getting up. He didn't seem to have a laptop or a tablet with him.

But how else to better explain this sense of completeness so early in the game? Not like giddy infatuation—that weird, crazed mess of longing, hope, promise, lust, perfection that soon morphed into something so less idealized as to be crushing—but rather a pure, calm, bedrock sensation of knowing. *Knowing.* Could this be what people meant when they spoke of kismet? Of being destined to be together?

It sure felt that way. Because even in her most emotional performances of Juliet in the balcony scene, no Romeo had ever turned her on the way this one did.

9.

HE WAS WAITING FOR HER IN THE LOBBY AT EIGHT IN
THE MORNING. He'd arrived at seven but sat in the lobby with the newspaper till he dared ask the front desk
to ring her room and announce him.

He had dreamt that an earthquake hit San Francisco, and a huge wall in his bedroom was falling
down, crumbling into bits of snowy shards of plas-
terboard onto his sawn-oak floors. Next, other walls
collapsed throughout the bedroom and then his office
and kitchen, shattered. He wasn't scared in the dream,
just shocked and, when he woke up, shaken. He would
think about its meaning later, as he'd been advised to
do by the therapist he saw briefly after Ruth left. "Keep
track of your dreams," he had said. "You'll find that they
can tell you a lot once you get how your unconscious
processes your feelings."

At dawn he had jotted down the dream, then looked
at the entertainment section in a *New York* magazine,
trying to figure out how to pass the hour after breakfast
before they had to leave for the airport. Libraries, mu-
seums, and bookstores were out—too little time. But
what? Something to share that they both would like
but nothing static, nothing that required words. *Movement!* The only things he could think of that actually

moved were the horse carriages in Central Park, and he figured she'd done that. Or the Staten Island Ferry. He was about to suggest the carriage but then thought, *Cars.* Yes. He'd take her to Manhattan Motorcars on Eleventh Avenue to view the new Porsches.

They merely looked at each other now, both a bit stunned. Morning, that spell-breaker, hadn't broken the spell. He found her as lovely as he remembered her. He knew he looked only slightly less ravaged than he had the night before, still mute with adoration and now bleary from lack of sleep. They decided to eat in the hotel restaurant. Again it fell to Eve to keep the conversation going once they sat down.

"Finish your coffee," Evan said. "Let's go to the Porsche place across the street. I'll show you around."

She downed the contents of her cup.

→

"Have you owned a Porsche before?" the car dealer, who looked like John Oliver, asked Eve.

"Me? No. Never." She glanced at Evan, who seemed to have perked up.

"What do you own now, if I may ask?"

She stifled a giggle while Evan attempted to look like he was coolly appraising a navy Boxster, the indulgent lover on a buying spree.

"Oh, just an old truck," she said, smiling sweetly.

"Well then, surely it's time for a new car!" The salesman was dressed in a perfectly cut pale yellow suit, almost beige, the precise color of the curvy 911 Cabriolet Turbo convertible he was showing her. Eve wondered whether the Porsche people gave out suits dyed in matching Porsche colors to their salespeople, and if so, whether it helped sales. He began pointing out the features he'd evidently been told would appeal to women.

"Note the inverted bathtub shape, resonant of the old Speedster."

"Beautiful," Eve said, exhaling, giddy as a teen mocking the nerdy science teacher.

"And the rear grille, which allows air through, to cool the engine. And note the banjo steering wheel, also taken from some vintage models. And the CD player in the glove compartment."

"They've evidently gotten wind of your breathing theory," Evan said drily.

"Nice," Eve allowed.

"But not nearly as nice as the vintage models themselves," Evan said under his breath. "Where are the baby moon hubcaps? The split windshield and attached bumpers and Reutter Coach Builder badge?" He shared these distinctions between the antique cars and the new ones with Eve, even as the salesman held her captive.

"Would you like to take a spin, madam?" the salesman offered.

Eve looked over at Evan, who nodded an approving *Go.*

"Um, yes. I would." She assumed he meant for her to ride with Evan.

The salesman handed Eve the keys, then sat himself down in the passenger seat. Eve began giggling again and walked over to Evan, car keys dangling from her forefinger and a look that said, *You figure out what to do.* He grabbed her hand holding the keys and pulled her to him a little less gently than he'd planned. Then he kissed her, as if he'd done it so many times before, as if it were the only decent response to a lady's dangling keys. She felt a deep rumble in her body, as though she herself were the car whose engine was being keyed to life. She kissed him back, boldly pressing her body into his.

The salesman, looking out the car window, seemed confused.

"We'll come back for a drive later, after lunch," Eve said smoothly, tearing away from Evan at last and poking her head in the driver's seat window to reassure the salesman.

"She's just a little excited," Evan said. He winked at the dismayed man. "Her first convertible. By the way, how much is this car?"

"A great price," the salesman crooned. "911 turbos with all-wheel drive are going up first of the year. This model is actually not even changing, except for the medallion on the steering wheel. If you buy it now, it's two hundred thousand dollars."

Eve shrieked with laughter.

"Thank you," Evan said solemnly. "Thanks very much. We'll be back when she stops laughing." Evan gripped Eve's arm. "Whatever is so funny, darling?" he asked, and steered her carefully out of the dealership.

"May I have it, honey?" Eve drawled. "I just *love* it."

Evan nodded magnanimously. "Of course, my pet. After lunch."

The snow had melted on the streets under a warm November sun. Evan looked at his watch, his mood darkening.

"It's time," he said.

Eve hesitated for a few moments. "I don't think so."

It seemed to Evan that she was appraising him, looking behind his eyes to his desire.

What was she saying?

"I can stay another twenty-four hours if you can," she said offhandedly, as though reciting weather from the Farmer's Almanac.

"*If I can?* I can."

"Good." She took his hand. "So then, you've shown me your way of moving through life. Tonight I'll show you mine. Since it's our last night, I'm taking you dancing."

10.

THE SNOW THAT HAD BLANKETED BURKE MOUNTAIN IN THE EARLY MORNING WAS CHANGING. It no longer floated down in cheery flakes that accrued into inches of powder, promising skiing paradise. What fell now was unrecognizable—tiny, rock-hard, elongated pellets, sharp and stinging as steel shavings. They blasted against Eve's chamois face mask, piercing it as though it were a sheet of tissue.

She had been one of the first on the mountain, eager to take a few runs in fresh snow. *I'm just an old powder hound*, she'd thought as she drove the twenty-minute stretch from Glover to East Burke, feeling the thrill, as she always did, of a morning alone on the slopes.

But this precipitation quickly accumulated into layers of corrugated ice and grainy snow. Skiing this erratic succession of hard and soft, sticky and slippery snow—skiers call it crud—was tricky, even dangerous, like trying to ski on children's mud pies, each frosted with cardboard and glue. She suspected that all ski classes on the mountain would be canceled; she would advise them at the bottom to close the runs, if they hadn't already.

The light above, more than the icy pellets and the junk under Eve's skis, was the worst problem. Instead of illuminating the meeting of sky and mountain, a molten opaque blanket erased the horizon and obliterated trees and trails, not to mention signs of other skiers. A lone skier passed to Eve's right and stopped no more than two feet away, all in white but for black gloves and a blur of blue. It waved to her, a massive, down-covered person looking like a masked burglar come to rob the moon. It held up its black-gloved hand to say hi. Only when it spoke to her was she sure it was a man.

Evan? Of course it wasn't Evan; how could it possibly be? He's in San Francisco.

"I figure we have a good two miles yet." The man's disembodied voice seemed to come out of the fog. "This crud is getting worse. So's the light. Want to follow me down?"

"Oh, thank you, yes," Eve said. "I was getting a little scared."

He came closer, stopping at the tips of her skis, a puff of blue face mask and black gloves still the only sign of a man in there. "We'll need to move," the man said. His voice was familiar.

"Jeb?" she breathed with a stab of irrational disappointment.

The masked figure bowed. "At your service."

"I didn't recognize you."

"That's where I have the advantage," he said. "I'd know *you* in a space suit." Even amid the banter, Eve could hear the concern in his voice.

Jeb Hobdy, a friend to everyone in Glover, sometimes seemed to track her like a hunting dog. He was a businessman whose generosity to the community made him a beloved local figure. He volunteered as the head of the mountain safety group known as the

Sweepers, consisting of only top-notch skiers, often former racers, who routinely checked all the runs every few hours to look for downed trees and anybody who might be stranded. Occasionally they had to blast avalanches. On days like today, Jeb was a skier's answered prayer.

"We'll make it down," he said. "I'd change my lenses to the yellow ones, though, for the fog."

Eve did so.

He adjusted his ski boots, mask, and gloves in preparation for a fast flight downhill. Eve did the same.

They started, Jeb at first just behind her so she could hear him calling out instructions. After a few careful turns, he told her to stop. He said he wanted to go ahead of her so she could see his tracks. He urged her to keep a close trail behind him, no more than two turns behind; any farther back and she might not see him and could get lost. As he made his first turn a few feet ahead of her, she could see nothing of him but his black gloves bobbing across her lenses. Looking ahead was like peering into a glass of milk.

"Eve?" he called.

"Yeah, I'm here."

"Ski ahead of me now. Better if I follow you." His voice was steady, but the storm was getting worse.

No longer sure of where the mountain was underfoot or how steep the terrain, Eve stiffened against the unknown—the worst thing to do on skis, she knew, and, like leaning back, a natural but disastrous response to gravity. She kept reminding herself that she was a good skier, as if that knowledge alone would loosen her up. The old ballet-troupe confidence and competitiveness rarely surfaced these days. When they did, as now, Eve saw them less as a signal of her spirit than as an opportunity for a moment of gratitude for her loose limbs, fast reflexes, and strong muscles—for the mental and physical toughness she relied on to take her power back whenever she felt it threatened.

They reached the crest; the hard part was over.

"Okay now, Eve? Think you can make it down by yourself?"

Eve knew he had to check the entire mountain for more lone skiers. "Sure," she said. "And Jeb, I can't thank you enough."

"Maybe we'll grab a coffee when this storm stops."

"Yes, or better, a drink."

Jeb had often tried to have coffee with Eve; everyone knew he had a thing for her. This time she promised herself she would take him up on it. On a day like today, though, Eve's greatest delight was the pleasure of being alone, then going home alone and taking a hot bath and making dinner. No après-ski for her.

It wasn't only that she had momentarily mistaken Jeb for Evan, she mused as she sailed down the bowl that ended the run. She also thought she had spotted Evan at the top, putting on his skis. And again halfway down, when she saw a man pulling his balaclava tight against his face. Who was it who said, "Out of sight, out of mind"? Whoever it was was wrong.

11.

EVAN WAS IN HIS STUDY, SUFFERING.

> *Dear Eve,*
>
> *The strangest thing has happened. My life seems different now. I want to turn to you and talk to you, and then I realize you're three thousand miles away and my heart begins to ache and . . .*

Evan crumpled the letter, a sorry companion to four equally maudlin and incomplete pieces of drivel he'd composed. He tossed it.

"*The strangest thing has happened.*" Good grief, a summer camp essay. "*My heart begins to ache.*" Yeah, indigestion brought on by his prose.

He remembered, in the years before Ruth, the ease of going to a woman friend's home at Christmastime, the comfort of her homemade eggnog and, later, her warm bed. But not this year.

Now the thought of any woman but Eve left him feeling moody, adrift, disconsolate—he couldn't find the right word for his edginess. His equilibrium was off. When he sat down, he longed to exercise. When he exercised, he wanted to sit.

He kept envisioning her in the blue dress she'd bought the afternoon before they went to the Latin club in Tribeca, saw it swirling around her legs as they danced the cha-cha.

Evan got up from his desk and began a little cha-cha of his own—front and a one-two-three, back and a one-two-three, positioning his arms as he had that last night with Eve, looking down just a bit the way he had then, to catch a glimpse of her beautiful legs. He remembered that it was not just her steps and style that were so good; it was something she'd done with her hands, some way she lifted her wrists into the air for a moment, spread her fingers as though to keep imaginary birds at bay, then brought them back in to her body. The same way she'd moved them to illustrate her point that night at the Russian Tea Room.

Her hands. Her body.

He went into the kitchen for some coffee, surprised that the stove clock read nearly noon. He'd wasted an entire morning trying to compose a simple letter to a woman asking if he could see her again. *And couldn't do it.*

Did she miss him just a little bit? Did she want to see him again this much? Was all that laughter, those kisses, that explosive erotic charge between them going to amount to just a promissory note? He had backed off reluctantly after their evening of dancing, wanting to make love to her that very moment but also wanting to wait until the moment was right—that is, right for her. He knew "right" would be the next time they were together.

He walked back to his study, picked up his pen.

Dear Eve,

*The strangest thing has happened to me. I
find myself unable to finish my book because
all I do is think of . . .*

Damn! Now he was paraphrasing ancient song lyr-
ics: *All I do / Is dream of you / The whole night through...*

He couldn't send such drivel. He imagined her dis-
gustedly tossing the letter into her wood stove, so he
destroyed it like the others. Failure number six.

He reached to call her instead but snatched his
hand away from the receiver as soon as he touched it.
If he couldn't write it correctly, God knows what he
would say. His throat constricted at the thought of trying to speak. *Hello, Eve? You remember me, don't you?*

With a sigh, he put on his coat and went outside.
The hazy winter light, the pedestrians lining the familiar path down Chestnut Street, even the cracks in the
pavement soothed him. He'd lived in his house at the
junction of Chestnut and Leavenworth since before he
met Ruth. They had taken this walk together hundreds
of times.

How Ruth had loved this area—loved their view of
Alcatraz and the water, adored their dinners of abalone
and sourdough at the wharf. He'd added more books
since she'd gone, replaced the couch, but it had retained
the overall look Ruth designed for it—slightly worn
now but intact. The same assessment, he thought, running his hands through his rapidly graying hair, could
be made about him.

Heading uphill toward the newsstand at the far
corner, he realized he'd thought more about Ruth in
the few days since he'd met Eve than he had in the year

since Ruth left. She was a splendid woman. Striking, smart, energetic. Sweet, too, when she wanted to be. Their life together had been a happy one. Yet he guiltily rejoiced in the fact that she was gone and he was free, that he wasn't being taken to task for his shortcomings. Maybe she had a new boyfriend. Maybe this one would marry her.

Only now, since meeting Eve, did he have perspective on how dissatisfied Ruth must have been. She'd wanted so much more for herself, so much more for him, than either had. Once she'd said she hoped that he would be the instrument of her self-discovery. He was not up to such a daunting task.

Would he be up to it now? He wasn't sure. He admired Ruth's fervor for improvement, of him and of herself, but it also went along with the "finding one-self" mantra that repelled him. All those lists she kept. *"Walk ten thousand steps today. Begin diet. Organize block party!"* As if she were essentially deficient and taking her life cues from magazines. It seemed to him, too, that she was always trying to burrow deeper inside him, to ferret out secrets of his soul he did not know existed. "What exactly do you mean?" she would say when he had thought his meaning perfectly clear. "Why are you sad?" she'd ask when he was contemplative and did not feel sad at all. "Do you love me?" she would beseech when, damn it, she knew he was giving her what he could; why else were they together?

She tried to draw out of him things he did not possess, feelings simply not lodged in his cells. He could not give what he didn't have, as much as he wanted to make her happy. But she was right: he didn't love her enough.

A few months after she left, he began to date again, pretty women who, like him, wanted nothing more than sex and their independence. And one day he realized he felt whole again. He quickly discerned which women would want too much, and he got out of the way.

Now, it seemed, as he walked back home, fun had all but vanished. He could not get Eve out of his mind. But, as he remembered her, she became ephemeral, mere mist. He could no more capture her than he could a snowflake. He bounded up the stairs hoping for a miracle. It remained as he had left it. Crumpled paper in the wastebasket, virgin stationery mocking him from the desk. A pen, a laptop—implements for writing beyond his power to use. And next to them, the manuscript.

He stared at it. An idea formed, neared, became clearer, like the headlight on an approaching locomotive.

He knew what he would do.

Dear Eve,

I may be blind. I looked for a long time at a head of reddish-brown hair and decided it was not yours. I would like to make an appointment....I hope you will be kind enough to make one with me—if you have not forgotten me!

— Evan

The very words James Joyce once wrote in a letter to Nora Barnacle.

12.

JEB WATCHED EVE SKI AWAY, marveling at her control even in these perilous conditions. He knew she was worried. So was he. Visibility was worsening, snow was accumulating, and the mountain was becoming more cut up and treacherous than she might be prepared for. Not everyone studied the weather in such depth; most people hadn't a clue about how to read conditions on a mountain.

"Don't go so fast," he yelled after her like the father of a reckless teenager. She's skiing fiercely for my benefit, to prove she's tough and doesn't need help. It seemed to him he'd had this same fatherly concern for Eve forever.

Yet he'd known her only three years. He'd left Rutland for Glover some thirteen years ago to escape the city. A private man and so taciturn that no one knew anything but fragments about him. He was rumored to have once had a wife back in the Green Mountains, where he used to live. But the story about the fate of their marriage, if indeed there was a marriage, had at least a dozen endings, depending on the source, not one of whom was reliable. No one knew him then nor the alleged wife. Certainly no scandal was connected to him. He had money; he was an expert skier, a skilled hunter, a fearless woodsman. Best of all, in the honorable tradition of Vermont enterprise, he still did business on a handshake. His reticence in personal matters was forgivable to the townsfolk not only because they shared that quality, but because in all matters except his private life he was accessible. Unsparing of time or muscle, he was there in a crisis, counted on to settle disputes, looked to for innovation, generous to local charities.

His business was selling farm machinery, everything from log loaders and dozer blades to maple syrup equipment and supplies. Eve had come to him the moment she moved to Glover from Boston. "I'm lost," she'd confessed. "I haven't been on this farm in years. My grandmother left me with an old wood smokehouse, funky buckets, props out of Hansel and Gretel. I need to modernize."

He had surveyed her property and advised her, guiding her through the maze of modern sugaring equipment, convincing her to buy the proper evaporators—steel troughs in which maple sugar farmers boiled the water out of the sap—and then installed them for her. He'd knocked 20 percent off the price, and when she protested simply said, "There'll be a lot more you'll need to buy from me as you go along," and she'd accepted gratefully.

It was that look he could never forget—as if whatever he said, she'd do—and he felt bound to help her succeed. She needed more than equipment; she needed sound advice and support. He found her resolute and indefatigable but ignorant of the basics and inexperienced with machinery. Many others could have helped her, but he took it upon himself to be her mentor, and, more and more, she turned to him. He spent hours at her farm, installing miles of tubing from trees to the sugarhouse, lecturing on drainage, soil, the winds, ways to prevent blight and defend against deer. Mostly, he worried about the weather. Sugaring, as his friends at Sugarmill Farm (considered large, with four thousand trees) down in Barton were fond of saying, depends on the weather the way poker depends on cards. And Eve's farm was smaller than average—fewer than a thousand trees but with excellent spacing between them—just enough to pay for itself and provide a small profit.

His motives, he told himself, were selfless. She needed a hand, and his hands were supportive. Simple as that. He looked forward to her visits to his store and his to her farm. One day, he approached her with a project.

"Want to help the Sweepers?" he asked. "I need to train more kids to police the trails."

"You're asking me to teach skiing?" Eve clapped her hands.

"Would you? It'd be for four weekends this winter. Little kids. You have the time?"

"No, but I'll find it."

"It's just two hours a day for the four weekends."

"Fine. Will you come with me the first day, in case the children decide to attack?"

→

The day glistened. Jeb took the boys and Eve the girls, eight of them evenly divided by gender but not in size or innate ability. It took little time for him to overcome whatever uncertainty he had about his ability to cope with so alien a group, and before long Bobby managed to get down Pussycat Hill falling only once, Nathan could actually snowplow, and Jonathan and Seth could stop without running into Jeb or each other.

He turned to get Eve's commendation, but she was bending over little Allison, the Cartwright's girl, who, he now realized, had fallen and was howling at the bottom of the hill. Eve had removed her own skis and was bending over the child, her gloved hand stroking Allison's head. The sight of that gesture, the curve of Eve's back, and the way wisps of Eve's hair blew in the breeze out from the sides of her ski hat made him take a deep breath.

"Wait here," he told the boys and skied over to Eve and Allison. "Everything all right?"

She looked up at him, her eyes merry. "Nothing broken," she said. "Just a little twist of the ankle. Right, honey?"

The girl whimpered. "I want more medicine."

Eve stood, took off her gloves, and from a pocket in her parka extracted a glass bottle filled with brown liquid. "Coming up," she said, winking at Jeb. "My medicine works magic." She uncapped the bottle and poured some of its contents on the snow. "Now you've already had four spoonfuls. One more and the pain should be all gone."

Carefully, Eve fed the girl with a plastic spoon and—presto!—the crying stopped. "Magic," Eve repeated, and led the girl back to her companions.

Jeb caught up with her. "Is that elixir of health what I think it is?"

"Dr. Eve's Cure-all Serum," she crooned, her confidence as clear as the maple syrup in the bottle. "If you ever come out with the kids alone, stop by my place first and I'll give you some to take with you."

As the months passed, Eve became adept around the farm and needed Jeb less. Their places at the ski classes were taken by other volunteers; both had plenty of work to keep them occupied. With the pressure to help her off, Jeb made do by seeing her, even at a distance, at town meetings or simply walking along Glover Road in the village. Occasionally he'd ask her out for coffee. Sometimes she'd say yes and sometimes no, but each time they were alone together, he was met by gratitude and a kindness as impregnable as any fortress, and he did not dare to breach it. It was only when she went to New York for that farmers convention and didn't return on the day she was supposed to—forgetting their coffee date—that he realized her negligence smarted and her absence disturbed him.

"Oh, Jeb, forgive me," she'd pleaded into his answering machine when she returned his call from a restaurant. "I'm still in New York. I got swept up in the city— I've decided to stay and look around a bit." She tried to sound both sorry and encouraging. "I hope you'll accept a rain check in a few days."

He hadn't seen her since. And today, when he saw her figure on the mountain and knew she'd come back, it was as though she had rescued him.

13.

In the cold Northeast Kingdom, where chopping wood and stoking furnaces were daily chores, a woman without a man was often considered seriously disadvantaged. Even Eve's grandmother, Big Eve, a widow who did her own wood-chopping, masonry, and bricklaying, had scandalized the town when, at age sixty-six, she turned down an offer of marriage to a local clergyman.

As one irritating neighbor who knew her family expressed it to Eve, a woman alone was seen as being "in danger."

"No," Eve had shot back, "as being dangerous."

Eve started her descent, adjusting the yellow lens inside her goggles. The fog was so thick she could taste the water in the air when she inhaled. She couldn't see ahead beyond the tips of her skis. On the side of a mogul she hadn't seen coming, she caught an edge, was thrown forward into the air, and fell on her stomach, facing downhill, skis flying off their bindings, feet splayed—like a cartoon character entering the Skeleton event. Eve hadn't fallen in a tummy-splat like this since she was a beginner, before Laddie forbade her to ski anymore lest it hurt her dancing. It took the wind out of her. The absurdity of the position she'd landed in made her laugh aloud, and she turned over on her back so she could make an angel in the snow. Looking up into the soupy sky, she saw a pinpoint of the sun peeping through two serious-looking clouds, its breathtaking light boring down on her wet, cold face.

"This is heaven!" Eve, still on her back, crooned to the sky. A bigger piece of the sun now highlighted a group of clouds so that they formed an enormous winged man with a halo all around his body and a heart-shaped object in his hand. "Must be the God of Love!" Eve decided whimsically. He stayed clearly delineated for several moments. She got up, brushed off snow that encrusted her jeans and parka like sodden cement, and put her skis back on, hoping to beat the sun down the mountain. She looked up. The sun was barely a red glow, but the God of Love had disappeared along with the clouds that formed him.

Mountains don't stand still, either, Eve knew. They aren't merely huge hulks of intractable sediment and mammoth lumps of rock; they expand and contract just as every other living thing does.

Eve was a mountain's conspirator. She felt its energy, breathed with it, didn't fight or fear it. Thinking back on her conversation with Evan four nights ago, she wondered whether he had understood this. Kids had no trouble imagining a mountain as energy, likening it to their own. They knew when the light changed, the winds blew, and the mountain contracted, to lean over their skis even though they were afraid, to bend their knees instead of straightening them. They understood the paradox of giving in in order to conquer.

Eve finished her descent within the hour. Although her toes and fingers were numb and her head pounded from the tension of trying to see where she was going, she decided not to go into the lodge to warm up. She went straight to her car. She wanted to go home, to a hot bath, a hot drink, a hot meal. The inchoate longing she'd felt when the sun came out, a gnawing at her heart at that moment, was gone. As she started her old Ford truck, she felt another wave but this time of exhilaration. *I'm in the most beautiful countryside I can imagine. I'm strong and healthy and alive. I have dear friends. I'm useful. I'm making my own way in the world. I give back. What more could I want?*

She was greeted at the foot of her driveway by her neighbor, Luann, poring over the contents of their shared mailbox. Luann, her lifeline.

"You've got mail, sweetie," her friend said cheerfully. She peered at the back of the envelope. "From a Mr. Cameron," she went on in a sing-songy drawl, at once teasing her and mocking the townspeople's mantra: If he's an ambulatory, unattached male with a decent job, grab him.

Eve laughed, happier still. "Gimme," she told her friend.

"What's so funny?" Luann asked, hugging her. "Oh, you are a cold, wet thing. Get inside right now!"

In northern Vermont, natives warm to you only after many winters together. Luann, though, was like a southern breeze, a neighbor as vulnerable and chatty and nosy as Vermonters were crusty and private and wary. She'd grown up in Georgia, majored in English literature at SMU, and now taught English at the local high school. It was her first teaching job in the Northeast, where she'd come for a change of scenery. Everybody in Glover, parents and students alike, adored her, but Eve loved her most of all. Lu was the first close woman friend she'd ever had who wasn't a dancer. They talked about literature and lip gloss, about men and #MeToo, about growing old and staying young. They checked up on each other, kept each other's secrets. They helped clean each other's chimneys, clear each other's thinking. They laughed together like loons.

Luann brought the mail inside, clearly wondering who would dare to write Eve, when the toughest men in the Northeast Kingdom would tremble at the thought.

Eve knew about her reputation as a loner and about the abiding wish of the neighbors to see her "settled." She'd come to take an almost perverse delight in witnessing their pains to match her with every available local, from the newly rehabilitated town drunk, aged thirty-eight, to the newly widowed appeals court judge, aged seventy-four. She managed, always, to convey the mythical sentiment that the mere mention of any man other than her dearly departed husband could bring on the vapors. She'd carefully cultivated the image of the still-grieving widow. The fact that his possessions still remained in their place at home, as in her heart, perpetuated that perception. She would keep that shrine to him, complete with pictures of him smiling down benevolently at his adoring dancers—for the neighbors' benefit, if not her own.

Even Luann, Eve knew, wavered on the man thing. As much as she mocked the notion of aloneness equaling loneliness, she'd been promoting Jeb to Eve for years. Their conversations were always the same.

"Just give him a chance, Eve."

"Why?"

"Why not?"

"He's not for me," Eve would reply. "But since you like him so much, why don't you take him instead?"

That would end it.

"I had enough man problems down south. Up here their hands are too cold."

This minor deviation from their solitary sisterhood delighted them. Within moments of poking around with the idea of fixing each other up, they'd dissolve in laughter, proving once again that despite their desire to protect each other and open all doors to future happiness, neither of them actually wanted to date.

Eve took off her boots in the doorway, peered at Evan's strong, direct handwriting, and felt giddy with desire. She ripped it open.

"What's he want?" Luann asked, hovering at the door of the bathroom while Eve filled the tub.

"Come look," Eve called out, smiling at the fine, deckled edge, the ecru-colored stationery, the Victorian formality mixed with a modern, masculine urgency—the elegant mix so much like him, so much like that note he'd given her at the ballet. Together, they studied his words.

An appointment? Eve smiled, remembering the word thing of his. "What man asks a woman for an appointment?"

"He wants an appointment with you, sweetie. Listen, you make that appointment, hear?" Luann shot back, cackling.

As Eve slid into the bath, slipping down so the water covered her ears, she was grateful for the fourth time this day. Grateful for her devoted Luann, of course, with whom she shared everything, but also for this big, mysterious and so far very proper anthologist, car guy, editor—whatever he was—who lived in another universe. She loved his courtly, old-fashioned manners. Who wrote things like "I would like to make an appointment…if you have not forgotten me"?

Suits me fine, she thought now, wanting again to touch those creases in his face, to draw them with her finger, trace them tenderly, study them, kiss them. *But I'd rather not go to California. Or to New York, for that matter.*

She shampooed her hair, dipped her head back into the bathwater to rinse.

Evan Cameron, you'll just have to come here.

There was a guest room—not that he'd use it, but he'd approve of that formal touch. She let the water drain out of the tub. She thought of Mrs. Schumacher next door, who'd never been outside the county. And the Turners across the street, who had become born-again Christians. She smiled. The only sure way besides grieving widowhood to evade the neighbors' meddling would be to provide a man for herself, all by herself.

Wrapping up in her terry robe, Eve delighted in what would surely become the talk of the town. *Yes, come, Evan. They'll all have heart attacks at the sight of you.*

IT WAS ONLY A COINCIDENCE. Really.

I was flying back from a royal castle in Belgravia earlier than expected (love-prone princes need only the slightest nudge in the right direction) when Eve, that glorious ballet dancer turned candymaker, spotted me. Usually I keep myself invisible to the human eye, but that morning, what with the fog, I was a bit careless. When the sun came out, there I was, caught in the act, so I did my disappearing fleecy cloud trick.

It took me a moment to recognize her as the woman my tongue-tied love anthologist selected in the Koch Theater lobby—a woman who still has the sap of love in her untapped. I was on my way to Montana, where a certain sheep rancher had put in too hard a winter without a bride, and was trying not to think of Evan at all. Then, on an impulse, I looked down and made eye contact with this skier, flat on her back and making wings in the snow, like a baby goddess learning to fly. She seemed filled with wonder and joy, and she was so pretty. The obvious symptoms of dawning love were so powerfully obvious that they reached to the heavens, reached me. Now that's love, Jove, human love. Great as Antony and Cleopatra's. Héloïse and Abelard's.

I love showing off when that happens; it happens so rarely.

I'm trying to keep my job, though. I'm focused on that heavenly 401k plan. I must concentrate on Evan and Eve. I have six months left. If they aren't together by June, I'll have to step in big-time. After all, a god's gotta do what a god's gotta do.

14.

EVAN BARELY SLEPT THE ENTIRE WEEKEND. A few naps, a couple of afternoon dozes, but nothing deeper. The anthology was due before Christmas—December 15, Scroopman decreed. He resented the fact that, despite the hurry everyone seemed to be in to receive the manuscript, the entire editorial staff would be off on Christmas break and thus would not look at it until after New Year's. He had decided nevertheless to get in all but the intro and the endnotes. Better the manuscript sit on his editor's desk than on his.

Evan could use his own Christmas break. Despite his passion for the likes of Keats and Shelley, Harriet Beecher Stowe and F. Scott Fitzgerald, he was growing tired of their tortuous love affairs. A book full of unrequited love, illness, and insanity was fascinating but hardly uplifting.

The endnotes represented drudgery, but the introduction was killing him. He still had no idea what to say. He'd read and reread every pink-inked word Lorelei Layton had scribbled on the letters in the files in order to understand her criteria for choosing or rejecting them. He could discern no coherent pattern. Why did one man or woman resonate in her mind as a lover, another as a loser? What made one man's passionate expression a keeper, another's part of her discard pile? Were her choices based on the author's artistic gift? Or were they personal, idiosyncratic—and perhaps biased? After all, her own lover was half her age! What could an eighty-something woman be doing with a forty-something man? She was as inscrutable, he thought, as love itself—although he now had felt a glimmer of what love was. Love was Eve.

He glanced again at the manuscript, felt a surge of panic. *Relax*, he told himself for the hundredth time. *You can't force it.* He thought again of Eve and wondered if the answer lay with her. A dawning suspicion that only his own experience could color what he wrote— could inform what he wrote—snaked its way into his brain. If he could breathe with Eve the way Abelard had with Héloïse, why, he'd experience the words, not just imagine their meaning! But at this rate, if knowledge of love magically arrived, it would still take months to articulate. The book would be in a second printing, still without an introduction. He'd be on to another West Coast woman, Eve wedded to an East Coast man. And love? As opaque as ever.

He was ready for a few light reads. A good thriller. He'd hole up over Christmas with an old Henning Mankell. He felt antsy: he needed a little physical action and straight talk, man talk—not all this…tortured passion.

Meanwhile, back on page two hundred sixty of Lorelei's manuscript, still trying to decipher what prompted her to include one entry over another, he landed in the middle of one of the most important social events of the 1795 season in France.

The elegant "Balls of Victims" were fêtes given at the end of the French Revolution for those who had lost relatives in the Reign of Terror. A person could get through the doors only by presenting a death certificate of a recently deceased relative. It was at one such odd ball—oddball ball—that two famous great lovers would meet.

Evan sighed, imagining the complicated emotions that filled the ballroom that night. It must have been an eerie festival of grief and greed and arrogance, of regret and anticipation and hope, for many of the victims on the dance floor were members of the French aristocracy who hoped to find new mates, even as they presented proof of the death of their former ones.

One guest was Joséphine Tascher de la Pagerie, also called Vicomtesse de Beauharnais, whose husband had gone to the guillotine while she sat in jail wondering what would happen to them both. Yes, that Joséphine. Her agenda on the night of the Victims' Ball was not only to have a good time (now that she was released from prison), but to find someone worthy of becoming her next husband. Such a man would have to be rich enough to pay off her debts and guarantee no financial problems in the future, for Joséphine did not intend to live in a manner befitting anyone less important than the viscountess she had been before she was thrown in the pokey. So she chose Napoleon Bonaparte.

Poor Napoleon! Evan mused as he made himself a ham sandwich. *He didn't know what he was getting into.* The next year, on March 9, 1796, Napoleon and Joséphine were married. When, two days afterward, the groom left for the military campaign in Italy, his bride did not accompany him. She decided that being alone in Paris was preferable to staying with her man in an armed camp.

Not a wise decision.

Bonaparte's letters to Joséphine were a mix of outrage and desire, of anger and passion. So smitten was the emperor, and so casual about responding was his new wife, that the intensity of Napoleon's emotions was heartbreaking.

> *I don't love you, not at all; on the contrary I detest you. ... You never write me; you don't love your husband; you know what pleasures your letters give him, and yet you haven't written him six lines, dashed off so casually!*

He was right. His wife hadn't written him as much as one measly line. Evan was outraged on the tiny tyrant's behalf.

→

The phone rang. Evan cringed, remembering that he was supposed to call Susan, a neighbor who had invited him for dinner. He dreaded having to tell her he'd forgotten—yet again.

"Evan?" the voice said.

"Speaking," Evan was already formulating his apology.

"It's Eve."

Evan fell back into his chair.

"Eve!" he said. "Eve. I wasn't expecting you to call!"

"You were expecting maybe Jennifer Lawrence?" she said in her flat Northeast Kingdom voice.

"Ah, me and Jen. I broke up with her."

"I got your letter," Eve said, "and I thought we'd make an appointment." She tried not to tease him. They hadn't spoken, it seemed, in centuries.

Evan, holding the receiver tightly to his ear in his effort not to miss a word, missed her facetiousness. "When and where?"

"Would you like to come here over Christmas? It's beautiful with all the snow, and I have plenty of room in this big old house."

"I'd love to." His introduction to the anthology would just have to wait a few days; there was no way he could concentrate on it now. "Maybe if I take some time away from this manuscript I'll become a normal person again."

"Oh, I wouldn't expect normal. By the way, do you ski?"

"No."

"Snowshoe?"

"No."

"Cross-country?"

"On what?"

"Oh dear me. Snowboard?"

"Uh-uh. Flexible Flyer?"

"You daredevil! Yoga? Please say yes."

"Yes. Er, nope."

He was as excited as when he was seven and his dad took him to a vintage car show, where all the contestants wore white gloves in an effort to prove to the judges how spotless their engines were. That was almost forty years ago!

"When?" he asked.

"Come on Christmas Eve, the twenty-fourth, and stay a couple of days after?" Her voice quieted into the question, as if a mention of Christmas Day itself were asking too much. "I'll teach you how to ski..."

"Yes," he said, his voice filled with emotion. "Let me check flights and get right back to you." He fumbled for his pen, his manila envelope.

"You'll fly into Burlington. I'll pick you up there. If you can get a really early flight that gets in by mid-afternoon, say, we'll have time to drive back and walk around while it's still daylight. It takes about an hour and a half to get here from the airport."

She was chattering away again, the way she had in the restaurant that first night, as though happy as he about their plan.

"I'll call you with a couple of possibilities," he said.

"Great!"

"And Eve?"

"Uh-huh?"

The old inarticulateness muffled him like a mouthful of wet, new-fallen snow. "I so look forward to it." Pathetic.

"Me, too," she said lightly. "We'll have fun. Bring ski stuff and loose sweats for yoga. We're going to do both." She paused. "Bye, then," and she hung up.

They both thought, at the very same moment, *Oh my God. I did it.*

Evan went into the kitchen, wolfed down his ham sandwich with a glass of beer, his heart still doing the cha-cha. He was wildly hungry and definitely could not face Susan for dinner later anyway. Meal completed in under sixty seconds, he spent the next fifteen minutes online finding a red-eye into Logan or LaGuardia, whichever connected to Burlington easiest and fastest. Then he called Susan to cancel.

His brain set aloft as if with helium, he returned to the frustrated emperor Napoleon. The emperor's letter fairly screamed his despair.

> *What do you do all day, Madam? What is the affair so important as to leave you no*

*time to write to your devoted lover? What
affection stifles and puts to one side the love,
the tender constant love you promised him?*

The poor man's crazed, Evan thought. *Insane with jealousy and hurt. And there she is, the elusive Joséphine, taunting
him with her silence, having a grand time in Paris!* Had Lorelei included the letter to show how even an emper-
or could succumb to love's madness? Evan suddenly
felt sorry for the delicate psyches of men. Men were
so inept at loving and yet so in thrall to the women
they loved that the merest slight sent them into parox-
ysms of murderous jealousy. He pictured Eve, her russet hair falling about her shoulders as it had the night
they went dancing, her body moving into his with ease
and delight, her tawny eyes gazing into his, and sure
enough he bristled at the thought of anyone else dancing with her.

*Indeed, I am very uneasy, my love, at receiv-
ing no news of you; write me quickly four
pages, pages full of agreeable things which
shall fill my heart with the pleasantest feelings. I hope before long to crush you in my
arms and cover you with a million kisses
burning as though beneath the equator.*

At one time, the feelings of the emperor would
have been to Evan as remote as a distant sun. Now they
burned hotly in him, searing his soul.

15.

EVAN HAD A FITFUL NIGHT'S SLEEP, filled with dreams he couldn't remember. He was dozing off yet again when a 7 a.m. phone call woke him. Irritated, he thrashed about and considered not answering it. He hated noise. He hated telemarketers. Even children's playful street squeals drifting into his office when he was editing. Or sleeping. He once moved away from a large house in the Presidio district to get away from neighbors who played jazz late into the night. He wondered how younger people stayed sane, with all those terrible electronics hanging off their belts, beeping and buzzing. Unwired was how Evan liked things. His publisher called him The Dinosaur.

The phone rang again. He picked up.

"Evan, hello," said a voice he knew.

"Ruth?" He was wide-awake now, his heart racing. "Well, hello," he continued, hoping she mistook the catch in his voice for mere surprise. Ever since Claire had told him Ruth was back in San Francisco, he'd imagined this moment, feared her intrusion. He wondered what he'd say, whom he'd be with, what he was supposed to do when this call came. Would they be warm to each other? Breezy? He always figured they'd say a quick hello at most. Once, early on after their

breakup, he even prepared a short speech, a noncom-
mittal two-liner he could utter if and when the run-in
occurred. But he'd long ago forgotten the words, snap-
py as they were, and even the sentiment, and he knew
he'd have become mute in any case.

So here it was. And it caught him off guard.

"Forgive me for calling out of the blue, but I—well,
I wanted to talk to you."

She was in trouble, he knew instantly.

"Sure, talk to me," he said, his stomach playing
tricks.

"Not on the phone. I have some news I want to tell
you face-to-face. Can you meet me at our place?"

News? Had it somehow to do with him? "Ruth, I'm
still half asleep. Does it have to be now?" He'd tried not
to sound as irritable as he felt—who but a telemarket-
er would dare call at this hour?—but then remembered
that insistence of hers, how entitled she could be.

"Please," she said.

He got up and reached for his jeans, thrown over a
bedside chair. "Silver Spurs in half an hour, then?" It
was the coffee shop where they used to meet for breakfast before she moved in with him.

"Bless you."

→

Ruth looked well in the dim light of Silver Spurs. Hair
pitch-black, cropped in the same spikey bob. Still slen-
der, still buxom. Gray eyes that took in everything.
Dressed even at this early hour in a stylish pantsuit—
deep gray, though, not the cardinal red or Kelly green
she used to consider her look. Over her shoulders, a
black trench coat he didn't recognize. The red beret she

always wore, which this morning didn't look jaunty but comically large, perched atop a woman more waifish, ethereal, than he remembered—more fragile than the fiery design consultant who had shared his life.

He flashed back to the dozens of times they had met in this booth, their booth, and the pleasure it had given them. For an instant it didn't matter why she had left him, or that she had left him; he felt a sudden regret in his bones. He had expected to see a ghost, a stranger for whom he'd lost all feeling, but here she was, Ruthie, whom he had loved.

"Evan," she whispered. He leaned down and she offered her cheek, turning her head so their lips would not touch. He sat across from her, slightly hurt, stung yet again by this woman he hadn't thought about in a year, and tongue-tied from the surprisingly moving memories.

"I'll have the pancakes," she told the waitress who had materialized by the table. "And black coffee."

"Coffee for me, too," Evan ordered. "And an English muffin."

"*Plus ça change*," Ruth said, extending her hand to take his. She looked at him intently, searching for what, he wondered. Was she moved to see him?

"Are you all right?" he managed. "Claire says you've been ill." He dreaded the answer.

"Ill. Yes," she said vaguely. She pulled an iPhone from her purse and placed it by her silverware. Evan fidgeted, reminded of her reflexive need for constant connection with the outside world. Even now, when they were talking one-on-one, even when she had blithely summoned him here out of the blue. He swallowed his annoyance, knowing the phone might be medically necessary.

"Trouble is I'm not precisely sure yet how ill. It's a rare form of hepatitis—neither viral nor contagious—that's why I'm in San Francisco. The doctor here is supposed to be the only one who knows what to do."

A rare form of hepatitis. "It's serious, then."

She smiled wanly. "Yes. Oh, not serious serious, I suppose."

When he met her eyes, he saw she was lying, but he quashed his impulse to get up and take her in his arms to comfort her. For the first time since he walked into Silver Spurs, he thought of Eve but couldn't make sense of his feelings. Was it guilt? Was it Eve he was betraying or Ruth?

"Tell me how I can help," he said. A voice inside him warned him not to get involved. A picture of Eve popped into his head, but it was too distracting so he willed it away. "Tell me," he repeated gently.

She dabbed at her mouth with her napkin, and he could barely make out her response. "Nothing specific. I'm in trouble, and I wanted you to know. Unfair of me, at this point. You loved me once, and I thought you might care."

"Of course I care. For God's sake, Ruthie, we shared…"

She smiled, brightly this time. "Say no more. I have my answer."

Not for the first time he felt like her vassal. "I'll do whatever I can for you."

She lowered her head, humble in victory. "Dr. Wade wants to do more tests to see if I'm a good candidate for clinical trials, and he's booked solid. The one time he has free is on Christmas Eve day, and he's agreed, miraculously, to see me then." Tears shone in her eyes, making them look like gray pearls. She'd rarely cried when they were together, and the tears produced a rush of sympathy.

"It's scary," she said. "His urgency. He doesn't want to put off the tests till after Christmas, which for doctors is after New Year's, I guess. Nice of him, no? Giving up his Christmas Eve like that? Maybe he doesn't celebrate Christmas. In any case, I'll be going back to Connecticut for three weeks, then coming here again."

Her fear, she who was never afraid, moved him.

"I just wondered what you'd be doing over Christmas," Ruth said, looking into her coffee mug and again at her iPhone.

"I'll be in Vermont," he said. "Way up in the northeast part of the state, near Canada." He'd determined before he came not to mention Eve. "Ever been there?"

"Jesus, no! I mean, not that I don't like cold weather, but I try to go south, not north."

Ruth always answered questions this way, abruptly, then softened them with a second less curt reply, only to find that the second one was inadequate and that a third, sweetly controlled, would be necessary.

"I mean, I'm sure wherever you're going will be nice." She cut a wedge off her pancakes. "I was hoping for some moral support."

She's going to die. The thought hit him so hard he could feel his legs tremble. There must be someone who can be with her.

Ruth the soldier, the warrior. He could taste her despair.

She was asking him to be with her for the operation. For Christmas. He would have to be strong now, in self-defense, even if he was too much of a coward to rub in how excited he was about being with someone else for Christmas. This was out of the question.

He had plans that were sacrosanct and had told her as much. No more games.

She had dropped eye contact and was sitting, her head down, hands in her lap, pitiable.

"Ruth, tell me straight-out. Do you need anything from the apartment? I have the feeling I'm missing something."

"The apartment? No, not a thing. I took everything I needed when I left." She took a last sip from her coffee cup, picked up her phone, and stood. "It was so good to see you, Evan."

Meeting over. He put twenty dollars on the table and helped her with her coat.

"You'll be all right?"

"Yes, of course." A fixed smile on a face drained of color under a red beret.

They walked toward the street.

"Good luck with those tests," he said. He wanted to hug her, tell her he did still love her but had moved on. "Tell me, why couldn't we have done this over the phone?"

"Because I wanted to see you. There was something I needed to find out."

"And did you?"

"Oh yes. It's made me happy."

He didn't ask what. Together they left Silver Spurs. He turned left and she, right. He checked his impulse to tell her it would be all right. She waved. But he, miserable, walked on.

16.

RUTH TRIED TO WALK A STRAIGHT LINE DOWN THE STREET, head held high, attempting a gait that would feel as brisk and strong as she remembered having at age thirty. She imagined herself then, in high heels, racing across Market Street to meet a client, aware of being assessed by others, and purposefully exuding confidence, energy, style, good cheer. She never let up her goal of being someone who conveyed, even from a distance—buying a newspaper at the corner or popping into a Starbucks—a person of note, a designer of splendor. She'd find her clients waiting outside the door of her office building. She'd shake hands and meet their eyes with confidence, assuming they were reassured by her firm sense of herself. This, she wanted them to understand, was the right person for the job. She knew it all began at that moment, at the first handshake.

She reached the corner, safe now to turn, certain that Evan could no longer see her. She felt a familiar whoosh of energy leave her body so quickly she could barely stand. It was as though a curtain came down, and her only chance of not falling, crumbling to the ground, really, was to find a corner of a building to lean on that second. When she felt safe, she reached in her bag for her pills and swallowed them quickly.

It was not lost on Ruth that today her disequilibrium had an emotional component. Couldn't every physical symptom, even her most bizarre ones, be exacerbated by what she was feeling? She'd walked into Silver Spurs with that peculiar confidence owned by the person she once was, the person in the couple who had initiated the breakup. She'd always fantasized that she, who stomped out and delivered the gut punch, could sashay back in again. Evan, she felt, was not a guy to jump into a new relationship quickly—he had dragged his feet with her, God knows, and she'd believed that now, a year later, he'd be a bit lost, a bit tentative and a bit available if she played her cards right. This was still who she was, she reflected sadly, a woman with so much pride she was deluded.

This was not the Evan she expected to see. Not the Evan she knew. This was an Evan with a plan, a goal, a bristling energy unfamiliar to her. It was as if they'd traded personalities. He was going to Vermont for Christmas, so her idea—of being together again—was shot. It was not just the mere disquieting awareness that there was no going back. He had moved on. Loving and caring as he seemed, he displayed not a hint of regret. No, her Evan was gone. She grabbed her bottle of water and took a big swig. What had she been thinking? That he was there for the taking, this lovely man she walked out on so brutally?

Ruth knew that Evan's heart was somewhere in Vermont.

17.

Evan's flight came in at three in the afternoon. Eve always found the trip to Burlington Airport soothing. Despite the trucks on the highway and a dearth of the foliage that lured tourists to Vermont, this hour-and-a-half stretch to the westernmost part of the state was just monotonous enough to let her mull over things she didn't usually have time for.

Like the sugaring business. The steely clouds that now loomed overhead had the distinct look of those that announced other freakish ice storms. One had ravaged New England while her grandparents were still alive and had left pretty much everyone they knew without power. Worse, it had destroyed countless sugar maples, stripping their trees of branches, uprooting them, reducing the nation's syrup production by close to 20 percent. It luckily had only grazed the farm, but still there was damage, and syrup prices soared. Her candies were unaffordable. Another price hike would make her syrup too expensive for a family's morning pancakes.

Why had she gone into this chancy business, one so dependent on precise timing and outguessing the weather? The need for that nightly freeze and warmer-than-freezing days for good tapping was harrowing in itself. Sure, her grandparents' sugarhouse and the delicious smell that permeated their whole farm had been a glorious memory, and she had loved to watch her grandfather drill the tapping holes. She'd help him pound in the taps, then later watch the sugar boiling. She'd been riveted by his stories of the early Abenaki's discovery of the sweet sap. She loved to hear how, before 1700, when sugar was rare and expensive, they and other Native Americans in the region would gather sap in bark pails, store it in moose-hide tanks, then hollow out logs, drop red-hot stones into them, and boil the sap into syrup.

But now, with acid rain affecting growth, and insects—aphids, parathrips, and horrible new ones like the Asian longhorned beetle—periodically decimating maple buds, Eve felt her sugaring experience was worlds away from her grandparents'. Her grandfather, after all, had used a team of horses to collect the buckets and transport them to the sugarhouse. Now, Eve ran flexible polyethylene tubing from tree to tree, the syrup fed by gravity into big galvanized tubs. And climate change was impacting Vermont terribly: the sapping season, compared to forty years ago, had grown shorter by at least a week, increasingly limiting the precious opportunity to harvest sap.

Sugaring was as exacting and ephemeral as ballet had been! Maybe she had a need to excel in a business that staked heavy odds against her success. Or maybe she wanted to be like her grandmother. Why didn't she opt for something foolproof and worthy to go into when Laddie died—teaching dance or yoga to underprivileged kids, say?

She'd come close to getting certified as a yoga teacher when she first decided to use her dance studio to hold a weekly class for her staff, because she couldn't offer them health insurance. So, two hours a week in her beautiful studio, with its mirrored walls and finely oiled barre and layers of sleek wood floors—crisscrossed and covered with linoleum so it duplicated the resilient stage floor Balanchine conceived for the old State Theater—was her gift to them. And by hiring Kitty to be the yoga teacher instead of teaching it herself, she got to relax and stretch for those two hours.

To feel this much for a man was a sweet surprise. But with every mile her qualms mounted. "The question is," she wondered aloud to her steering wheel as she pulled into the airport parking lot, "what kind of fool drives an hour and a half to pick up a man she just met—even if she'd gone mad for him? What woman hasn't learned at my age what it costs in effort and emotion to spend an entire weekend with someone— anyone, even a lover one knows well?"

She had an out. If she took one look at him and the magic was gone, she'd simply bring him home and set him to work in the sugarhouse. She could put him out there in the newly painted shed with the fire going full blast—let him stoke the wood every five minutes to keep the sap aboil and smell how wonderful Northeast Kingdom winter is. All the others would be out there working, so he'd simply be an additional hand.

She'd offer him the guest room. Not as a pretense— they both knew what the true sleeping arrangements would be—but for his privacy. It would be his room, a place where he could vanish and read, or edit, or be alone. Didn't he say he liked a lot of downtime? And didn't she?

Walking to the arrival gate, Eve's legs felt leaden, as if she were heading not toward pleasure but to an unnamed doom—like the nightmares she used to have of being onstage and dancing a part she'd never learned. She considered getting a drink. No stage fright had ever left her trembling like this.

She spied Evan walking down the gate in the gray overcoat he'd worn at Thanksgiving, his manila envelope tucked under his arm as if it were stapled there. Seeing his smile—and those hiking boots—her whole body relaxed and her heart revved. She remembered why she'd come.

This was no ordinary attraction. She had changed, deeply, like it or not.

She ran toward him, all hesitation gone, and he threw his things down to swoop her up. Only then did she feel something deep in her chest unlock. When he held her face in his hands and kissed her and she kissed him back so naturally, so spontaneously, as though they were lovers already, a sensation new and momentous gripped her. It was a kiss so erotically promising, pleasure poured down though her like warm maple syrup over snow. She fought back tears. Sure, she'd please him! And please him and please him. She would do anything he wished.

18.

ONCE BACK HOME, Eve felt the job of becoming a hostess begin to weigh on her. It had been a long time since she'd waited on a man—on anybody. When she heard herself ask, "Want a short tour before dinner?" her tone was formal and strained, as though her home were the Oval Office and Evan a visiting dignitary. Crumpets for you, Mr. Ambassador?

"Sure," Evan said, still carrying his bag in one hand and his manila envelope in the other.

The guest room was on the third floor, next to her dance studio. "I don't use the studio as much as I thought I would when I built it, but I love it," she said, stroking the shiny wooden barre as though it were a kitten. "I do hold our yoga classes here. You did, of course, learn yoga since we spoke on the phone—right?"

He nodded dully. She picked up on it and realized that it couldn't have lasted, that ecstasy at the airport that continued for much of the drive home. The ease they had with each other was undeserved, after all; they weren't lovers or even friends, and they had no history, no common references—nothing to say, really, once the excitement of being in each other's presence mellowed.

The guest room was a sedate deep green and featured a single bed with a red-and-green plaid flannel bedspread. He dropped his envelope and suitcase on the bed and turned on the rickety brass candlestick lamp. Four books, their pages yellowed and torn, already lay on the bedside table: *Walden, Silent Spring*, a biography of George Bernard Shaw written in 1931, and a 1947 dog-eared manual called *Successful Marriage*. Either the same books had lain there unnoticed for years, he decided, or Eve had placed them there specifically for him—figuring, no doubt, that this guest would be most comfortable among books at least half a century old. Successful Marriage? He decided the title held no hidden meaning.

Does she mean for me to sleep here? Evan shuddered. *To dart in and out of her bed and then return to...camp?* He felt weary. *Did I get this all wrong, somehow?*

Evan saw her grin as he thumbed through the marriage manual.

"Here's a section title for you," he said. "Persons Not Prepared to Fall in Love."

"Oooh, tell me."

Evan skimmed the page. "Seems to be a discussion about the immature person who can't distinguish between infatuation and love, how he's likely to experience his superficial responses as real love. But he is wrong, you may not be surprised to learn."

"I would imagine."

"The immature person is not a good candidate for the profound and permeating type of sharing found in its most fully developed form only in the marriage relationship."

Eve laughed. "Written in 1800?"

"Close. Every living thing that grows is subject to the influence of time, and love is no exception. It grows slowly, in a variety of circumstances...while infatuation may come suddenly." He yawned and patted his fingers over his mouth dramatically.

She took the book from him, placed it down on the bed, then took his hand and led him from room to room, arriving finally in her bedroom. It was a bright room, with three large windows, an unused fireplace rimmed in colorful mismatched tiles, two chairs and a sofa in wild colors and patterns—altogether a cheerful décor serving as dramatic evidence of the changing epochs of her life. One white wooden bookshelf held what appeared to be hundreds of old dolls—mostly little dancing girls with pale pink legs and long hair. Another held boxes of worn-out pink toe shoes and black ballet slippers, their ribbons frayed and falling over each other, and in the box beside it: colorful ballet costumes—scarves and tutus and magic wands and tiaras. Books on dance filled an entire wall of shelves—biographies of Balanchine, Makarova, Pavlova, Farrell, and Golyakovsky himself, as well as picture books of the New York City Ballet, the American Ballet Theater, the old Kirov, the Bolshoi, the Ballets Russes. This section of the room was all pastels—the palest colors, the frailest fabrics, everything faded and fragile, like cherished old sepia photographs.

Next to that bookshelf was another, jammed with books about the trees of New England: the blue spruce of Maine, the firs and evergreens of New Hampshire, the sugar maples of Vermont. A dog-eared *Birds of North America*. Antique tins lined the shelves above her bedside tables; a few patchwork quilts; old five-gallon transfer tanks; stainless steel drums and syrup cans; diaries and notebooks; piles of a tabloid newspaper called *Farming: The Journal of Northeast Agriculture*.

A gilded cabinet held his eye. "I learned about American furniture for one of my anthologies," he said, touching the ears of the rococo lions leaning out like flying buttresses from the corners of the cabinet, their gilded mouths formed in a roar. "But I never saw anything like this."

Eve, hands on hips, seemed to be contemplating it for the first time. "A present from Laddie. Our tenth anniversary. It once belonged to Diaghilev," she said. "Kind of wild, don't you think?"

Inside the cabinet were twenty or so glass, porcelain, marble and ormolu objects probably valuable, probably also Russian, mostly anniversary presents from Laddie, Eve explained. A few gifts from Balanchine, a few from Lincoln Kirstein, a thin gold necklace from Osipova, her favorite dancer of all time. These were the gifts she had mentioned during their first dinner together: a soldier, a sugar plum, a match girl, figurines Evan could not identify but obviously characters in The Nutcracker. In a place of honor was a miniature canopied bed, and next to it a ballerina no more than six inches high—loving tributes, Evan realized in a wash of dismay, to the exquisite grown woman who was Laddie's bride. To witness this shrine to their marriage in Eve's rustic bedroom was like coming upon a pillow book in an otherwise antiseptic Japanese model home.

He began to imagine what they did after the presents were opened.

"Marvelous," Evan lied.

He wondered how he would be able to make love in this room. Would the contents of the gilded cabinet explode in fury? Would the nutcrackers start marching in revolt? Would the ghosts of Balanchine, Diaghilev, Danilova, Makarova, Golyakovsky hover like the Russian army over their heads and over her heart? The Kirov Conspiracy would be a good name for a juicy Cold War spy book, he mused. If there were still a Cold War.

Ah, but the real bed in the center of the room was not something out of the Kirov. Where everything else was a hodgepodge of clutter, it was wide—enormous, actually—with a gleaming, curled antique brass headboard tarnished to a rich red-brown gold. The top of the mattress arched upward at its middle, as if hundreds of pillows were buried underneath. The layers of white sheets, pillows, blankets, throws, and duvets looked like a snowy mountain valley Eve might ski on.

"Why three comforters?" Evan asked.

"In Vienna, at least when I danced there many years ago, they had the most amazing eiderdowns, lighter than any quilt or pillow I've ever felt before or since. See? Feel it. Light as air.

"I had one made for my grandmother, but she refused to sleep with anything but heavy woolen blankets," Eve explained." The other was for the guest room."

Evan continued reading: "Today in American society, five stages in the relationship of the sexes finally culminate in marriage. If any stage is omitted or slighted, the chances for a happy marriage may be correspondingly decreased."

"Oh dear."

"The five stages are Dating, Keeping Company, Going Steady, Private Understanding, and Engagement."

"Where are we?"

"Pre-stage one, I think. Recklessly infatuated and with no chance of gaining the maturity needed to move beyond superficiality, idealization, sex, and self-centeredness." He glanced at her. This was where they were.

"Excellent," she said. "Onward."

19.

EVE'S HOUSE WAS SCENTED WITH BLUE SPRUCE, HOT SPICED CIDER, MULLED WINE. Fresh eggnog whipped with maple syrup, sugar cookies made with fresh-cut vanilla beans and maple sugar sprinkles abounded on the kitchen counter. Gifts for neighbors and friends, outbursts of red and green wrappings lay under the enormous tree Eve had picked up earlier in the week at a Glover tree farm. Festooned with her collection of antique Victorian ornaments—stars and angels and Santas and Gabriel's horns and tinsel— the newly cut spruce was unearthly in its silvery grandeur.

Evan's impatience for the shimmering evening to come to an end so they could go to bed was soothed by this atmosphere. Sleigh bells rang in the distance. Snow fell lightly, solemnly, on the old farmhouse, maple syrup boiled on the stove, ready to be poured on the newly fallen snow, a trick Eve promised would make the most delicious maple taffy he'd ever eaten.

"I've never had taffy, so it will be the best I've ever eaten," he said, impetuously hugging this woman whose skin, warm from the kitchen, smelled like a spice cookie. At that very moment—impossibly, Evan thought—the sound of "The Little Drummer Boy" wafted through the living room windows. Shall I play for you? Barumpapumpummmmm...

It was too perfect.

"Oh, good!" Eve said, disentangling herself from Evan's embrace. "The Younts are early!" She waved to Diana and John, then Natalie and Christopher Rachelson, Linda and Rob Gordon. Ryan, Sarah, and Eileen O'Toole. "It's good when they're early," she said. "It means they'll sing here longer."

"Where can it go from here?" Evan asked. "Will tiny tots appear at the hearth and put out cookies and milk for Santa? Are Donner and Blitzen out back? Will Santa fill our stockings in front of us?"

"The stockings!"

He followed her into the pantry off the kitchen, where Eve began rummaging through a stack of boxes. "Where are they?" she asked, suddenly serious. "They happen to be gorgeous. Needlepointed by my grandmother—the first one when I was six, and then another one for Laddie, which I buried with him because he loved it so. And then another one, the biggest of all, that she made for me just before she died."

"Sort of a hint? Like, time for you to start thinking about finding another man?" Evan knew that such an idea would irritate Eve to no end.

"Yeah, right, and needless to say, it's never been touched. I threw it in some box or another, and now that there's a flesh-and-blood guy in my house to fill it for, I can't find it. We have to have them."

For some reason, this thrilled him. He began rummaging with her.

Eve pointed to a box behind a rusted-out, unused freezer and said, "Try there. That's Christmas stuff, too."

Evan cut open the taped top of the box and, looking inside what seemed to be endless fluffs of crumpled pale blue tissue, declared it otherwise empty.

"Look again," Eve said.

Evan reached down to the bottom, over in the far corner, felt a hard object with round sides, and brought it up. It was wrapped in pale blue velvet cloth with a thick navy-blue satin ribbon. A tag hung from a gilded pinecone. Gold ink declared: "For E from E, with love."

Clasping it to his chest, he said, "For me?"

"No, another."

"Oh, Eve, you—"

"I know, I shouldn't have. Now open it before you start thinking there's something valuable in there and get all excited."

"Can we at least sit down? I'll spike that eggnog. I bought some fine stuff."

He made his way to his suitcase and brought out one bottle each of bourbon and cognac.

She eyed him warily. "Are you going to do to me what you did in New York?"

"Hope to."

Inside the blue paper was an old-fashioned VHS tape. Evan stared at it. Finally he looked up. "I know what it is! It's you. Am I right? Is it you?"

"Yup. Age eleven, in *The Nutcracker.*"

"Let's play it now."

"After dinner."

"No, now," Evan said. "I'll make drinks. You set up."

Evan whipped up the eggnog with cognac and bourbon and handed Eve her drink. "Yum," she said, and shut the lights.

The scene was Christmas morning. The little girl with red curls bouncing to her waist was sitting up in her bed, dressed in pale pink tights and a high-buttoned nightshirt. She had exquisite skin, delicate arms, strong legs. She yawned, stretched, and then leapt off the bed and down the stairs, strawberry hair flying, to find her gifts under the tree: the toy soldier, the match girl, the nutcracker. Her movements—bold, light, elegant—and her mood wrapped the viewer into her excitement, as if this and only this young girl could express the essence of childhood at Christmas, its longing and fulfillment. Other children were dancing with her, but it was impossible not to focus on this gifted ballerina, the one who could fly.

A shining gold tiara held her ringlets off her face. The lights went down and she bourréed up the stage and joyfully pirouetted around the tree. The screen went blank.

"You were...brilliant," he said. "A heart-stopping little angel."

"That's what got me into the Boston corps," Eve said matter-of-factly, taking a sip of eggnog. Her eyes, he noticed, were the color of the bourbon. "And noticed by Golyakovsky."

"And to stardom."

"Sort of. At least not a moment of free time till I quit."

He was moved, and groped for words. "I'm honored. Thank you."

"I wasn't sure..."

Evan got up and, erasing her doubt, lifted Eve out of her chair and hugged her. "Wait here."

He went to the guest room, then came down the stairs solemnly, like a child bearing a handmade card for his mom. He was afraid she might not understand his present—or worse, hate it. He'd thought about a traditional house gift—scented candles or flowers—or, at one point, a silk scarf but decided on something from

Anne's Antiquities, a shop owned by his friend on the wharf.

Should've gotten the scarf. Too late now.

Eve opened the note. It said, "For Eve, who did it all herself. With admiration and love, Evan."

Inside the box was an ivory mortgage button. Eve had told Evan when they met that it was the custom for families to put this emblem of their just-paid-off mortgage inside the newel post of their stair's banister. It was a badge of success and pride. She'd added that there had never been one in her grandparents' house.

"How did you know?" Eve's voice cracked.

"That you paid off your mortgage? You told me at great length, remember? When you were drunk?"

"You could get arrested for buying ivory."

He smiled. "Not if it's over one hundred years old and imported prior to nineteen eighty-two."

"Smarty pants."

As Evan watched Eve roll his gift over in her hand, she tilted her head as she had as a tiny dancer, when she'd held the nutcracker. She put it inside the newel post at the bottom of the stairs and then said, with a deep curtsy, "No one else but you understood."

Evan felt he was witnessing in her face and her curtsy the eleven-year-old dance prodigy, the thirty-five-year-old farmer, the seventy-year-old beauty Eve would one day become.

He took her hand and escorted her, minuet style, up the stairs. Courtly or no, Evan could wait no longer.

20.

"How's a man supposed to undress his lover in this minefield of down?" Evan asked, gently reaching for the top button of Eve's cardigan.

"He doesn't do it alone," Eve whispered, pulling him into the center of the bed beside her. "She helps."

In moments, her clothes lay in bunches on the floor like discarded Christmas wrapping. She sat up, facing him. Evan said nothing as he looked at her adoringly. He removed his own clothes slowly, methodically, from top to bottom—shirt first, socks last—folding each garment at the foot of the bed.

"I thought so," Eve said.

"What?" He was putting his reading glasses in their case.

"A neat freak. Scary."

Evan bent over and started to kiss her throat, moving slowly down her body, as if to feel the skin on his lips and tongue, to savor the scent of her. He kept moving downward, cradling the small of her back with one hand and holding himself up with the other, murmuring about her beautiful skin, her wonderful smell.

He moved back up, kissing her lightly along the side her of her neck. Once Evan's clothes were off, he became different, so loving and sure, that she slowly let her catalogue of worries, mostly about herself after all this time of abstinence, boil away like syrup into sugar. How did he make her so comfortable so quickly?

Evan slipped effortlessly into his element like a lumbering, land-bound seal slipping into the sea water he craved. He'd always found lovemaking easy and natural; Ruth, he recalled, had long been puzzled by his ability to express himself so fluently in bed—but not, she pointed out endlessly, outside it. It seemed vaguely annoying to her, his sexual assurance, as if it foiled the picture she wanted to have of him, the decision about his ability to be intimate.

Eve brought him back: "I'm so hungry for you." He began moving gentle kisses down her breasts, to her waist, and below, once more. She appeared to tighten then, and Evan seemed to intuit that she felt they must hurry or she'd be left stranded, without satisfaction. So he tried to slow her, promising her with his sure, easy tempo that there was no rush. And that she would most definitely be satisfied.

Eve relaxed. She began to feel delicious currents flashing throughout her body, streams of warming waters flowing into her chest first, then her belly, her loins, right down to her feet—a river with currents growing ever stronger until she was rocked in its rapids, and she held his shoulders with both hands, pushing him now to arm's length as the river claimed her whole body and flooded her mind and soul with pure sensation. Evan was speaking to her in a language of pleasure that had no use for words. His own language, she thought.

He had his hands under her now, and as he kissed the inside of her legs, she said something, but it came out as a guttural moan. Finally she managed words, crying out, "Oh, Evan." He slowly pulled away. "No, no, don't stop," she said. "I've never been here before."

Eve felt a pleasure far beyond dancing, beyond this world, even, pulsating through her until she was helpless to stem the tide spiraling through her. She felt boundless, the oceanic joy coalescing into one ecstatic, unendurable moment that went on till she seemed to leap beyond the boundaries of consciousness. Only then did her breathing soften. She could not speak.

Evan held her close.

"Evan I—you didn't get to—I'm sorry."

"I got to just fine," Evan said, shushing her, tucking a damp strand of her hair behind her ear. "Don't you worry."

Eve said nothing. There was time, she knew; she only hoped she was up to delivering the same ecstasy. "This is unbelievable," she whispered. "Lovemaking was never like this. I mean, sex was just not—"

"How do you know this is good?" Evan asked. That look again. The innocent, with the merest hint of meanness. "We haven't even made love yet."

Eve laughed. But she was also crying, so it came out as a sort of snort. "So, when?"

"After my snack," he said, rolling her on top of him to kiss her throat again.

Eve looked at his eyes, his kind, full lips. "I like your skin," she said, tracing his forehead, his cheeks with her fingertips.

"You do?" He reached his face up toward her hands for more.

"It's so...I don't know. Craggy." She smiled. "And your legs. I like them, too. Those big calves."

"You like worn-down and beaten-up, eh?"

"If you put on that robe there and then go downstairs and find us a wonderful snack, I promise when you come back I'll reveal the secret of cleaning goose down," she whispered.

"Can't wait."

He took his glasses out of their case, put them on.

"There's turkey in the little drawer in the fridge down on the left, and mayo on the door."

She decided that tomorrow she would take him to her favorite spot in town, the former parking area at the foot of Burke Mountain, where the kids' rope tow used to be. There, at the entrance to the bowl for beginner skiers, was where she went when she needed to be alone. She'd share her private spot with him.

As she waited to see what Evan would unearth from her refrigerator, Eve's thoughts were in the future. *He leaves in three days.*

He came back with a sandwich cut in half and a bowl of ice cream. "Eve," he said—he had not spoken her name before, and she liked the touch of drama, and even discomfort, in the way he said it so earnestly. She thought about all the years she'd spent craving this easy connection, cozy intimacy, and unselfconscious desire they shared. She wondered if it meant as much to him. Had he, too, yearned for closeness but not had it? Or was intimacy always available to him? Probably it was. He had a magical ease about him. But for her it—he—was a miracle. And suddenly something came out of her mouth that she regretted as she said it. "So, this girlfriend of yours..."

"Former girlfriend," he shot back.

"She's sick?"

"So I hear." He took the last bite of his sandwich.

"Where is she again?"

"Well, at this very moment...Oh Eve, don't go there. Please, darling. It's over." He sounded weary, whether because of the abrupt change in mood or a familiarity with possessiveness she wasn't sure. He slid into bed beside her and stroked her hair.

She tried to make light of the surprising flood of jealousy that had seized her. She removed some mayonnaise from his lower lip with a napkin. Then she began to stroke his chest. "So. Will you still love me tomorrow?"

"C'mere," he said.

Eve was still ruminating about the girlfriend and the number of hours she had left with Evan. She looked up to find him taking off his robe. It was an old terry cloth robe the color of faded rose, clearly washed a hundred times, probably bought for him by the girlfriend for some long-ago Christmas. It was, she thought, a what-shall-I-give-him present from a humorless person with no taste who didn't know her man. He probably wore it, dutifully, around the same humorless, tasteless woman, when it was thick and stiff and still a deep burgundy. And only years later, when it emerged from a thousand washings, and he lived alone again, and the woman was as remote a memory as the cloth's original color did he actually grow to like it.

Eve looked at his legs, his shoulders, his back. She knew every kind of male body from her ballet days, but Evan's was rounded, not sinewy and elongated as dancers' usually were. He'd acquired this muscular body not by stretching, not with weights and reps at the gym but outdoors, and not by working at it but working—carrying backpacks, hustling under car engines, hiking up and down mountains. An athlete's body, "beaten up," he'd said. She adored it. Most men with husky, compact builds like Evan's looked and felt impenetrable, as if their muscles were armor. Those bodies scared her, as if their emotions were as dense as their sinew. Though Evan's powerful legs were defined, they were not hard to the touch. She was enthralled.

Now that is what all the fuss is about! Eve smiled in anticipation of the next hour or so. Whoever told women that infamous lie "Size doesn't matter" must have been a man.

She looked away. He seemed to see her do so, and gave her a look that said, Are we to eat sandwiches all night?

She opened her arms.

"You are the most beautiful woman in America." He was hungry for her, and she knew it—she felt an undercurrent of roughness, of impatience, that he tried to control—and she herself was so ready for him that she felt agitated by the desire exploding in her. She pulled back slightly, trying to control herself, to manage her own urges and his, but he wouldn't let her.

"C'mere," he said again hoarsely, as if to say, Yes, I might be teasing you with my tongue, but I'm not playing games.

She was thrilled; she wouldn't have to sacrifice a moment's pleasure. She could feel his body become taut, ready, poised—just waiting for her go-ahead sign. "Only in America?" she asked. "Not in the whole world?"

She let go of fear. She let go of the girlfriend, too, and the fact that he was leaving, and the possibility that she might not reach orgasm at the proper moment. She let go. Her release was as much spiritual as physical. *Yes, come in*, it said. *Come in and we'll move heaven and earth.* And just then, as they choreographed a dance she'd never mastered, she felt him arrive so deep within her she could only cry out with pleasure at their accomplishment, marveling at the newness of it all.

"Let's go," he said.

"Let's go," she moaned.

Eve felt infused with an immense gratitude, a global sensation of thanks. The pleasures and successes to which she had until now given her life seemed to pale next to this feeling. She understood at last the price, not just the pride, of artistic sublimation—why she'd for so long felt a nagging loss in her heart, in her bones, in her skin. It was not just a hunger for another kind of love; it was a need to feel part of the world, of the universe, even. It was a need for this.

"What was that?" he managed to ask her, teasing but also serious, when their breathing had returned to normal.

She took a moment to find the right words. "That was us."

21.

"So far, yoga is just as ridiculous as I thought it would be," Evan grumbled to himself. Plunked down on a rubber mat in some New Age universe inhabited by too many females—just as he'd imagined. He didn't want any healing white light pouring in through the top of his head. He didn't want to twist himself into weird poses. He'd already found bliss.

Eve dimmed the lights. She walked over to Evan, whom she'd tucked in a corner in the back, he figured, so no one could observe him.

"Warm enough?"

"Yeah."

"Sit on this. It'll be easier." She tucked a block under his sitz bones. "Breathe that lovely Vermont air deep into your belly," she said softly, laying her cool hand on his stomach to indicate where to focus his breath. She seemed entranced.

He got weak remembering how insanely intimate they'd been hours earlier. He opened his eyes long enough to look directly, coolly into hers in an unflinching gaze that said, *Go lower.*

She seemed to want to and gently squeezed the flesh above his hip to let him know this, then returned his gaze and whispered, "You are to focus on nothing else but that slow, deep breath coming in and going out of your abdomen."

"Of course." He restrained himself from grabbing her. She placed her hand an inch lower to make sure he was doing as she said. He wasn't. Again, in his ear: "Even a frog needs more oxygen than you're getting. Now breathe into my hand."

He gulped some air.

"Through your nose. Take in the air way back in through the nostrils so it makes a sound like the ocean—it's called an Ujjayi breath—and let your belly fill up slowly. Puff out your belly as the air goes in." She was standing over him. She poked his navel.

He inflated his belly with air. But another part of him, below his pelvis, also rose.

He fixed her with an accusing look. *See what you've done?*

Just as she was about to draw her hand away, he grabbed it and pulled her down hoping for a quick, subversive kiss before the torture of the class began. But he pulled too hard: She lost her balance, tripped over one side of his stomach, and fell on top of him, both her knees crashing into his diaphragm.

"Oh fuh—" he yelped, and then stopped short, gasping unsuccessfully for air.

Eve scrambled to her feet and bent down again to tend to him till he coughed and inhaled a jagged breath. The whole class was staring.

"Is he okay?" Lu asked. "Can he breathe?"

"Are you okay?" Eve asked moments later when Evan was breathing evenly again.

He gave her a grim look. *What fun yoga is!*

"I'm fine now," he assured everyone.

"Want to go downstairs?" she whispered. "You don't have to stay, you know."

"No, no, I'm fine." The grim look again. "Wouldn't want to miss a minute of this!"

When all was calm again, Kitty saluted the class with a "Namaste, everyone," her hands held together in front of her chest like a church steeple. "We have a guest, as you no doubt have gathered. He's new to yoga."

Everyone laughed. And then applauded.

"Namaste," Kitty said, bowing to Evan. "We sometimes trick people before taking them to Nirvana. Now, class, any new injuries I should know about? Besides our guest's?"

"My hamstrings..." Luann.

"New injuries," Kitty said sweetly.

Silence.

"Evan, anything I should know about your body?"

Evan could see the skin on Eve's neck redden. He shook his head.

"No operations? No back or hip problems?"

Nope.

Evan, still looking at Eve, ostensibly to imitate her alignment, observed only her hair tied loosely at the place where her long neck curved into her shoulders. He imagined her sitting just like that, cross-legged—but naked and facing him. He wanted that. Tantric sex with Eve. He wished Annie, Bea, Luann, Ned, and Kitty would go away and this ridiculous class, with its phony-baloney calm and its pretentious Sanskrit names, would end.

They were instructed to get on all fours for Cat and Dog poses.

But Evan wasn't watching the instructor. He was watching Eve, admiring his lover's perfectly shaped derriere, mesmerized by the rhythm of it going up and down, up and down.

He thought of James Joyce's erotic love letters, the ones kept under lock and key in the author's grandson's archives. The one he'd seen was sexy as all get out, and vulgar, too—unsettlingly so. Joyce, he thought, understood everything about us, our raunchy as well as our saintly instincts.

Nothing remained of the sunset they were celebrating but a hazy red glow, the color of dimming coals in a dwindling midnight fire, poured in through the studio's dormer windows. The wind whined. Clouds were swelling, moving around, and clustering together, assuming odd shapes. Evan was in a sexual reverie, and Eve was dreamily watching the clouds take the shape of dolphins.

The evening became still, almost warm. This could have been Maryland, even Georgia. After a long resting pose, the class quietly left. It was part of the drill that socializing be kept to a minimum afterward. Eve, looking at the one guest who remained, sat beside him.

"I can't believe what I did to you."

"Me either."

"You'll never want to do yoga again."

The look said, Right.

"Did you enjoy it at all?"

"Your knees digging into my gallbladder or watching your behind?"

"Oh, Evan."

He pulled the clip out of her hair. "Get naked," he said.

She considered this un-yoga-like command while observing the spot on his stomach she'd been focused on earlier, the silky swirls of hair moving downward.

She complied and he joined her.

22.

THEY SPENT CHRISTMAS MORNING INDOORS, in contented togetherness. Loneliness, tight little knots that
had long lodged in each of them unawares, had begun
to loosen. When they reluctantly agreed that they had
to get out of bed sometime, Eve made breakfast and
showed Evan the grounds—her grandmother's favorite maple tree out front, hundreds of years old; the rest
of her sugar bush, including the white canoe birches,
bent down as though with too many cares; and a shed
in the middle of the back lawn. He noted idly that the
shed was just the right size to house a Porsche.

They took a hike on the walkway behind her
neighbor's sugar farm. These were the Ryans, famous
throughout the state for having switched from regular
oil to used vegetable oil—UVO, it was called—to run
their operation. Eve wanted to show Evan the beauty
of the sugar maples in the area. They would take a two-
mile-long route behind the Ryans' at the foot of the
Green Mountains.

They walked side by side, not speaking or holding
hands but comfortable in the silence. Occasionally
they both stopped while one of them looked around
or touched a plant or tree, or together looked at the
clouds now forming a mackerel sky—a sure sign of an

impending rainstorm. Eve felt renewed faith in their ease with each other, their harmony. "It takes the Ryans seven-tenths of a gallon of vegetable oil to produce a gallon of syrup," she said, noticing that Evan had moved ahead a few yards and was leaning down over a squirrel plant to stroke its feathery leaves. He seemed to be trying to figure out what they were. She didn't tell him, and she didn't resume her lecture on the Ryans' business, either, remembering the glazed look in his eyes when she droned on about the coverlets. Soon he got up, and they resumed their desultory walk, coming together sometimes, touching sometimes, and holding hands now.

She took him to Burke Mountain. It was here, with its view of the calm hill and the changing sky, that she could see into her own heart. "It's where my brain turns off and my heart turns on," she'd told him while they were still in bed. Here she said, "Now it's ours."

In the late morning, they prepared Christmas dinner for Luann and five other friends and neighbors—ham (covered thickly with a mixture of Eve's maple cream, mustard, and ground cloves), yams (stuffed with butter, cinnamon, and Eve's maple sugar), and pumpkin pies (sweetened with Eve's syrup).

"Heaven help you if you don't like the flavor of maple around here," Evan remarked, pouring the thick pumpkin mixture into piecrusts.

"Gives you energy for skiing," she said. "And for lunch at the Inn afterward." All morning she'd begun alluding mischievously to the ski lesson she was to give him. "Hope you're up to it," she said.

"If it means we can get back to bed sooner, I'll learn really fast."

"Swell. Nothing safer than a chunky old guy who can barely snowplow, careening down a hill. Ever been hit by one?"

"Not in this country."

Eve laughed. "Oh you sophisticated Europeans."

The day had grown warm. The front of the mountain, where the bunny slopes were, faced the sun at midday and had turned to corn snow, a sign of spring that now, oddly, came about even in winter. They rented ski boots and poles for him at the little shop at the foot of the mountain. The repair kids in the shop adjusted a pair of Eve's old skis to fit Evan's boots, sharpening them first. "Aren't they too short?" Evan asked, noticing how much longer Eve's new ones were. "Not for a beginner," was her curt reply. Evan wore jeans and two big sweaters over a white cotton turtleneck he'd brought for the occasion, and a blue wool hat that, Eve observed, made his eyes dreamier. They stopped outside the shop.

She looked at the sky. "Dammit."

"What's the matter?"

"It's going to snow."

"That's bad?"

"Real bad," she said, "because it's too warm for snow—remember how balmy it was last night? So it may actually rain."

He smiled. "No problem. I'll be wet anyway from the number of times I fall."

She frowned then squinted. "If it rains and then gets cold tonight—and that's the forecast—there could be trouble."

He caught her concern. This was a different Eve, one he had not yet met. "What kind of trouble?"

"Ice," she said. "But never mind. I refuse to be gloomy on Christmas."

Puzzled, he followed her to the ski area. If it got icy, what was the difference? They'd be off the mountain. Still, she kept looking at the sky, and her usually buoyant step was slow, like an animal checking for hidden prey. Then she shrugged, turned to him, took his hand, and squeezed it. "Here's where we put on our skis. Toe in first, and then step hard into the heel. Here, hang on to me so you don't fall."

"In skiing as in life," he said, and was rewarded with a look that told him her spirits had revived.

Eve had warned him that this was to be a no-nonsense event; if he wanted to learn, he'd have to pay attention and follow her orders exactly. But he didn't want to learn; the only reason for doing so was to please her. So he endured her perfectionism without comment, pretended he didn't mind the snow on his ears and neck when he fell, and valiantly struggled to his feet for more instruction.

"You'll fall if you're scared of falling," she told him. "When I say lean forward, I mean from your ankles, bending your knees like this, not straight-legged, leaning over from your waist." She imitated the faulty position. "If your weight's behind you, as it is if you're like this, your skis will shoot out from under you. And you'll fall on your backside again. Understand?"

"Yeah, boss. I get it." Snow slid from his neck down his back.

"The steeper the slope, the more you push forward over your skis," she continued. "Your impulse will be to stiffen and straighten against speed or to bend forward at the waist."

Hadn't she just told him to lean over? What was the difference between bending and leaning? He experienced a flash of resentment. This wasn't the gentle, pliable Eve of her bedchamber. This was General Patton.

"I'm going to be asking you on this first steep section to throw your upper body down the hill over your skis, to focus on keeping your weight over the balls of your feet, and to keep your poles in front of you like this."

Who could remember all that? Who wanted to? He'd contorted his body in the yoga class, awkward and humiliated, and she'd teased him. Dammit, now she wanted to make him a skier without thinking how he might feel about it. He remembered Ruth, who'd tried to transform him into something he wasn't, and how much he'd hated it. Would it be the same with Eve?

He followed instructions: lean, bend, focus, push—ankles, knees, feet, weight. In five seconds he had toppled like a tree, his mouth and nose awash in snow and ice.

"Oh dear," Eve said.

He got up, red-faced and furious. "Fuck, Eve! You're trying to kill me."

"You'll get it," she assured him. Was she smiling? How dare she!

"Yeah. When hell freezes over. You can give me lessons there."

"Really. It'll come naturally in no time."

He took his pole straps off. "That's enough for today," he said brusquely, thrusting his poles into the snow.

"We'll try again tomorrow. Come on. Your reward is a cup of coffee. There's a snack shop at the base of the chairlift. Follow me."

He began pulling off his skis, a galley slave released from his chains. "No. You go on down. I'll catch up."

"I'll walk with you."

"No," he growled. "Ski."

23.

EVE WORRIED ALL THE WAY DOWN THE HILL. It would take him twenty minutes or so to walk down, and he would be in a horrible mood when he got there. Something had shifted as quickly as the cloud cover over Burke Mountain. The warmth between them had turned as frigid as her socks. Evan would not tell her what was going on with him, and she was not about to spend her time imploring him to. She wondered for the first time whether he was clueless or if he had the capacity to communicate his feelings outside of bed. He had, after all, warned her of his infamous sudden-onset inarticulateness under pressure.

In the cafeteria, Eve chose a little table overlooking the bottom of the slope so she could see Evan when he came down. Twenty-five minutes later, he did. He peeled off his jacket and goggles, tossed down his gloves and hat, unbuckled his boots. His hair was matted and glistening with sweat.

Eve brought them coffee and chili. They didn't speak for a while.

"I can go fast, you know," he said. "In a car. Wait till I strap you into the passenger seat. Then I'll show you fast." He wasn't smiling.

She was overwhelmed with relief nonetheless. "Not if it doesn't have a passenger-seat airbag, you won't."

"It's a '53 Porsche. The Germans, like the rest of the world, hadn't yet heard of airbags."

He stood up then, looking at her with a cool, distant expression. The rift may not have solidified, but it was still there. If he hadn't wanted to learn to ski, she thought with some annoyance, he could have said so. Had she kidded him too much? Was being a newcomer to both yoga and skiing bad for his ego?

"Never tease men," her grandmother used to warn. "They don't like it, and they never think it's funny. They will repay you by becoming defensive and withdrawn."

She'd teased Evan from the moment she met him. The man probably had a right to major hostility toward her. And she should have remembered from earlier conversations that he'd be unlikely to volunteer what he was feeling. She'd known him long enough to be familiar with that one defense. *No wonder Evan wasn't laughing at himself,* Eve thought. *He was not amused.*

He stood with his big shoulders squared, his chin up, looking down at her. It wasn't clear what he felt; all she knew was that he looked as if he wouldn't budge. He'd been cool all morning, distant, now that she thought about it, and she had ignored it, thinking he was only playing along, wryly acting the beginner role she'd assigned him. Wrong.

"C'mon, let's get out of here. I'm cold." Evan took a last swig of coffee, zipped up his parka, buckled up his boots, and headed for the door.

"Darling, please." Whatever hope Eve had that Evan was over it or would be anytime soon was now replaced by the certainty that he'd hated every second of those ski lessons. And he'd likely hold a grudge.

She was crushed. They walked in silence to the truck.

"Evan," she called ahead to him as he opened the door. "Wait."

She walked up and threw her arms around his big trunk and pleaded for mercy. "I'm sorry for being so bossy. You did great!"

"You're patronizing me."

"No, just trying to get you in a good mood again." She still had her arms around him. He still hadn't budged.

She took Evan's goggles from him and began polishing them. He was watching her, but his expression was unfathomable. Was he nervous, too?

"There's no comparison," Eve said out of the blue.

He looked at her suspiciously. "Comparison. Between what and what?"

"Between you and them. Other men. In my life." She hoped he'd be touched by her attempt to reengage, even if she'd gotten it all wrong. And evidently she had, as he didn't reply. "Never mind," she said, and put the goggles on the windshield and climbed into the truck. This was hopeless. She turned on the ignition.

He sat back in his seat and rested the back of his head in his hands. "Since you brought up other men, tell me more."

She had already chosen to walk the gangplank blindfolded, so she decided to jump. "There was only one man, really, besides Laddie. I'll tell you about him another time. To everyone else it seemed clear: I was the desirable young thing and Laddie the lucky older man. Oh, how he must worship her, everyone thought. How he must want sex with her every minute of the day."

Eve gunned the motor as if to explain something in her heart. They still weren't moving, but the heat had come on. She was cold. She stifled a sneeze.

Evan nodded for her to continue.

"The truth is…" She was unnerved. "Why did I start this? Okay. Our relationship—Laddie's and mine—was so much about creative collaboration, so focused on art and not us, that sex and even food and drink wasn't important. Travel was for guest appearances. See what this life was? How feelings were exiled? What do you need to know that isn't clear?"

"I need to know about when there was trouble. When all this idealized perfection and artistic triumph just exploded."

She seemed stymied. She took a few moments before trying again.

"Okay. One day, just before my debut in *Firebird*, when I was twenty-two, a friend of his from Moscow came to stay with us. She was a former Bolshoi dancer, about Laddie's age, I guess, somewhere in her late forties at the time. I remember thinking happily that she was a little fat, but I had crazy standards then. He'd mentioned her before, said she'd been a fine dancer in her time, not technically brilliant but a crowd-pleaser, like Maria Callas was as a singer, he said, and clearly special enough to earn Laddie's approval. Anyway, we had a dinner party for her the first night she came.

"The night of the party—it was a Friday, and I remember Laddie sent me up to bed early because I was dancing the Saturday matinee—he became a different man. Instead of stern and preoccupied, the way he was with me, he was warm and funny, sweet and excited as a pup, wine and jokes for everyone. After the guests went home, he and Sonya stayed at the table, drinking and smoking, exchanging long, apparently hilarious stories in Russian. I watched him ply her with rich desserts, something he would never have done with me!

He didn't come to bed that night. He told me the next day they talked all night."

"Did you believe him?"

"Yes. I did and I do. But the thing is, the thing is—" Eve could hardly catch her breath. "I was so jealous! Because they might have slept together? No! It was much worse, what I felt: I was envious of the fun they were having! I wanted to laugh like that, play like that! Eat like that! I thought, someone in his life makes him giddy! What about me? Who will make me laugh, tell me jokes, keep me up all night, enjoy me?" She took a breath, startled by her own words. "Who," she said, her voice sounding like a child's, "will want to know me? Me, Eve."

Evan remembered the night they met, how she'd been overcome by the dancers onstage. His rage on her behalf plunged away from him now into a landslide. He moved into the center of the seat and pulled her onto his lap, stroked her hair, still melted-ice wet and uncombed. "That life is over. You and I will laugh and have fun. You will work as much as you want, and I will work as much as I want, and we will play as much as we want. I swear it."

She leaned her head into his, pulling a handkerchief from her sleeve pocket. "And also?" she said after she blew her nose.

"Mmmm?"

"Don't you dare leave me," stated General Patton.

Evan whispered in her ear, "Champion skiers never leave their women."

She sniffled. "What about lousy skiers?"

"I wouldn't know."

24.

By NIGHTFALL, THE RAIN HAD TURNED TO SLEET, pounding against the window like a live presence demanding to be invited in. Eve grew anxious, distracted. Her agitation was momentarily quelled by the arrival of Luann, who declared that the storm was "not that bad"—but then, Luann, still not used to the vagaries of climate change on the Northeast Kingdom, was always optimistic, if too naïve, about the weather. Soon the other guests arrived, a woman named Natalie and two men, Fred and Jeb, who negated Luann's cheery assessment. Jeb was a rugged, large man with a ruddy face who glared at Evan like a pit bull. "The forecast's bad," he told the group. "If it gets much colder, we'll be skating home."

Competition? Evan wondered, and kept a close eye on Jeb's interaction with Eve. Friend, he concluded tentatively, intuitively, and went back to wishing guests would all leave so he and Eve could be alone. Eve, though, seemed in no hurry to be alone with him. Her good mood restored, she dominated the room, Evan observed, like an oft-photographed San Francisco socialite hosting a charity ball. She was beautiful, graceful, elegant—but surely not thinking, as he was, of

the two of them in bed. Merging, he thought grumpi-
ly, that wonderful undifferentiated mass of happiness
when our borders become fluid and our defenses crum-
ble has its downside.

The group exchanged presents—scarves, cook-
books, CDs, the latest in sugar molds. Excluded from
their exclamations of pleasure and their serious talk of
yields, equipment, and weather, he felt vaguely miffed,
as though he were a city slicker amid a convention of
farmers. So that's how they keep outsiders at bay! Instead of whipping out his bona fides as an outdoors-
man and a macho contender to any Vermonter, he
overate and overdrank, falling at length into a pleasant
torpor from which he was aroused only by the departure of Eve's guests.

Eve opened the front door to usher her friends out.
The sleet had stopped, but it had grown noticeably
colder. Fifteen degrees, in fact, according to the thermometer on the door. A blast of freezing air revived
Evan—and Eve's embrace, after she returned to the living room, rekindled the warmth in his blood. He felt
his grumpy mood lift, giving way to something less
gripping and sour. They began cleaning up. She was
jumpy, though, worriedly opening the door several
times to stare out into the darkness, even as she tried
to cover her agitation with smiles and touches. Not until they were back upstairs at last did she undress and
become more relaxed. It was she who moved in to kiss
him, she who initiated sex so that at last his own defenses—more like caution, really—melted.

The more they made love, the hungrier they became for each other until what they already knew was
there for them was clearly there again. And again. At
last they fell asleep, snuggled into the spoon position,

Evan's hand cupping her belly, the sound of the wind a lullaby.

He didn't know how much later it was that he awoke and instinctively reached for her. But she abruptly pulled away. She was sitting up, now getting up, now switching on the light and pulling on long johns, jeans, a lumberman's shirt, a sweater. He looked at her bedside clock: 4:48.

"What is it?"

She barely glanced at him. "Listen."

Evan heard a series of thunderous cracks, a fusillade. He sat up. "Who the hell has a gun around here?"

Eve was climbing into her boots. "Not gunshots, Evan. Ice. Ice on the trees. The boughs are breaking under the weight!" She rushed out of the room, slamming the door behind her, shutting him off as effectively as if she had slapped his face.

Not gunshots, Evan. His brain worried at her impatient tone, then tossed it aside. *Don't take it personally!* It had taken him a minute to realize, first, the significance of snapping branches and then the meaning of her rejection, but once he did, he was up and reaching for his own jeans and sweater. He pulled on his socks and then his boots, opened the door and started down the stairs. He heard her on the kitchen phone.

"I'm scared I'm going to lose my trees," she was saying to someone on the other end. "Is there anything you can do?" A pause. Then: "You're a blessing, Jeb."

25.

JEB COULDN'T SLEEP. This was unusual, unprecedented. He was a large, easygoing guy who carefully led his life focused on productive work and community activism. "My mind sticks to business," he liked to say—meaning it was a mind free of the emotional complications that plagued the nights of so many of his peers.

He thought of himself not so much as a happy man as a contented one, a distinction he felt to be reasonable and mature, and a condition essentially unwavering since childhood. He was busy, but laid-back—more type B than type A—another distinction he was proud of. No heart attacks for him. No anxiety meds, either, or antidepressants, or blood-pressure drugs. He had friends and admirers of both genders, no enemies he knew of. He was prosperous—his rustic, restored Victorian home on the crest of Bean Hill Road was West Glover's grandest—and his community work brought him another, more valuable kind of satisfaction. He had a laconic passivity about him that people might have mistaken for dullness. But he didn't see it that way. Great joy might be unknown to him, but so was great sorrow. There was drama enough, living so close to the Canadian border, in the vicissitudes of wind and weather.

Yes, contented. But on this yuletide night, discontent lay beside him like a child without a Christmas stocking and would not let him rest.

Every time he closed his eyes, he saw Eve's face beaming at the man she introduced as Evan Cameron. She seemed transformed, hostessing her friends with a radiance that could only have one source. She's given herself to this stranger from the West.

His brain reeled, refusing to accept it. *And why not? What have I done to prevent it?* Evan seemed nice enough, gracious, smart, unimposing amid the talk of the storm—well, hell, what would such a man know of an ice storm's potential consequences? You had to live in ice to understand it. Good-looking, too, Jeb supposed; he had a lot of hair—women seemed to like that— though not all that young...must be forty-five. An ordinary guy, really, and even if a gentleman, no one to set Eve ablaze—though he was obviously on fire, too.

Jeb got up and went to the window. It might be the wind rattling the glass that was keeping him up, though he'd slept through worse storms than this. No, not the wind, he acknowledged, but a curious disequilibrium, as though his world had been reshaped without his knowledge. Was it a stomach ache? *No, no, face it: you should have courted her, damn it! You've acted as if some day when the velocity of the wind is right, it'll all happen naturally with Eve.*

The understanding came with the force of a religious revelation. Of course! He should have recognized that she was not a fact of his life, like the predictable palette of October or the soft April rain. And that she could be taken away—or could take herself away—leaving a void as black as this night. He took her for granted without ever having told her he truly wanted her, and all he felt now was stupidity and her possible absence. He didn't know if what he was feeling was love, but whatever it was filled him with both loss and surprise, as if he'd awakened from a joyful dream and couldn't hold on to it. He, who never desired anyone enough to write a poem about her; who never got lost in a love song; who never chased her down the way he might, say, an appealing merger possibility. He now remembered the loneliness that burned in his chest when she stayed in New York.

Jeb was forty and for the first time aware of an uncharted part of himself. He and his wife, Anabel, had been teenagers when they met. They came together for a moment, married in haste, and separated by the time they were both twenty-one, feeling fortunate both for their time together and the effortlessness with which they agreed to part. He had loved her, as she had him, but they had married in order to sleep together. When they began to talk about having a family, they realized their affair was long over, that they didn't want to spend their lives together, and that they both had a chance to move on without rancor and without hurting others. So they did.

The knowledge that he might now be in love—there was no other phrase for it, and he said the words aloud—rang in his ears.

Maybe it wasn't too late. Maybe he could take on this Evan Cameron and win Eve from him. He would have to wage a war with unfamiliar rules, on terrain as alien as desert sand. But he'd never shunned a battle in his life. If victorious, he would show Eve this surprising new facet of himself. Maybe then, seeing him on fire for the first time since they'd met, she'd want him, too.

He turned on the light and stared at his face in the mirror above the dresser. The same high forehead, the same dark hair slicked back without a part, the same jaw his mother liked to call "the Hobdy jaw," receding enough along the chin line to benefit greatly from the beard Jeb had worn since he was in his twenties. A slight pout to the lower lip, which he worried would one day make him look like Alfred Hitchcock. Even the eyes were the same, small, deep-set, hazel brown, and now looked back at him with an expression at once sympathetic and mocking. A down-to-earth face many a farm woman had found appealing.

But Eve was not a farm woman, not really. He found the face looking back more florid than usual, as if he'd gotten too much sun, or had too much to drink.

The phone rang. He raced to pick it up.

"It's Eve. I'm scared I'm going to lose my trees. Is there anything you can do?" Her voice was breathless, terrified.

You bet there was.

"Don't worry," he said, convinced beyond all logic that this was kismet and that if it meant chopping his hand off in the process, he would still save the trees. "I'll be right over."

26.

EVAN ENTERED THE KITCHEN, hands in pockets, shoulders slouched. Eve hung up the phone and turned to look at him, her eyes wide. The ungodly rifle shots were still popping. She was pale. He moved to offer her comfort, but she took a step back. "The maples are in danger," she said with a tremor in her voice. "If the heavier branches break, they can rout out the life blood of the tree, and next year's crop will be ruined. I'll be ruined." She started to pace. "Jeb's coming over. We're going to try to figure out if there's anything we can do."

He remembered the guy with the beard. "Can we get the ice off them before they break?" he asked.

"What, with a hairdryer?" she shot back. "I'm sorry." She gave him a wry smile, the kind mothers reserve for children too young to understand why they were upset, and her voice softened. "Four hundred trees? Even with four hundred workers—four thousand— what could we do?"

The realization sent a shudder through her, and at last she came to him and let him put his arms around her so she could press her cheek against his chest. He kissed the top of her head, but she did not look up, did not return his embrace. Her grief lay beyond his ability to comfort her, he knew, and he stood stiffly, helplessly, searching for practical words that formed no part of his vocabulary, his powerlessness an ache in his chest. Finally she broke away and filled a kettle for tea, and as he watched her pace the room, it was as if he were seeing her disappear to a place where he had no bearing.

They sipped their tea in tense silence until, not ten minutes later, the front doorbell rang and she rushed to answer it.

The huge, ruddy man, Jeb, had arrived. Eve hugged him and led him into the living room, leaving Evan alone, hunched over the kitchen counter cupping his mug of tea. The man grunted a hello at Evan and hovered awkwardly in silence while Eve fetched him some tea. Evan said nothing but nodded a meager acknowledgment.

She returned and motioned for Jeb to sit beside her on the wooden settle her grandfather had built so guests could sit and speak with whoever was cooking. She had cleared the farm table of everything but her plot plans and maps, pencils and scale rulers. Evan waited for a similar invitation, but she didn't offer it; she was already discussing strategy with Jeb, leaning in to tell him what she suspected was happening. They made no attempt to include Evan but sat with their heads together, hovering over a map of the region, or maybe it was a weather map.

Evan fumed. Prevented from joining them, he sauntered into the pantry where, amid jars of pickles and canned tomatoes, he could see and hear them. Jeb talked and pointed and circled areas on the map with a grease pencil.

Evan felt a rush of hate. Then, immediate regret. I shouldn't be thinking of myself now. They need to talk.

"I don't know about the whole sugar bush," Jeb was saying. "It might already be destroyed. But you've got a bigger problem."

The sag of her body spoke of despair. "What?"

"That sugar maple in your yard. If the main branch breaks, it could fall on your house. That's about a ton—"

"We've got to save it! That maple was my grandmother's favorite! Her grandmother planted it."

Jeb put his arm around her shoulders. "I've got grappling hooks and a chain saw in the truck. Soon as it's light, we'll tie the branch back, try to brace it somehow so it doesn't fall, then cut it off if we have to. Then we'll see what the ice is doing to the maples in the grove."

Jeb spoke as animatedly about conditions outside as a television weatherman, and Eve gave him her absolute attention, hopelessness now replaced by resolution.

Jealousy settled over Evan like dry ice, chilling him as it burned. He dared not move, dared not even breathe. He felt banished, a voyeur, witness to an act more intimate, more binding even than the love that had engulfed Eve and him only hours before. He took a step back in angry defeat. The hushed words Eve now spoke felt more meaningful than her whispers when they were in each other's arms.

At last Eve stood. "It's getting light out," she said to Jeb, picking up the map and heading for the front hall. "Let's go look."

Jeb plucked her hat from the coat rack and helped her into her coat.

"Evan," she called over her shoulder. "We're going out."

"I'll come too," he said. "Maybe I can help."

It took her a few seconds to decide. "Sure. Great. But hurry!"

The trees surrounding her backyard were sheathed in ice, as though they had been shrink-wrapped for delivery and not yet opened. Several birches, unprotected from the wind, bowed like a king's courtiers almost to the ground. It was bitter cold, windy, the air whipping with a stinging mist. The sugar maple itself, a black silhouette in the gray predawn light, stood over them, menacing as an executioner. Even with a spray of frost slicing into his neck, Evan could see ice several inches thick on the branches. Some of the limbs had snapped off, exhibiting deep wounds to the tree, and he could hear Eve's breathing quicken with anxiety. Jeb lugged a steel cable to the bottom of the tree and stood looking up in puzzlement.

"I don't think it'll work," he said. "I can tie it around the base, maybe bring it up to the branch. But I don't see how I can get it secured higher up the trunk. We'll have to go to plan B." He ran back to his truck and returned with maybe twenty yards of heavy rope, handing one end to Eve, who began securing it around the base. Jeb put on two enormous black gloves, climbed up the trunk, waited for her to finish, then crawled precariously onto the damaged branch, lassoing the rope as close to the base as he dared reach. One of his gloves stuck to the tree. The end of the branch was so heavy with ice it threatened to crack off.

"It could leave a cavity so big inside that it'll never seal up again," Jeb shouted to the wind. He worked his way back to the trunk, shimmied higher, and wound the rope around it, creating a kind of pulley effect, the branch at its fulcrum. His movements were precise and assured. Evan stood indecisively below him, arms held out ridiculously as though to catch him if he fell.

Eve stood next to Evan, still as a statue. "There's a chain saw in Jeb's truck," she told him. "Know how to use it?" She'd pulled on a ski mask against the cold, so all he could see were her eyes, bleak as the overcast sky.

"Sure." Chain saws, his father once told him, were as temperamental as lawn mowers, with idiosyncratic glitches only the owner could fathom. He recalled vividly the time his father, a car restorer, had to crank one up before the choke was on and then cajole it, like a cranky toddler, into budging. Evan had used it a few times.

He couldn't start Jeb's chain saw. It wouldn't turn on. Exasperated, Eve went to find Jeb. He arrived, merely touched the thing, and it started up, leaving Evan to rage silently at this display of his own incompetence. *You didn't have to go through this. You could have told the truth: "No, I don't know how to use a goddam chain saw."* He stood motionlessly, looking up at the maple, his body useless as a snowman's, until Eve returned.

"Don't use it yet," she cautioned. "Maybe Jeb can save the branch."

Evan heard the sound of tractors and moved to the side of the yard so he could see the front driveway. Maybe a half dozen vehicles stopped near Jeb's truck and disgorged a phalanx of men and women, evidently Eve's neighbors who, shouting to each other, moved into the yard like a platoon to see if lines were down, power out, cars frozen shut. Jeb must have called them. They carried braces, ropes, chains, sand, and salt, and Evan could hear Eve's welcoming cry when she saw them.

He felt at once tremendously moved and insignificant. As these able, organized people flowed past him, united in emergency, he imagined himself growing smaller and smaller, without substance. *At this moment, I don't exist for her. I have no place in her world.* Of all the various indignities he'd experienced, insignificance was not one of them. Evan, the man who could handle anything! Mindlessly, he watched Jeb jump down from the tree, heard him greet the newcomers.

"We're okay here, I think," Jeb said, putting a large reassuring arm around Eve yet again. "The cutting can wait. Where we're really going to need you is in the bush." He turned toward his truck. "C'mon. Sooner we get there, faster we'll salvage something."

Evan remembered standing in his father's garage when he was eight, bewildered by the strange tools surrounding him. It had taken him only a few years to master those tools, and he knew that, given time, he could become as adept as Jeb was out here in dark Vermont. Then he could help. Then she would turn to him. But a cold sorrow encased him like the ice on Eve's maples.

There was too little time.

27.

JEB HAD SAVED HER HOUSE. No one knew what to do about the maples. Fueled by hope and adrenalin, Eve watched her friends run toward their tractors. She took a deep breath, her only defense against such stress, and inhaled gratitude. Without them—without Jeb—she'd be lost.

Lost because she had spent Christmas morning in bed with Evan, then wasted the whole of Christmas day giving him—insanely—those unwanted skiing lessons. She'd been aware of the rain and its implications, aware of the forecast of subfreezing weather that night, aware that his body alone was luring her away from responsibility.

There was her lover of the night before, standing helplessly by the maple, outlandish in his new ski hat, a cartoon farmer at a loss now that there was urgent farmwork to be done. When they last had sex, she'd told herself that she would never lose him, must never lose him, so the current workings of her heart, yanking her back to life before Evan, shocked her. But her body belonged as much to the finicky sugar bush as it did to her frozen lover; her blood flowed with its sap. If it came to trading her farm for him—if the trees all died and he asked her to go back with him to California? She could not. Vermont was her home. If it meant replanting, starting all over again, being alone forever, she knew she would choose that.

Her agitation rose, devastating her further at its furtive aim of betraying Evan and sabotaging this love. The sugar maple now seemed to her a beast of burden, stooped under the weight of its ice garments, and it was her task to relieve it—to relieve all her trees—of suffering. She had no choice but to cut Evan's suffering short.

She walked resolutely up to Evan, noting with a pang his obvious pleasure as she approached, his instinctive reach to embrace her. She stopped short, tried to drop some of her irritability, and steeled herself.

"Evan, dearest, I think you should go back."

"To the house? Sure. What do you need?"

"No, back home. Your home, I mean. Today, now, instead of tomorrow." She looked down at her feet. "You're only going to feel more helpless if you stay, whether you're out here or inside. And I can't be there for you in either place. I just can't."

He cocked his head, smiled patiently, and tried again. "No problem! I may not be the chain-saw king, but I can help out. Put me to work!"

"I can't. I don't...want to. I want to not think about you or us while this horror is going on. It's too hard for me and will only get worse for you. So please, please understand: I need you out of the way."

She winced, hearing herself. But how could words say it otherwise?

Out of the way? The words struck his heart like the gunfire sounds that had driven her out of his arms that morning. "No."

She put her hands on her hips. "No?"

"No. You need me with you. And you need to allow help from less perfect sources." He was trembling, not from the cold but from the racing of his blood.

"Please. What I need are my trees." She was crying.

He had given in to Ruth's needs. This gallery opening, that dinner with clients, this antiques show, that debut of each "exciting" new designer. He hadn't minded at first—compromise, he thought wryly, was part of relationship—but accommodation eventually wore him down, and he'd rebelled. Well, he'd stand firm now, before it went any further. "I can help," he said sharply.

She turned. "I don't have time to argue. Evan, I want you to go. Do it for me. We have time, but my trees don't." She walked off in Jeb's direction, then stopped and came back. "You can call my car service." Her voice was gentle, supplicating. "The number's on the fridge. They'll take you to Burlington. It's not expensive."

"I have cash, thanks."

She shied from the rebuke and reached for his gloved hand. He let her hold it. "Can't you see how bad this might be for me?"

He considered briefly. "Yes. For me, too. For us. What I don't understand is why you want me gone. I'll stay out of your way."

"You'll be in my brain," she said, "and I can't have you there now."

They glared at each other.

"You invited me, remember?"

"I remember very well."

"So?"

"I'll invite you again, of course!"

"When it's convenient."

His sarcasm went unnoticed.

"When the farm's back. When the trees are well."

His throat seemed to have blocked, as he could hardly get the words out. "Swell. Sometime between now and summer."

"Soon. Soon as possible." She looked up at a birch tree.

"Be specific," he demanded. "I don't want to lose you to"—he took his hand away—"to a bunch of trees."

She winced.

"Listen, Evan." Her voice turned as ragged as the edge of Jeb's chain saw. "You don't get this. I'd like to be able to say, 'My love, we'll meet in spring when the sapping's done,' but there may be no sapping—this spring or ever! The future of our romance? What about the future of my livelihood? Do you know how much I pay to cover one evaporator? Do you have any idea? If this storm wipes the trees out, I won't be able to re-build this farm. Ever. It's not like Laddie left me money for this, you know. I'll be finished."

Her face, rosy from the cold only moments ago, was white as the bark of the birch tree she'd been peering at so fearfully.

Evan seemed to form a sentence but stopped, as if stunted not by her anger but his own. He was still trembling.

"Got it," he said. "I'm outta here." He turned away from her abruptly.

She looked anxiously behind her at Jeb, waiting for her. "Please, please understand," she begged. "Text me when you get to the airport. Okay?" She looked like a child, squinting up at him with her arms down by her sides. "Say something."

His voice came out a thin rasp: "Yeah, okay. Or I'll call."

She remembered something and touched his shoulder. "No, you can't call. At least not right away. Jeb says phone lines are down. Not sure about cell reception, either."

Her words were yet another reproach, one more farm disaster he didn't know about and Jeb did. He shook his shoulder away from her touch. He didn't look back.

→

She watched him stride off toward the house. Furious, and who could blame him? She'd waved him away as if she didn't care, turned on him with a rant about property insurance as if it were his fault! Sent him to the bench, or, as Laddie would have done to lesser mortals, to the back of the corps. *What have I just done?*

Fear pressed in on her chest—whether of losing him or her trees, she didn't know—even as the sickeningly loud gunfire sounds that had blown her out of Evan's arms earlier were now blessedly absent. As she ran toward Jeb, her knees buckled. The answer came back in a flash. *You're trying to save your life. There's no time for anything else.*

She joined Jeb, and together they drove out to the sugar bush, where they separated, in tune with each other, needing no words. The trees surrounding her in serried ranks reminded her of a revolutionary army: bandaged in ice, woebegone, and stalwart. She began to inspect them closely. There were wounds where some of the smaller branches had broken off, but for the most part, the main branches, complaining under the weight of the ice, held steady. These trees at least—she didn't know about the ones farther into the bush—could still be sapped. If, that is, there was no more icing. If snow wasn't added to the weight (and the sky above looked ominous). If the accumulated pressure didn't, after all, destroy them.

It was noon, then two in the afternoon, and still it grew more frigid. The thermometer in the truck now registered seven below zero. Jeb and her friends removed as much heavy snow and ice from the trees as they could. Fatigue, for hours held away by sheer will, overwhelmed Eve. She sat down in the crusted snow, shivering, not caring how cold she was. She sneezed. "Stop, Jeb," she shouted, knowing he was too far away to hear. "We've got to rest. My feet are numb." *And I'm hungry*, she thought, feeling that familiar hollow tug below her ribs. She recalled how ravenous she'd been as a teenager, when her budding breasts and hips began to alarm her and when Laddie, who had noticed, too, had said to her, "You will know what it means to be hungry. But it will be for a higher good." Art, art, art. What a dope. I'd rather have had a trayful of buttered muffins.

She could hear the shouting of her friends, but she had never been more conscious of her solitude. She plunged deeper into the forest, hardly able to feel her feet.

A cry from her left: Jeb, calling her name. Startled, she limped toward him.

He pointed to the eastern sky. "Look!"

Clouds that looked like cottontails skittered above them where blackness had been moments before. It began snowing—not rocks of ice but angel flakes that fell gently, lightly, then stopped and, as Eve put her hands out to feel them, became thick droplets of rain. Eve's sugar bush poured off hunks of ice, big as toy boats, from their branches. Instead of devastated, the grove was now ashimmer. A warm wind touched her face.

Warm? How could it be? There, breaking through a distant cluster of clouds, was sunlight! Eve closed her eyes. Red and green dots danced beneath her eyelids, and she yelped with delight, feeling the impossible combination of frozen feet and the sun's intense heat on her face. *Was it too late to stop Evan? But the cell phones were out. Oh God.*

Jeb took her hand and led her to the nearest maple. She took off her gloves, reached out to caress a branch. Water fell from it in sheets!

"The ice," Jeb said. "By Jove, it's melting. This is impossible! The trees are…raining. Well, I'll be."

YEAH, YOU GUESSED IT: it was me. And it was The Big One. My one and only intervention.

And not easy, by the way. Politics are as intricate up here as down there. I had to consult Aquilo to be authorized to command his warming winds, and Aquilo always has to be bribed. So I promised him a date with Pleasure if he'd heat up his breath and help me out. "You know how to do it, don't you, Aquilo?" I said. "You just put your lips together like this and...blow."

He didn't get the reference. (By the way, Bogie and Bacall? I did that.) Moreover, he refused. Not because he didn't want to date Pleasure but because Aurora would have knocked that hot breath of his right out of him along with his teeth.

I had to go to Jove. I had no other choice. If the storm had continued, Evan and Eve would have been decimated as surely as were those maple branches in Eve's lawn. So, to save the trees, the lovers, and my heavenly butt, I went off to see the Wizard.

Jove chided me for being antiquated, washed-up, a supernumerary in the battle of the sexes. Lulu blinked back a tear in her chocolaty eyes and hid under Jove's desk. So much for godly paternal love.

"You want me to melt the ice?"

"Yes sir."

"You're sure of this, now."

"Sir." (See how he makes me crawl?)

"Then consider it done." He banged his scepter on his desk, the better to hear himself make a pronouncement.

I reached for Lulu, still cowering under his desk. "Father, you wouldn't try to sabotage me, would you?"

"Moi? I'll intervene for you this time, but the progress of this affair remains solely up to Evan and Eve, so let's hope they're not saps."

He laughed at his wordplay.

"Sapling love can grow into a solid tree only with a little maturity," I said, as if Jove, the Pan of Mount Olympus, the sex addict whose own mother couldn't stop him from philandering, would take the hint.

"Do you want my help or not?"

I forced out a "Thank you, sir," and went back to Psyche to tell her the news. She was sympathetic about my contretemps with Jove but stiffened when I mentioned Eve and Evan, leaving me with a perverse father, an unhappy wife, a lovesick eagle, two stubborn and possibly disenchanted lovers, and a migraine.

28.

Evan slumped into his seat with a fiery brew of fury and relief. He'd been the last standby passenger allowed on the flight. Once seated he found it would be delayed two hours for de-icing. Slim chance he'd make his connecting flight out of LaGuardia to San Francisco, the flight that would take him definitively away from Eve.

He'd stay in New York for a night or two if he missed it, courtesy of John Scroopman, who'd promised him anything he wanted if he'd just finish the anthology's introduction. He'd neglected his work on it, work he'd hoped to do in time for the already strained deadline.

In each of her earlier anthologies, Ms. Layton had written long, personal and heartfelt introductions; in one, Love Letters of Victorian England, she'd charted her reasons for gathering her precious notes and letters, material she collected and then, mysteriously, hoarded for four decades. She also had a file on the specifics of love-letter writing—a primer on the most elegant words to use for intimate parts, should the writer be interested in sending an erotic letter, and on subtle ways to express anger or hurt. She evidently had some sort of "how-to" section in mind at some point but may have abandoned it.

He still needed to know far more about her and her intentions for the book.

Scroopman underestimated the difficulty of this introduction. To grasp the author's view of love well enough to offer the proper tribute, Evan knew, he would have to grasp love itself. And at the moment, he had never felt further from that understanding, after thinking himself never closer to it.

He'd consulted the dictionary to get, as Scroopman put it, "the lay of the land" at the beginning of the project. He was horrified to find that love, in Oxford's dictionary, began: "1. n. fondness, warm affection; sexual passion; sweetheart, beloved one; colloq. delightful person or thing."

So tepid, he'd thought. The folks at Oxford and Webster never met Lorelei Layton. She'd have wept at the pallor of these words. Fondness? Not in her book. Not in Evan's, either.

"Are you all right, sir?" The flight attendant took one look at him and then mumbled, "Oh dear."

"A double Scotch. And three aspirin."

"We're not allowed to give out medicine. And the Scotch—oh hell, I'll get you some, even though we're supposed to wait until takeoff."

"Then make it a triple."

He burned with humiliation. Had he stayed, he'd right now be alone under the massive covers on Eve's brass bed, or else fumbling about following on-the-spot forestry tips in the freezing rain. At the same time, he was flooded with images of Eve's fairy-tale house, her joyful face when he gave her the mortgage button, the warmth of her in bed. And that declaration of love: "Don't ever leave me!" When he heard it, what came to mind was a letter from George Eliot to Herbert Spencer—he even remembered it was from July 1854:

I want to know if you can assure me that you will not forsake me, that you will always be with me as much as you can and share your thoughts and feelings with me....I find it impossible to contemplate life under any other conditions.

A flicker of nausea reminded him of the thrill he'd felt at her command that he never leave, and then the nightmarish outcome—her ease at letting him go. Rage prickled inside his temples.

He whipped down the first Scotch.

He never questioned the fact that the farm was her life. Yet she behaved as if he didn't have the wits to fathom her priorities—as if, instead, he would only sabotage them! What kind of dopey feminist box had he been hurled into? Couldn't she have begged him to stay, if for no other reason than to see what this new lover of hers was made of? Or was he nothing but a part-time passion slipped in over the holidays?

The Scotch was doing its work, finally, and his rage was subsiding. Let her be consumed by her farm, her memories of stardom, the vagaries of climate change on the freakin' syrup industry. He'd bury himself like-wise in his own work. His copyedited manuscript, which he'd receive after New Year's, plus the introduction—which he'd not yet solved—could well take all his energy. He'd breathe in San Francisco, play at Big Sur, hike at Point Reyes, surf at Dana Point, sun in Laguna, and stay far away from that infernal New England ice.

As familiar images of himself going solo replaced the more recent coupled ones, the weeks ahead promised a respite. He leaned back in his seat and put his earphones on, found some Bill Evans on the box, and downed more Scotch.

Weeks? Or would it be months?

Months without Eve. The thought, which had not seeped through his anger until now, seared him. What if there's another crisis? Insufficient sap? New trees to be planted and overseen? A Nor'easter that takes the roof off the house? Will she keep postponing our next meeting? "Let's wait until June, Evan. Until October. Till next Christmas…" And with each delay, diminished feeling, increased guilt, faded memories, buried reproach. Until what they'd had was no more than a sweet interlude.

Images of the man with the huge red face and his gargantuan chain saw began to taunt him. *Get over it, man!* Evan's anthology was filled with bitter expressions of precisely this sort of jealous fantasy, suffered by far nobler men than he. For an instant, he felt like Napoleon when he'd heard no word from Joséphine and had no recourse but to imagine himself a cuckold:

> *Of what sort can be that marvelous thing, that new lover who absorbs every moment, tyrannizes over your days, and prevents your giving any attention to your husband?*

Evan had been too confident to worry about Jeb until just now. *Damn! Why didn't I suggest a specific date? We have to see each other as soon as possible. Then we'll know where we are and hammer out the fears and the logistics and—*

The seat-belt sign went off.

"Ladies and gentlemen, this is your captain. I want to welcome you to the last flight out of all Vermont airports."

The passengers clapped.

"The fine folks down at the weather bureau are mighty stumped."

Evan gulped the icy remains of a second drink.

"The temperature in northern Vermont went from six degrees Fahrenheit at two p.m. this afternoon to a record high of sixty-two degrees at four p.m. That's a rise of fifty-six degrees in two hours. Ladies and gentlemen, that is one astonishing event."

Evan listened, motionless, remembering the minus six degrees of early morning at the farm. The farm! The ice would melt now. Eve will be all right!

"I guess we've got Santa to thank for saving New England this Christmas!" the captain crooned.

Evan could hear the beeps, rings, and songs of cell phones turning on around him, like an electronic choir. The woman in the aisle seat next to Evan had finished using the aircraft's telephone, now nestled in its cradle between his seat and hers. He took out his own phone, eager hear Eve's happy voice, to hear her say how horribly she missed him, how badly she regretted sending him away. He dialed but got nothing.

He had left her a note on her kitchen table as he rushed out to catch his plane, just a howl of pain, really, a quick farewell to briefly say everything he couldn't say:

Eve,

One of the hardest things in life is having words in your heart that you can't utter.

Evan

The words were originally written by the actor James Earl Jones, and Evan couldn't think of a better way of saying it.

He remembered he couldn't call her. Jeb said phone lines and cell reception are out. He'd have to write instead, tonight, on the plane, and mail the letter the moment he arrived. He took a piece of stationery from his manila envelope, but the Scotch and his shyness combined to blur his brain.

This has got to stop. I can't be afraid of expressing myself, or I'll lose Eve—if I haven't already. This letter has to say more than what a thrill it is that the ice melted.

So he began.

> *Dearest Eve,*
>
> *The captain just announced the news of the thaw. It's a miracle. I'm as happy as you must be. But I wish I hadn't left so abruptly.*

Words spun around in his head, but a tumult of conflicting emotions consumed him until the familiar shame and shyness won. Evan found himself once again borrowing from the masters to ward off paralysis.

This time it would be Beethoven.

> *I have to write to tell you what I feel: Letters have souls; they can speak; they have in them all that force which expresses the transports of the heart; they have all the fire of our passions. They can raise them as much as if the persons themselves were present. They have all the tenderness and the delicacy of*

speech, and sometimes even a boldness of expression beyond it.

And as for you, my love, I am resolved to wander so long away from you until I can fly to your arms and say that I am finally home, send my soul enwrapped to you into the land of spirits.... Your love, this weekend, makes me at once the happiest and unhappiest of men.

Evan

There. Not all the words were Beethoven's, actually; there was a dash of Héloïse, written to Abelard, thrown in for emphasis. Not a word of recrimination, no hint of jealousy, no mention of his chain-saw massacre or his unfair banishment.

Satisfied with everything but the sign-off, which he'd decided to omit altogether after an agonizing hour of alternating between Ever yours and Love always, he settled back for the remaining few hours of the flight. In the middle of reading a dazzling love letter of Proust's, Evan drifted off to sleep.

He awoke to the shout of the passenger next to him. "Did you see that?" she asked, gripping his leg.

Evan blinked. "See what?"

"Out your window! A plane, I thought! Flew up from below, passed inches away from our wing. Our windows blackened for several moments, like night had fallen, but only on this side!" She rang for a flight attendant.

Moments later, the agitated attendant admitted she, too, had seen the winged vision and was mystified.

Several passengers had risen out of their seats to hear her account.

She sounded stunned, as if in a trance. "It looked like a rocket shooting toward space, but our radar picked up nothing. I swear, what I really thought when I saw it? That it was a giant...eagle, soaring straight up to heaven."

→

Evan made the connecting flight in New York and arrived at San Francisco Airport without further incident. He found a mailbox in the terminal near baggage claim, dropped his letter in it, and waited no more than a minute for a cab.

He saw a letter awaiting him on his doorstep, his name handwritten with a large black felt-tip pen, without an address, stamp, or postmark—just Evan Cameron. It had to have been dropped off. The handwriting was ominously familiar: Ruth's. He dumped his bag in the hallway, his heart filled with dread.

29.

EVE AWOKE IN A SWEAT.

In her nightmare, Laddie had been cursing her, shouting, "You shouldn't have gone skiing!" and ranting about how he should never have let her go back to Vermont to visit Big Eve, that he would never again let her out of his sight. "Evisha, how could you disappoint me so?" he'd asked, looking as morose as he always did when she let him down by risking injury. Even once she was awake, it took her several moments to realize that Laddie was not, in fact, still alive.

A nurse was applying a damp cloth to Eve's forehead. "It's okay, dear. You're having a bad dream is all."

"Will my foot be okay?" Eve was still disoriented enough to imagine she was speaking to her grandmother.

"It'll be fine," the nurse said. "You just got too cold for too long today."

"It's not broken?" She opened her eyes and saw a strange, pale blue room drenched in sunlight. The curtains, once probably light green, looked like dirty aprons.

"No. Frozen."

Eve focused on the large woman sitting beside her, someone she didn't know. "Where am I?"

"Glover Hospital, dear. Mr. Hobdy brought you in. We have to warm you up after that terrible storm."

"Yeah, only a crazy woman like you would stay outside hacking at the ice for over eight hours." It was Luann, smiling from the other side of Eve's hospital bed. "Lucky you fainted and that Jeb was with you. Or heaven only knows what could have happened!" She was rubbing Eve's hand gently between her own two hands.

"Just like you to miss the greatest event in Glover history," she went on. "The ice melted."

Eve sneezed and glanced up. "It did?" She vaguely remembered having felt the heat of the sun before collapsing. "The trees?"

Luann looked away. "Jeb's talking to the insurance people right now, so don't you fret." Luann always made insurance companies sound like neighborly sorts likely to send flowers. "You have pneumonia, sweetie."

But Eve was asleep again. On the farm with Big Eve. Her grandmother was ushering someone in to see her. A man. He came into the front hall, and Eve raced to him. She was in his arms and could see the pores along his nose and forehead, a blue vein in his neck, a cleft in his chin, the dearest things she ever saw. She was kissing the man as if he'd just walked all the way from Boulder to Birmingham, as Emmylou Harris would do, and thanking him for coming, begging him to stay, inhaling his sweet male scent, a mix of soap and sweat from his long journey. She was deliriously happy, her senses overwhelmed.

Eve rose to a sitting position and gripped Luann's hand, which had never left hers. "I dreamt I loved someone," she said. "But I couldn't have him."

"Why couldn't you?"

"I don't know."

"Hmmm. Who was it?" Lu asked softly.

"I don't know."

Her friend smiled wryly. "Well, hell, honey, that ain't no fun. So then what happened?"

Eve was too dizzy to continue speaking. She remembered having once breathed in a man she loved, just the way she had with the mystery man in the dream. She tried to sit up again, intent on explaining this to Luann, but the thought evaporated just as the dream did, and she slumped back onto her pillow.

"Shh," Luann whispered. "They're only dreams."

But Eve, awash in sorrow, remembered that she had kissed Evan Cameron in real life just the way she kissed the man in the dream—opening her whole heart to him. She had breathed with him, too. And yet in this dream she'd been worrying, worrying. What had she been worrying about?

"Tell me, tell me," said Lu, wiping her friend's forehead. "What's going on?"

But she was feverish and exhausted and once again fell asleep. This time, Lu coaxed her: "You're going to have a good dream this time. You're going to have what you want in this dream, do you hear?" Lu believed what people said about speaking to someone in an unconscious state.

This time there was no mystery man in Eve's dream. And this time the dream had no ghosts from the past— no Laddie, no Big Eve, no childhood terrors—no one who could claim or control or hurt her. In this dream, she was an adult. With Evan. In a small car, a sports car—she knew that because she felt close to the ground, which felt bumpy under her as they drove. It was a convertible with the top down, and she felt the clean breeze against her face. This must be the car he loves, she thought, but couldn't remember its name. All she could recall was that it was German. And all she could remember in German was Ich liebe dich, a meaningless phrase to her right now, although again she thought she should know what it meant. Was that the name of his car? An Ich liebe dich?

Evan was driving. They were evidently on a trip, which filled Eve with happiness. He wore a yellow baseball cap. His skin was tawny and his eyes a deep sea blue. Everything about him seemed glorious in its maleness; he seemed, as she looked at his profile, painted by the gods. Yes, he seemed to her more alive than a mere man. Not mortal—heaven-sent. They were singing along with the radio—it was "Stormy Weather"—but it wasn't the real song that she knew, the one about stormy weather; it was upbeat and modern, jazzy—with David Sanborn playing sax and Mark Knopfler on guitar.

Outside the car were maple trees, but they weren't maples as she knew them, the kind in Vermont; they were big-leaf maples only found in the redwood forests of California. So that's where they were! Among the giant sequoias! They stopped. "That tree there is a sequoiadendron giganteum," Evan said, pointing out the window, "and it's three thousand years old." He pulled out a map. "That's how long our love will last," he began, as he hugged her to him to show her the topography, and circled the spot. "Can't get deeper into redwood country than this."

He put up the top of the convertible. "Hold tight, my love." He was laughing. She saw they were driving straight into the tree, and that everything began to get dark as they entered a tunnel. The last thing she felt before they drove straight through to the center of the tree—the tunnel—were the leaves of the maples brushing against her face.

"Darling, wake up, wake up. You're all right. No, no ice storms. Everything is fine."

But it was not Evan speaking. It was Luann. Eve looked at her friend, disoriented, bewildered. She spoke carefully, oddly, as though translating from another language. "I was inside a tree. A giant tree."

"So I gathered."

Eve began to sob.

"It was a dream! And a good dream!" Luann said, trying another tack. "Dear one, tell me why you're so sad."

Eve stared down at the dingy green waffle-weave blanket covering her knees and the dreary, wrinkled flowered gown covering her chest. She took in the spotted bandage in the crook of her arm, the one covering the glucose drip, and then her eyes landed again on the curtain hanging from the tiny window, grayed from years of dirt and bleach and sadness.

"He was so…real," Eve said, knowing her words fell as short to communicate what ailed her as *Ich liebe dich* fell short to describe Evan's car. "Real as you."

30.

BEFORE HE COULD BRING HIMSELF TO READ RUTH'S LETTER, he poured himself a double scotch.

He had never drunk so much as in the last few days, but this promised to require serious sedation. Some homecoming. He tried to calm himself till the liquor took effect by riffling through other mail, but finally ripped it open.

> *Evan dear,*
>
> *So grateful for our breakfast; it meant a lot to me to see you and to know you're well and happy.*
>
> *The results of my tests show that I'll need to be in San Francisco for the next few months. Dr. Wade gave me the boring news that I must stay around for even more tests, more treatment—with interferon, apparently, and for ongoing dialysis.*
>
> *Do you know anyone who might rent out space by the month, or who needs a house sitter? Affordable. From January, say, till mid-April.*

*I'll call in a few days. Again, dear Evan, many
thanks.*
—*Ruth*

Evan rolled her words over in his mind. He should
be concerned about her dialysis, he knew, but he
felt something odd and familiar going on. Ruth was
straightforward, but he'd often felt manipulated by her,
as if she withheld any information to which she suspected he might not respond well—and then reformu-
lated it to get it past him. He felt that spoonful-of-sugar
response now. He was being handled. What she meant
was that it was his apartment that was affordable, he
who might want a "house sitter."

No such luck. No more visits. He would extend
whatever kindness he could, but his apartment, which
now conformed to his psyche the way his manila envelope did to the crook of his arm, was henceforth open
to only Eve.

His home phone signaled messages. He listened to
several grumpy ones from his editor ("Evan, where the
hell's that intro? You promised.") before coming to two,
one right after the other, from Claire Barrett. This was
the first he'd heard from her since he'd thanked her,
with more gratitude than she could understand, for inviting him to the ballet.

One, dated December 25—yesterday—simply said,
"Call me." Another, earlier today: "Guess you're not
home yet. Please call me as soon as you arrive, no matter what time."

And a third message, from this afternoon, wasn't
from Claire but from Eve! "Evan, my love, the sun
came out...that terrible ice...it melted as if summer

had come. It was a miracle." Her voice sounded so far away that he wasn't sure the word she'd used was actually miracle. Static had cut her off, so he caught only a few syllables at a time. He pressed the receiver to his ear. Was that a goddam chain saw roaring in the background? His rage at Jeb flared as his humiliation rose up like an allergic reaction. "I'm calling from right here in my own sugar bush...I'm on [garbled] cell phone... can't talk long...others need to use it...[garbled] lines are still down... I just wanted to tell you. Oh Evan [garbled]." Then it went dead.

Oh Evan what? Evan pounded the rewind button and played it back once, twice, to make the end of that sentence emerge. Was she sorry? Consumed with regret?

He threw the phone on the sofa.

He tried to calm down by reminding himself that the call was, after all, the blessed and welcome event he'd been waiting for. It had come at 4 p.m. From a J. Hobdy—which must be Jeb's cell phone. Had Eve been out in the storm since dawn? He tried to call her back but couldn't get through. The cell line was dead. He calculated that she'd get his letter the next day. He put a Beethoven string quartet on his stereo and sat down.

Then he remembered Claire's messages. Knowing the urgency had to be about Ruth, Evan would pretend he was still away—he could postpone his response till tomorrow. But the music reminded him of Beethoven's message to his brother: "Recommend virtue to your children; it alone, not money, can make them happy. I speak from experience." He didn't approve of his wish to avoid helping Ruth. But Ruth herself once said, "You're too good, Evan," embarrassing him in front of her father with praise Evan knew was faint. "People can confuse your goodness with weakness."

Maybe Claire was calling to say she'd found some friends who could give Ruth a place to stay. Not a chance.

He washed himself as though his soul had to be scraped clean. When he finished, he called Claire.

"I'm so glad it's you," she said. "Have you spoken to Ruth?"

"No," he answered, "I've been away. But she left a note."

"She told me. Sit down. There's something you should know."

"I'm lying down," he said, shivering, though the room was warm. "What?"

"She's in desperate shape. Her tests results are terrible. There's no way to stop the degeneration this weird disease has caused. Dr. Wade told her that her liver's so mangled she can barely process water, let alone food. She hasn't much time, she's broke, and she has to stay in San Francisco."

Ruth had looked healthy when he saw her at Silver Spurs—just a little thin. No indication of the "desperate shape" Claire spoke of—though Ruth had used the same word in her note. He sat up feeling embattled. This room, where he hoped Eve would soon sleep by his side, is to be invaded by his "desperate" ex?

"Claire, why are you involving me?"

"You must give her a place to stay, Evan—you must."

"What about her friends? She used to live in this town! What about Martha, or Pat?"

"You're still the one she trusts most," Claire said gently.

"And you, what about you?"

"I'm in Connecticut. Dr. Wade's in San Francisco."

Part of his brain reassured him that he could still look for some other place to put her up, somewhere he could visit occasionally while leaving the apartment free for Eve and him.

"She can come here for five days," he announced.

Claire hesitated. "What, are you negotiating?"

"You bet I am." He wanted to tell Claire about his new love, one so urgent it had consumed him to the point where a dying woman he once loved could not move him to charity. Silence on the line.

"A week, then." He spat it out, then hung up on her.

A book of letters he'd been reading before he went to Vermont still lay near the phone, open where he'd left it. "*Circumstances are like clouds, continually gathering and bursting,*" wrote a frail John Keats still in his early twenties. Evan turned the pages idly and landed on a letter the poet wrote just a few years later. "*While we are laughing, the seed of some trouble is put into the wide, arable land of events....While we are laughing, it sprouts, it grows, and suddenly bears a poison fruit which we must pluck.*"

It brought to mind the poison figs given to the ailing husband of Caligula's mother in ancient Greek lore, the treacherous Livia, who had so desired the throne for her son that she murdered her own husband. Evan wondered whether it was while the poor old guy was laughing.

"I'll need a day to get the place ready," Evan said, his compliance leaving him breathless. "But Claire, I'm serious. One week."

And remember to be very, very careful while she's here, a voice whispered in his head. *Don't eat the figs.*

31.

EVE HATED HOSPITALS. "They just make you sicker," Big Eve had warned her, usually when it was necessary for her or Granddad to go to one. "Stay out and you'll stay well." Whenever Granddad landed in Glover Hospital for high blood pressure or gout, her grandmother would wait in the truck while Eve snuck him out without the doctor's discharge papers. Now that Eve was feeling better, she wished she had like-minded friends around her who would do the same.

"Don't even think about it," Luann said, when Eve suggested they escape.

Eve rubbed gel on her hands. "Want some? Destroys germs," she said. "Haven't you heard that hospitals can kill you?"

"You're not going to be here long enough to get sicker," Jeb said.

"My point exactly. Can't we just—"

"No," they said in unison.

"Some friends." Eve grabbed the bed's remote control so she could sit upright.

"Anyway, I have things to talk to you about," Jeb said.

Eve saw Luann and Jeb exchange a look.

"I'll go get us all some lunch, be back in an hour," Luann said too cheerfully and scuttled out. Something was up.

It crossed Eve's mind that they might be dating, a fantasy too good to be true. She looked at Jeb suspiciously. "Okay, shoot."

He pulled papers from his briefcase. Their edges were already dog-eared, as if he'd been poring over them for weeks.

"Now hear me out, okay?" he said. "And for Pete's sake, don't talk while I go through this." Jeb put Middlesex Mutual Insurance Company papers on her lap. She knew they covered her flood insurance and hoped her docile smile was proof of her openness, evidence that she would listen. She was feeling woozy, hardly able to talk business, but trusted he couldn't tell.

"I'm just going to say it straight. Many of the trees on your farm were wiped out. It's going to take money to replace them." He shook some of the papers. "These people had a clause...ever since the storm of '97, they've included a rider...they're no longer responsible. I wanted to wait till you got home to go over all this, but we've got to move now."

"We?"

"We. I wanted to arrange a remortgage for you, to get you the money quickly. But after working it out on paper with your insurers and my people, what works best for you is for me to lend you the money." He said the words quickly, like a child admitting to doing another kid's homework. He watched her reaction carefully, then resumed. "You will have nothing to pay back. I can put as much money into the farm as you need with no tax implications and no interest."

She looked as weak as she felt.

He continued, "I have the money, Eve. This is no hardship for me. You won't have to worry about further loans until after reconstruction."

Reconstruction? Eve went ashen. "It's that bad?"

"Yes." He looked her in the eye. "I love you, Eve. But I wouldn't try to win you by buying you. This is the only way you can move right now to get the farm up and ready for sapping."

He couldn't believe he'd said it.

Nor could she. He what? Loved her? Well, maybe, if he knew what he was saying. But when she compared Jeb's matter-of-factness to Evan's strangled near-silence on the matter, she felt such sorrow she nearly wept. She forced herself to respond. "This is what you've been doing since I've been in the hospital? Just thinking of me?"

He reached to take her hand, thought better of it. "If you let me help, I swear you won't regret it. There are no conditions attached, nothing about...us."

She knew this couldn't be true. She would be in his debt forever, another man to whom she owed a part of herself. Eve felt a flicker of pride for having paid off the mortgage in the first place, then leaned back in her bed, cranked it down so she was lying with her face averted, and looked gloomily out the dingy window.

"No, Jeb. I can't. No. You're wonderful, and I'll have to think of something...but not now." She was bone-tired. The idea of starting over on her own was as absurd, she knew, as returning to ballet dancing. But she could not take his money.

"Eve, it's me. I'm offering help is all. It's a debt, yes, but to me..." He sounded defeated.

A debt to Jeb. He wanted it to sound like no debt at all—a gift. Like any friend would do the same. To her it felt like a debt.

"I've watched you work the farm," he went on. "I know how much you love it. It's the first time in my life I've been this thankful for having money. Now, if you have enough energy, let me go through the reasoning of this again."

"The reasoning of it," she said, woozy with fatigue. "Yes, my kind friend. But could we do it tomorrow?"

32.

"SHE MEANS NOTHING TO ME," he'd told Eve, "you must believe me."

How would he now explain to her that this woman who meant nothing to him and who was no longer part of his life would be living with him for a short while? And arriving just moments after his return from Vermont? It sounded like a lie. Evan could imagine the letters flying back and forth parsing what "means nothing to me" means. He recalled Eve's no-nonsense summation: "Sure," and imagined more of the same.

He tried to envision Keats sending a letter to Fanny Brawne proclaiming, in dazzling words of love, that he adored her with all his heart, but, um, well, he had, um, this houseguest...

No, it was absurd. He couldn't do it. He wouldn't tell Eve. Ruth would be staying only one week, and in January, so why mention it? Would he dream of asking who was staying at her house? Of course not. For all he knew, Jeb was there right now. And that was her right. His mind seized on this defensive strategy, so bent on reassuring his heart that the single best benefit of a bicoastal romance was that both partners could still have their independence.

His logic gave him heartburn. So then I'll have two secrets from Eve: the one about Ruth's visit and the one about "borrowing" the poets' words in my letters to her. He got out some Alka-Seltzer. And Scotch.

It wouldn't work. This wasn't just some woman he hoped to see a few times; this was...Eve. He wouldn't dissemble. This was going to be different from a lighthearted affair, so he would have to be different. No secrets between them.

He again tried to call her and again couldn't get through. He'd write tomorrow, when he was fresher, tell her everything—his use of the others' words, his offer to Ruth—and hope that Eve cared for him enough to see through the words to his heart.

He tried to compose the letter in the morning and again in the late afternoon, and finally got it right by the time he reached for a second Scotch. Pedestrian writing, but at least he'd stated the truth simply, in his own words.

Dear Eve,

Thank you for your message—it was filled with static, but just hearing your voice and knowing the trees are saved makes me happier.

You know by now how inadequate I feel when trying to express deep feelings. Because I've been reading about famous lovers who have won over each other through their letters, I thought I could do the same to win you over—using their words. Borrowing from poets, bards, esteemed statesmen—not whole paragraphs but words, phrases—was a way to do so. My words seemed so pale.

I was angry. I decided if I couldn't win you over by chain saw, I'd just have to with words—no matter whose. Hence my letter from the plane.

Eve, I'm sorry. I will use my own from now on, no matter how feeble.

I also need you to know I've offered my home for seven days to my former girlfriend, Ruth. It is as I told you it was: we're through. But she's very sick. She must stay in San Francisco and has neither money nor family. It would be inhuman of me not to offer her shelter until I can find her another place to stay.

These truths look harsh on paper. I hope you'll forgive the first and understand the second. I hope you know, too, that I love you so very much. I want to make plans to get together as soon as you can—anytime, anywhere.

I pray you're fine and that you were spared the worst of the storm. Please call me when you get this.

Love, Evan

He thought of asking her to meet him somewhere, but it felt too presumptuous on the heels of the Ruth thing. She'd need time to think about what he said. Or get a gun, he thought ruefully.

He read over his letter one last time. Satisfied, he addressed the envelope, put a stamp on it, sealed it, and tucked it under his desk lamp. He'd mail it in the morning.

Please let her believe me, he thought, speaking to a god he hadn't asked too much of before. He hoped for his sake it was the God of Love.

33.

RUTH ARRIVED EARLY THE FOLLOWING DAY dressed in a long down coat, somber as sorrow, a scarf tied under her chin like a babushka.

She looked different. The tiny woman was shriveled beneath her coat, as though she had borrowed a giant's before leaving San Francisco. He choked down a sob, shocked at the surge of emotion. "Welcome."

"Evan," she said, voice low, "I'm so sorry. I had no other place to go."

He had determined to be helpful. He'd make her comfortable, then go back to work on the introduction to the book. Still in his robe, he took her bag. "Come on in."

She pulled back the hood and raised her face to look at him. "Thank you."

Good God, what had happened to her? A month ago, she'd been a vibrant woman. Now her once suntanned skin appeared so pale and dry that when he leaned over to kiss her cheek, he might have been brushing his lips against tufts of cotton. He'd heard of people whose hair turned white overnight from fright. Could fear have transformed her so? No, he realized with breathtaking awareness. Illness had.

"I'll stay out of your way," she was saying. "I won't be a burden. Believe me, I know how you must feel about this...invasion. Soon as I can, I'll be out."

Her solicitous tone annoyed him, and he chafed at "soon as I can." Had Claire not told her specifically how soon, the one week? He felt a pang of self-disgust: Ruth was dying! She had but months ahead of her. Was he so selfish that he couldn't give her a few weeks of comfort without resenting it?

Still, he had no more time. The introduction was due in a few days, and he was ill-equipped to write it. Love, he'd concluded, hardly yet an expert, combined passion and despair, acceptance and rejection, pleasure and pain, hope and dismay. But it wasn't just a feeling; it was a behavior. Passion required careful nurturance, or it vanished. Certainly the letters in the anthology reflected this textured idea that love is a delight but also a discipline—would Lorelei Layton agree with this definition? It was her views he was supposed to project, and all he could conjure up from the clues she left were his own. Right now, despair, rejection, pain, and dismay had triumphed over all the good stuff. Remembering his brutal departure, he thought of using the introduction as a warning to uninformed readers. DANGER! LETHAL MATERIAL. DO NOT PRACTICE AT HOME!

He doubted that this was the lesson Ms. Layton wanted to convey, let alone the one John Scroopman was waiting for.

If worse came to worst, he'd make something up, something pink and pleasant, like Lorelei's handwriting. If he coated his words in metaphorical maple syrup, he was sure he could get away with it, betraying both Lorelei and himself, true, but freeing himself to pick at his worry, as he would a blister, without distraction. He'd stay clear of Ruth and, dammit, work.

"I've made the den into a bedroom for you," he told her. "I know you like light, so I brought in a few extra lamps for you to put wherever."

"Evan, I just want to say—"

He raised his hand to cut her off. He didn't want to hear her gratitude. He didn't want any words that would take up more time, any exchange that might consolidate their arrangement. They'd managed under difficult conditions to stay friends by keeping their interaction polite but distant. His pity and her guilt were strange enough partners. He'd settle her in, then go about his business.

I'll work through New Year's, he thought miserably, trying to comfort himself, while Eve is partying among the defrosted trees.

He led Ruth into the den and turned to set her suitcase next to the couch, where she would sleep. He heard her give a little sigh and wheeled around to see her crumple to the floor like a marionette whose strings had been snipped by the puppeteer. She slumped onto the carpet silently, almost gracefully, all her limbs giving out at once. She lay gazing up at him, blinking.

"Jesus! Ruth! What happened?" He knelt by her, afraid to touch her.

Her voice was clear and preternaturally calm. "I don't know. One moment I was standing, and then I was felled like a tree." She raised herself to her knees and cautiously made her way to the couch. "I'll be all right. I feel okay now." She tried a smile. "It was scary, though."

My God, what she must be going through. Has this happened before? He moved to touch her, then pulled away, not sure of what degree of comfort she might want, or how she might interpret the gesture.

"Nothing like a dramatic entrance," she said. "I'll try not to add an encore."

He pulled a blanket over her legs and sat by her side. "I should get you to a hospital."

She held up a hand. "No, please. No hospital. I'm going to see Dr. Wade tomorrow, and I promise I'll lie still till it's time. Then, if you could take me…?"

"Of course."

"And now maybe a glass of water?"

He stood. "Right away."

She reached to take his hand. "You're the best, Evan." Her eyes filled with tears. "Imagine if I'd been alone and fallen like that."

It was precisely what he was imagining, and he knew now there was no choice: she'd be staying with him however long it took. Surely Eve will understand! I'd do as much for anyone so fragile. So would she.

He brought her the water. She was lying back on the couch with her eyes closed, her breathing rapid, her hands clutching the slipcover. It hurt him to look at her.

"I'm going to get us some lunch," he announced too cheerfully, eager to flee.

"I've eaten," she said faintly. He knew she was lying.

His claustrophobia intensifying, he said he'd be back in an hour and put her water glass on the night table. He'd get them tuna fish sandwiches. Everyone, even sick people, liked tuna fish.

→

Ruth was exhausted but could not sleep. Every time she closed her eyes she could see herself falling—it was like watching a movie in slow motion—so she forced herself to stand, as a test and, when that went all right, began to walk carefully around the room. She kept a hand outstretched, her heart pounding with fear, and stopped to lean on Evan's desk, winded as though she'd been sprinting.

She thought of the concern on Evan's face, the comfort of his voice. He had always been the dearest man— with qualities she'd underappreciated, so involved was she in making him competitive, powerful, tough. When he finally told her that he genuinely had no use for these alpha traits and was happy with his own nature, she became frightened. How could she marry a man who was going to go his own way no matter what her wishes were? To be a real loner, emotionally and professionally—when her own design career required a booming social life? Her youthful injustice and stupidity haunted her now. Without Evan's strong convictions and commitment (to her, especially!), who would have been there? Without his kindness, where would she be right now? She still loved him, she realized. More than ever.

Her hand touched a pile of Evan's bills tucked under a lamp, stamped and ready to go. He had always been religious about bill-paying, she remembered, attending to them the moment they came in. Hated being behind. Typical that he'd get to them first after only a few days away.

In the pile was one letter. It was addressed in Evan's handwriting to an Eve Golyakovsky. Ruth saw the address was Glover, Vermont—Vermont, where Evan had been over Christmas. She looked at the back. It was sealed.

The letter was to a new girlfriend! Maybe a new lover! Ruth grabbed the back of the chair to right herself. *What if it said he was going back? What if he was asking* this Eve person to San Francisco? Where would that leave her? In a hospital? In a dingy hotel?

She began to cry.

→

"Ruth?"

Was Evan back so soon? Could it have been an hour already? Yes. She could hear him in the front hall, hanging up his coat.

"I got us tuna on the city's best sourdough." Evan entered the kitchen with concerted jauntiness.

"Mmmm," said Ruth, her face flushed. "I've been making tea."

They ate their sandwiches and talked desultorily about the news, movies, inflation. Evan mumbled something about getting back to work. Ruth said fine; she'd go out for a short walk.

"You promised you'd stay in bed till it was time to see Dr. Wade. If you need errands done, I can do them."

"No, I'm desperate for some air. I need to breathe."

That word again, he thought.

Ruth got up, went to her room, retrieved the black duffel coat, which now looked more like a shroud than Evan had first thought. She had letters in her hand.

"Your bills. I'll mail them for you, okay?"

"Sure. Thanks."

"See you in a minute."

"Yep. Be careful."

When Evan realized the letter to Eve was among them, he had a moment's panic—it was irretrievable now—followed by a flutter of relief. He couldn't have improved it anyway. Now everything that needed to be said was said. And in his own words.

34.

NEW YEAR'S WAS THE WHITEST NORTHERN VERMONT HAD SEEN SINCE THE WINTER OF '87—light, dry snow that vanished quickly once the sun warmed the mountain slopes then returned at dusk. This regular dusting thrilled eager skiers, who, piling onto the gondolas before breakfast, floated down the four or five inches of fresh, untracked powder—a delight akin to catching the perfect wave.

The rest of January and February would be ideal for local sugarhouses. Even the murderous frost from the Christmas storm had been deemed by local experts a glitch in the trees' health—external, like a skin rash, nothing that would hurt the sap. Some went so far as to say that because of the icy morning and the subsequent uncanny warmth that afternoon, sap would flow even better than usual. In any case, late February to mid-March was tap time, and Eve's sugar crop, despite her substantial losses, had been miraculously saved from the storm—as had she, except for a little twinge in her foot from time to time. She would turn out grade A medium amber syrup that could win an award in the next International Maple Syrup Institute competition. Maybe snag the coveted Stitching Award Blanket given to the "Best of Show" winner in Burlington in the fall, if she met her quota. Quality tests of her hot syrup, the moment of truth at the hydrotherm, would only prove that Christmas Eve Candies met Vermont's highest standards, right up there with the major players.

For now, she was grateful her foot was okay. It had taken her a full day to warm up in the hospital; her pervasive chill had been unresponsive to the endless hot packs put in her bed, the orthopedic ice contraptions on her legs. She had promised her doctor she'd stay put for a week. Out of the hospital just one day now and with a few weeks left before sugaring started, she was doing her calculations, opening her mail, listening to music. Christmas cards that had arrived late, while she'd been in the hospital, now got arranged on her mantel. Evan's letter from the plane reassured her that she had not hurt him too much, and—thank God—that they would see each other soon. In response, she sent a hasty text: "Great. Yes. Love you too." He didn't need to know about her frostbite or the pneumonia; she could tell him later.

Nor did he need to know about Jeb's financial offer—surely she'd made him hate Jeb.

And the mortgage button Evan gave me: thank goodness I turned down Jeb's offer!

He'd come up instead with a financial plan—one that would take her years to pay off. She knew he'd worked on it for days and, she suspected, had used his substantial clout with the banks to arrange the best possible deal for her.

A light snow fell outside. Eve rubbed wintergreen oil into her foot, and Emmylou Harris sang on the stereo about a sweet dream of love, filling Eve's home with the twangy harmonies she loved.

Laddie had hated Emmylou Harris and Patsy Cline, all the country music she treasured, in fact, so

Eve had listened in secrecy. Sometimes she thought he'd just resented the fact that Emmylou's songs of love and heartbreak spoke of an emotional world he knew she missed. Not to mention travel. Or, just reminders of her youth that might lure her away from him.

She didn't want to think ill of Laddie. But she reveled in the freedom from a deep, knotty complication she'd never before dared to undo. With Evan's letter in hand, the world was fine again. She yearned for him, simple as that.

The phone rang. "Hey, Eve, it's Jeb. I have a whole mess of food here for you."

It was the wrong voice, but she would never casually rebuff him again.

"Jeb! Hi! Sure, come over tomorrow—okay? Anytime. I'll be right here with my stocking slippers on."

"I'll come early then, say around nine?"

"Great."

Eve felt a wave of agitation at both her cheery deference and her sense of obligation. Just his voice alone reminded her of the money she'd have to come up with over the next twenty years. She felt ashamed. *Poor Jeb*, she thought. *No good deed goes unpunished.*

She wanted Evan.

How many days had it been since his letter from the plane?

Five days and three hours, in fact. She was beginning to get more than apprehensive; she was frantic. What if he'd had an accident? In that sports car? What if he (like she) had been injured?

She picked up the phone. The lines were back again.

She dialed his number and listened to the rings, her heartbeat loud in her ears.

"Hello?"

It was a woman's voice. Soft, frail-sounding. Groggy, as if she'd been sleeping. Sleeping! Oh my Lord! In the background, a television was on. A reality show?

Eve was paralyzed. She tried to say hello back but couldn't. A sudden cowardice, hearing that proprietary "Hello?" repeat itself in her ears, made her hang up. This was not the voice of a visitor. It was someone who belonged on the other end of the line.

Was Evan with a woman? The girlfriend?

She felt sick—and ran to the bathroom in time. *What an idiot!* In her head, she rewound one scene: the moment in her bedroom when, drenched with their lovemaking, she asked about her. She now felt her cheeks get hot.

"So, this girlfriend of yours…"

"Former girlfriend."

"She's sick?"

"So I hear."

"Where is she again?"

"Well, at this very moment…Oh Eve, don't go there. Please, darling. It's over."

Sure, she'd thought.

She'd hated her refusal to believe him, the snarky sarcasm she'd almost blurted out. But had she been right? A new picture was forming.

Evan and Ruth were living together! She wasn't his former girlfriend at all. Could Evan be one of those men who simply pulled off his ring when he was away from home? Was he a player? No, no.

Her foot began to throb. Flashbacks of their intimacy, their vulnerability with each other, their magic flooded her: Evan's handkerchief in the lobby, the roses in the snow, the mortgage button, his eager touch on Christmas Eve, the promises on the slope, his humiliation and then devastation at being banished... Were they all false memories?

What about the note he left? And the loving letter from the plane?

And her words to him—feelings she'd never admitted to anyone! Her utter trust in him, the pleasure she took in sharing her body and her secrets! The parts of his body that she loved—how she'd told him so, kissing them one by one. Yes, she'd been hard on him during the storm; she'd reverted to old strategies and she regretted it and vowed to make it up to him. But this pain of his possible betrayal now made her double over. She stayed that way, head down between her legs, for a long time, until finally the dizziness subsided.

She went to the kitchen, still hot with shame, splashed her face with cold water, and put on a kettle for tea. Evan's face, smiling down at her, clearly loving her—she could see it now as if he were inches in front of her. That sweet, tough-guy smile, a little hesitant even as he was so obviously offering himself to her, as though the man wasn't sure such openness was a good idea. As though love sneaking up on him like that was treacherous.

Could a man radiate adoration and not mean it? Wouldn't he have to be disturbed to pull off such an act? A sociopath?

For the first time, she understood why Big Eve so approved of Laddie. He was an icon, not a man! He was trustworthy precisely because he was beyond passion—or, more accurately, not interested in it except as a sublimated urge expressed only through art. He would worship and idolize Eve but not love her. The two of them—her grandmother and her late husband—shared a passion not for love but for idealization! And precisely because Laddie wasn't Eve's heart's delight, Big Eve must have felt her granddaughter would never be subjected to…this torture.

Luann, too, was leery of love—always talked of its inevitable wretched outcome. "Men are scum, darlin'. Simple as that," she'd say with wicked delight.

Eve reached to call her best friend but hesitated for a moment, fearing the predictable interrogation:

"You slept with a man like that?"

"He's not a man 'like that.'"

"You know this for a fact after, what, sixty hours with the guy?"

"Yes. At least I thought I knew. Within minutes, in fact, not hours."

She took her chances and dialed Luann anyway.

"Eve! How are you?"

Eve fell at the mercy of her friend. "Oh, Lu, I'm terrible. Could I come over?"

"Of course, sweetie. Come right this instant."

She hung up, gathered Evan's letters, stuck them in her bag, and threw on the fisherman's sweater Luann had knitted for her two Christmases before. But first she redialed Evan's number. She wasn't even scared this time, just wild to nail the truth.

"Yes?"

It was the same voice. Entitled. TV still on in the background. Owned the joint.

"May I please speak to Evan Cameron?"

"Who's calling?"

Eve's instinct was again to hang up, but she forced herself to press on. "Eve Golyakovsky."

A pause. "Eve who?"

"Golyakovsky. If you tell him it's Eve, he'll know."

Another pause. This time, a long one. "My husband isn't here right now, Miss Goly…"

Eve enunciated it: "Golyakovsky."

"Yes, well. He'll be back later. But we're leaving at six sharp for dinner. Shall I let him know you called?"

"Yes, do," Eve said crisply, and managed to leave her phone number before she hung up.

My husband! Oh dear God in heaven. Not his girlfriend at all. His wife!

35.

"Honey, you look awful. What on earth happened?"

Luann took Eve's jacket and led her stunned, ashen-faced friend into the kitchen.

"It's Evan."

"Has something happened to him?"

"He's disappeared. I mean, I received these from him." She groped around in her bag. "And then I found out something. I want you to look at these again, because I just don't get it."

She pulled out the letters—the first inviting her to dinner, the next when he got home, the note after yoga, his parting words at Christmastime, the one from the plane swearing love forever—all five sheathed in a blue velvet ribbon. Eve yanked the ribbon off and threw it into the trash.

"Tell me how a man could write these—and be married."

"Don't be ridiculous. He couldn't."

Eve described her phone call to Evan's home. "She sounded like she owned the place. He had told me about a former girlfriend, an 'ex-girlfriend' is what he said. A sick person."

"What makes you think it's his wife, though?"

"She called him 'my husband.'"

"She called him her husband? Truly? Used the word?"

"She did." Eve began pacing, then crumpled into a chair. "I really won't be able to stand it if—"

"Oh my God," Luann said softly, pulling her friend to her and hugging her. "I didn't know for sure how you felt. Now sit for a second, you hear? Let's be sensible about this."

Eve smiled wanly. "I got this last letter five days ago. This line, 'Your love, this weekend, makes me both the happiest and unhappiest of men.' I thought it only meant he missed me. Now I think it meant something terrible, something ominous. What besides having a wife would make him so unhappy?" She threw his letter down on the table.

The two friends looked at each other with foreboding.

"Sit while I read these again," Luann commanded, "this time with no mercy." And she read each letter, taking her tea in little methodical sips. The last two letters she looked over twice. Then she disappeared into her den. Eve got up and continued pacing, too depressed to wonder what her friend was doing. She wasn't sure she wanted to hear the verdict anyway.

Luann returned, letters and a book in hand, and sat down, her lips pursed in disapproval. "I have bad news, kiddo." Luann's voice was low.

"He doesn't love me?" A voice as earnest as a twelve-year-old's.

"He may love you, but you may begin right this minute to find a way not to love him back. It breaks my heart to tell you this, but the man's a fraud."

"A what?"

"A fraud. A fake. A quack, a charlatan, an imposter. A phony." She said the words slowly, as if to a person who didn't speak English. "These letters are...fables.

They're filled with the words of everyone under the sun except Evan Cameron! Why, see this part?" Luann pointed to a brief passage in the second letter: '*I may be blind. I looked for a long time at a head of reddish brown hair and decided it was not yours. I went home quite dejected. I would like to make an appointment but it might not suit you...*'

"Darlin', the moment I saw the words, I had a feeling I'd seen them—in a letter from James Joyce to his wife! And here it is in the Ellmann biography. It's famous! And it made me suspicious. How come this man didn't tell you he was quoting Joyce?"

"He's an editor, an anthologist," Eve said lamely. "He's editing famous love letters."

"He has no damn business using them to seduce you! Can't he find his own words?"

Eve was at the kitchen door, her back to her friend, looking out. Big soft clouds danced little tour jetés against the azure sky, the whole outdoors a magnificently choreographed ballet complete with a divinely extravagant set design—about the clash between the gods and man. Shame, like furtive insects, crawled down her arms. She wrapped it around herself, as if to hide it from Luann. What if the other letters were also Joyce's—or someone else's? Suddenly she knew why a woman might want to be a goddess. No mortal could then touch her, con her, hurt her.

Eve longed for the pedestal her iconic husband had once put her on, above other women, where she wouldn't be touched by betrayal. She longed—for the first time in years—for the world in which art was all that mattered.

"I can't stand it." She sighed. "I wasn't brought up for this."

"Who was?" Luann shot back.

The two stood silently for several minutes, unable to find their usual laughter or tears. "I know, my sweet girl. I know. This is agony for anyone, but most of us have been through love's tortures since we were teens." Luann's voice was so gentle that Eve had trouble breathing.

"And it'll all work out—it always does. But first we've got to know the truth. I'll bet he didn't write these other letters, either. I'm not an English teacher for nothing. But dear girl, do you want to know?"

"No. Yes."

"Give me some time on Google, then, and we'll see."

At four thirty, Luann showed up at Eve's house looking disheveled. "I wish I hadn't offered to do this," she said, making her way into Eve's living room.

"Too late now," Eve said, her voice steely.

Her friend sat down on the couch, pulled out her notes along with the letters, and plumped the pillow next to her so Eve would join her. "Okay, then. This wonderful first letter to you, '*How can I see you?…When will it be convenient to present myself?*' Stendhal! Honey, this guy's no dummy. Keats, Byron—nothing's too good for him! This one he says he wrote on the plane? Unbelievable! And this one—'*Letters have souls; they can speak; they have in them all that force which expresses the transports of the heart; they have all the fire of our passions?*' Brilliant! Written to Abelard from Héloïse. And look, in that same letter: '*I am resolved to wander so long away from you until I can fly to your arms and say that I am finally home?*' It's none other than Ludwig van Beethoven. Really! The famous unsent letter to the mysterious woman no one's ever identified, the Immortal Beloved! It was found in a cashbox after Beethoven's death."

Eve gave a little gasp and stepped outside the front door for some air.

Luann followed her. "Oh, and the note he left after yoga? John Keats to Fanny Brawne, March 1820. Here, want to see it verbatim?"

They stared at each other as though they'd just discovered a corpse in the closet.

"In fact, even his parting shot was uttered by someone else: James Earl Jones. How dare he play games with you! He's like Christian in Cyrano de Bergerac, wooing you with the words of others, but for no reason. Did he think we didn't know our literature and theater here in the Northeast Kingdom? Did he think he could sound like a great poet? But the question is, why would he need to? Where did this creep come from?"

"From San Francisco," Eve said. *From hell,* she thought. And her vision of the world, and her own place in it, burned in flames of disappointment.

36.

EVE TRIED FOR A WEEK TO DIGEST WHAT SHE'D DIS-COVERED: Evan was married. He lived with his wife. He was a fraud. He had been toying with her; he didn't love her at all.

Evan didn't love her. Every nerve ending refuted it, and every part of her that loved every part of him cried out in pain, but the evidence was overwhelming. That wasn't just jealousy that had seized her when his wife answered. That was her deepest intuition confirmed.

By nature, Eve was not a revenge seeker. If someone behaved badly, no point in behaving badly back and prolonging the toxic interchange. Give the event no vital energy and it will wither. There was no power in revenge, only wasted time and sadness.

Except, of course, for the satisfaction. .

She'd made a foolish mistake and knew there would be no closure to this sorry episode until she did something. He had invaded her bloodstream like some intractable virus that never leaves, just finds someplace within to lie dormant, and now she had to figure out a way to cure herself. In time, her work would make her well—she understood that. Her body rebelled against making no gesture of protest. She couldn't stand still, never could.

Once, when she was barely twenty, she was given a chance to dance the difficult double role of Odette and Odile in *Swan Lake*. It was hardly a piece of choreography usually offered to an inexperienced ballerina. The minute Eve began rehearsing it, she realized she was not capable of fully executing the dual demands of precision and emotion implicit in all ballet—and obsessively demanded by Laddie in this work particularly—and she began to clip out little pieces here and there that would fudge it a bit.

Odette, the beautiful peasant girl who changed into a white swan every night under the evil spell of Von Rothbart, could break the spell only if she could induce—really, trick—Prince Siegfried into swearing his undying love not for her, the white swan, but for a black swan named Odile. Eve felt unqualified to embrace and convey the extraordinary emotional maturity demanded to play the two different females. Relying on her physical expertise to become the most graceful bird in the world, she concocted an ending to her adaptation that would allow her to start dying a fraction earlier than the famous choreography prescribed—and eliminated a step from the difficult pointe work that she feared might trip her up. This would allow her plenty of time to emote on her way to her final death scene. She pulled off her brilliant new ending just once. The audience went wild.

But Laddie was livid. "What? You think you are the new Makarova, child? You think the audience cares more about your dramatic interpretation, your feelings, than what Balanchine and Tchaikovsky together intended? You're an amateur, a prop! A baby! You'll never be a great dancer until you put precision before emotion."

She decided to write Evan. This very moment. In the middle of the night. Precision? She'd show him precision.

Every time she tried to put her pain into words she cringed at what appeared on the page. Precision before emotion, Laddie had said.

Right.

Rife with rage, she decided to write the letter but to conceal her feelings—lest she grant Evan perverse pleasure in her pain. Why should he know he had broken her heart? As to the matter of his having a wife, and for stealing words from the poets, well, this was not news to him, so why waste time? Stay away! was all she wanted to say.

Stay away. She found the perfect way to say it thanks to Luann's research: the way Sarah Bernhardt had when she blew off an obsessed lover. The Divine Sarah, a famous commitment-phobe, had zillions of lovers, most of whom accepted her status as a courtesan. But one of them, the actor Jean Mounet-Sully, wouldn't take the hint, even after she broke up with him. So Bernhardt wrote, in January 1874:

> *I've told you distinctly that I do not love you any longer....Why do you reproach me? Surely not for a lack of frankness....I have been loyal. I have never deceived you; I have been yours completely. It's your fault that you have not known how to hold on to what is yours....What can I do? You demand my love and it is you who have killed it!*

Good stuff, but using someone else's words didn't sit well under the circumstances. No, she wouldn't play Evan's game, even if he wouldn't recognize the source of her letter any more easily than she recognized the source of his. In the end, her stripped-down letter was the essence of steely precision.

Evan,

Do not ever call, write, or try to see me again. If you do, you will get no response.

Eve

She was satisfied with the brutal simplicity: why talk about heartbreak to a pathological liar? He wouldn't know she knew about his theft of poetry, nor that she'd phoned him and found out about his wife. This stark note, a do-not-complain, do-not-explain itemization of her heartsick decision, was all the man deserved.

Early in the morning, she read it to Luann over the phone.

"That's it?" Luann said.

"That's it."

"Want me to add a few words for you, for heaven's sake? Like about the teensy business of a wife?"

"Thanks sweetie, but no thanks. I think goodbye pretty much does it."

"Not even the plagiarism?"

"Nope."

"Okay. Well. You've got to do it your way. At least you did this much."

"Right." Eve tucked the letter into an envelope.

"You're well out of it," Luann said lamely, sounding, she knew, like a supportive friend offering up too readily the most knee-jerk of platitudes.

"Right," Eve repeated, "your thoughts and prayers are with me. Sorry, Lu. I love this man," she said, as she tried to think of ways to murder him. All those ballets with all those vengeful creatures came to her now—the furies, the gods and goddesses and witches with tempers that were a match for no man—and she wished she could cast an evil spell, as had the Wilis over Albrecht in *Giselle*. Yes, force him to dance and dance and dance till he dropped exhausted to his death. While she watched on, unmoved. Or maybe just a little drop of poison, perhaps, like in the vial Romeo takes. Or cast a spell like the one in *Swan Lake*. Or something more visceral—a knife, perhaps—slicing through those beautifully developed muscles and then straight through into his heart!

"I'm sorry!" he'd say as he fell backward.

"I'm not!" she'd reply coolly as he took his last breath and fell to the ground.

→

She made an early morning call—a local number. "Jeb?"

"Eve! Hi."

"I have an idea."

"Shoot."

"Since you've been the one plying me with food these days, why don't I take you to dinner at the Inn tonight? I'm in the mood for roast beef."

"You got it! What time?"

"I'll reserve for eight."

"Great. I'll pick you up at quarter of."

Never had she heard a man so delighted to hear from her.

Never could she remember such sadness.

37.

Jᴇʙ ᴡᴀs ɴᴏᴛ ᴏʀᴅɪɴᴀʀɪʟʏ ɢɪᴠᴇɴ ᴛᴏ ғᴀɴᴛᴀsɪᴢɪɴɢ, nor to second-guessing his actions. He rarely regretted his past mistakes and only occasionally worried about the future. It wasn't as if he'd trained himself to live in the moment—he neither meditated nor did deep-breathing exercises, and "mindfulness" was, to him, mere jargon. No, Jeb was simply equable by nature and didn't think too far ahead. Blessed with little anxiety, few mood swings, rare and fleeting moments of circumstantial depression, he believed his life was set.

He liked the predictable. And he liked being in control. Glover was too remote for real estate speculation by outsiders, so it would not substantially change. Farmers would always need machinery. There would be good years and bad years for crops and for the outdoor sports that brought needed income to the community, but there would always be New England fine dining and Vermont itself. There was no need to anticipate calamity and, if it came, well, he would deal with it as he'd always dealt before: calmly and efficiently.

Still, Eve's call evoked feelings of such force and beauty that he paused over his morning coffee to contemplate them further. He was unable to concentrate on the morning paper, although he noted a new recording of Prokofiev's *Romeo and Juliet* that he would tell Eve about this very evening.

She had never before asked him to dinner. Was it simple repayment for his offer? No, she had surely long ago seen beyond his bank account to what lay in his heart—but now, maybe now, would permit him to speak of it.

He toured his house, preparing his words. He found himself inspecting its interior carefully, imagining her reaction. Too masculine by far, he knew, with its worn brown leather chairs, mounted deer heads, skis from every era since he was a boy, nondescript curtains, cast-iron pots and pans. He loved its authenticity, the fact that each piece was skillfully made. Seeing it through her eyes, though, it looked dull and unoriginal, a staid prosperity. It looked too much, he thought with a stab of shame, like him.

His clothes, too. There was sobriety in the plaid shirts from Brooks Brothers, not Eastern Mountain Sports, and the loafers by Ralph Lauren, not Rockport, but the distinction was important to Jeb. This flicker of snobbery (and, yes, wealth) made him feel a cut above the ordinary fine and successful Vermonter—as if he'd taken the attributes and the look of the region and ratcheted them up a notch. Not enough to be seen as fraudulent—like that Californian playing Vermonter—but to distinguish himself as the man he believed he was.

None of this was lost on Eve, who had long observed with fondness those finicky details about him he took such obvious pride in. She knew that he liked to talk to her about dance and film to let her know that he was familiar with her former world and with the world itself. She indulged in these discussions more to reassure him, he suspected, and she accepted his subtle form of intellectual flirting because he was dear to her.

Later that morning he took his best sports jacket to the cleaners to have it pressed, got his hair cut, called the Old Cutter Inn to make sure Champagne would come to the table (and be put on his check), and arranged with the florist to have a dozen red roses delivered by 3 p.m. to her house. He took pleasure in his gallantry, particularly on this unprecedented day.

Evan Cameron, he reflected, had not been to Glover since he mysteriously disappeared in the middle of the ice storm. Did this mean the path to Eve's heart was clear? *I can offer you a bountiful life,* he began his imaginary speech, *and, if you don't yet love me the way I love you, know that if you will have me, you will be cherished and protected. As you deserve to be! And that perhaps you will find over time that you'll grow to love our life together, and me as well.*

His little attempt at drollness, he thought, was not half bad.

He pictured Eve's vivacious, teasing eyes. No, the words sounded like his house looked: like an American antique. He had to do better than that.

Bathed, attired in his finest, hair and nails trimmed, palms sweating and heart revealing its arrhythmia the way it hadn't since his high school prom, he set off at seven fifteen to pick her up. Filled with unaccustomed anxiety, he practiced a more compelling speech.

38.

THE ENDNOTES FOR *BE MY GOOD ANGEL* WERE FIN-
ISHED. Evan was free to eat, drink, and work according
to a schedule that reserved his evenings for Ruth. Work
was a torment. His plan to write a sugar-enriched introduction fell apart when he couldn't stomach his
own prose, and he spent most afternoons composing a
few sentences, then erasing them, much as he had destroyed his fumbling early efforts for Eve. *I can't write of
love*, he concluded, *let alone speak of it*. He became more
and more disheartened. The distance between his and
Lorelei's sensibilities had become a chasm. *Why hasn't
Eve answered me?* he asked himself obsessively. The answer never varied: *She can't forgive me.*

In late afternoon on the eighth day after Ruth's arrival, he grabbed the latest *Car and Driver* and decided
to put aside the intro. The cover featured a famous ac-
tress's Porsche Continental, painted a deep rose-red
instead of an authentic shade from the original Porsche
palette. At the stroke of six o'clock, he put down his
magazine and went to check on Ruth.

They discussed the contents of the *Examiner*. This
daily ritual—the news, the weather, the political scan-
dals—had the feeling of homework. There was a kind of
virtuous agony to it; neither of the two former room-

mates could find one thing wrong with their good behavior toward each other. But neither could they find
anything to recommend it. Both knew it was all they
had. One day Ruth spoke up.

"I haven't told you this simply because I haven't
been able to express it well," she began carefully.

Evan felt his neck muscles tighten. The conversation was promising to deviate from the contents of the
newspaper. He sensed a show of thanks coming.

"I know you hate to talk about your feelings, but
you have to admit, we know each other pretty well.
And your refusal to let me thank you for all you've—"

"No, please. Don't. I'm doing what I want to do."

Ruth was adamant. "You're behaving like"—she
smiled at this—"a dutiful wife. I know the signs."

The words forming in his head seemed to come
from nowhere. "*My last and only request shall be that my
self may only bear the burden of your Grace's displeasure*,"
wrote Anne Boleyn to Henry VIII from prison, shortly
before he had her beheaded. Poor doomed Anne, still
trying to save others around her from suffering the fate
of her husband's trumped-up charges, still trying to
"*erase a foul blot on a most dutiful wife…*"

Ruth persevered in spite of his obvious foul mood.
"Leaving you was a terrible mistake."

"It wasn't. Really." *Really.*

"I mean, for me it was." Her voice was barely a whisper. "I came to value your brand of success; your kind of
life; your solid, unspoken affection. But too late."

This was a stranger talking, and revealing too much.
She continued in a monotone.

"Then I learned I was sick, with this hepatitis that
no one knew how to cure. And the only person I could
trust, the only person I could turn to was you. Even

Claire doesn't know me like you do. Did. I fantasized that you still needed me. So, as a kind of pathetic ruse, I asked you to meet me, and saw that you were just fine without me. I knew then I'd die alone…and that I'd ruined my own life."

Evan stood and placed his hand, which felt wooden, on her shoulder. She threw her arms around his waist, her head against his stomach, and began to cry.

The doorbell rang. He gently pulled away and went to the door.

"Mr. Cameron?" It was Evan's neighbor.

The mood was broken. "Jen, hi."

"Hey, I gotta run, but the mailman came by earlier today with this, and he wouldn't leave it unless someone signed for it. So I did, as usual. You sure get a lot of mail."

"Yep. Business. Thanks, Jen." He shut the door.

The letter was from Eve!

A week had passed since he'd written her. Despite his repeated assurances to himself that she'd answer immediately, he'd been left in suffocating suspense, wondering how she'd react to his admissions. He'd purposely not called her, wanting to give her a chance to digest the news about Ruth. He kept telling himself that she'd told him she loved him, and she knew how much he loved her, so… Surely his sins weren't so terrible….

"This is important," he called to Ruth, taking the letter into his bedroom. It took less than ten seconds to take in Eve's two-sentence statement. Then he stumbled to a chair. *What's she saying? What's going on?*

He went to the phone, ignoring Eve's written command. He got her answering machine.

"Hello, you've reached Christmas Eve Candies. We're either on another line or not in at the moment.

Please leave a brief message. We'll return your call immediately."

"Eve, it's Evan..." His voice was barely there; he could feel so little air in his lungs. "I just opened your letter. What's this about? Please call back."

Had he been able to see her now at her kitchen table, ignoring his message and sipping wine, he'd have had his answer.

But all Evan knew was silence.

He made his way back into the den. Ruth had gotten up from her chair, looking ghostly and distraught. "Are you all right? Who was at the door?"

"I can't talk anymore tonight, Ruth. I got some mail. See you in the morning." With that, he walked past her, poured himself a glass of Scotch, gulped it down, and left the room.

Ruth started to ask whether there was something she could do but stopped herself. *I may be cruel, but I'm not hypocritical enough to pretend I can't guess what was in that letter.* She mumbled a shaky good night to Evan, shuffled back to the den. Haunted, she leaned back in her chair and shut her eyes. She'd get no sleep, she knew that.

Evan waited till three in the morning and, with still no response from Eve, called her again. It was 6 a.m. in Vermont, and he knew she'd be up. He prayed she was not already out at the sugarhouse. He wouldn't last till morning without speaking to her.

"Hello?"

"Eve, thank God you're home. It's Evan. Did you get my message? You must talk to me. I don't understand this letter."

He said this so fast it took him a moment to realize that at the sound of his voice Eve had hung up.

"Eve!"

She was gone. He dialed again. "Dammit, Eve, pick up! Talk to me!"

This time, all Evan heard was "Hello. You've reached Christmas..." and suddenly, he was furious. "Answer the phone, for Chrissake. Don't leave things like this."

But she didn't answer the phone. And she didn't call back. Not that night, not the next night, not a week or a month later. All his attempts to contact her by phone, text, email, facetime, Facebook, even, were futile, as her letter had warned.

A bizarre panic unlike any he'd experienced seized him. Half blinding fury, half crushing dismay, there was no letup. He managed to get himself to his car, and drove recklessly down Pacific Coast Highway through the night. But the drive served only to heighten his fear that he would never get her back; it did nothing to solve the riddle of why she reacted with such cruel finality. He thought about the plagiarism, which was merely his misguided effort to win her favor. And about the welcoming of Ruth, an act of humanity none but the vilest of men would have refused. Why was Eve was so steadfastly impregnable to attempts at goodness? She would not give him a chance to explain. So he drove faster and faster.

He became a lunatic hiker, with his backpack, his energy bars, his water, his bellyful of mystified rage, trying to shake his frustration and fury.

What was he to do, go to Vermont and bash her door in? Tie her to a chair until they'd both said all they had to say? Hang out in the local Glover tavern and beg people to get her to come have a beer with him so he could talk some sense into her?

His independence, so long his refuge, now seemed claustrophobic; the more space around him, the more he felt confined. All of Big Sur was but a vast prison. But if retreating felt like a hollow recourse, so did fighting for his woman—who evidently was not his anyway. An image of the ruddy man with a chain saw arose in Evan's thoughts and sickened him. He knew at once that Jeb had fouled up everything, and he hated him.

THE FOLLOWING AD WILL APPEAR in the Classifieds section in next Sunday's *Olympus Omniscient*:

SEEKING EMPLOYMENT

Extraordinary matchmaker. Eons of experience. Heavenly results. Full time or part time. Will relocate. Reasonable rates. References, testimonials, credentials on request.

Box L.O.V.E.

39.

RUTH WAS DETERIORATING DRAMATICALLY. She barely ate, just sucked on ice chips. Her breathing was labored; the pain broke through the morphine patch every few minutes. Evan hired a hospice-trained nurse, Marge, to be with her during the night, and another nurse recommended by St. Francis Memorial Hospital to relieve him three days a week.

But there was no relief from his obsessive thoughts, no way to stop contemplating ways to break through the barricade Eve had built between them.

His calls were futile—she hung up instantly on the rare times he reached her, turning him into a madman each time.

Oh, hell, why should she answer? he brooded, his despairing brain tired of the tape repeatedly running through it. He slumped over the galleys of Lorelei's book—a book still missing its introduction.

In his mind, the letters in the anthology and his own letters to Eve stood opposed to each other like warring armies. The anthology's battalion contained the contents of the writers' souls. The other, his, were lies—worse, cover-ups—since a man with real feelings, capable of real love, would never hide behind another's voice. Indeed, such a man would be unable to contemplate such a thing.

He had dissembled to win Eve and, in a pathetic effort at literary self-aggrandizement, enhance his own self-portrait. He'd become an emotional con man, an imposter. No wonder he couldn't write the introduction! He would have to fill the hollow; un-dam his blood; reshape his heart; become a whole man and not this cowardly beast, this human effigy.

Still he yearned for Eve more desperately than ever, felt her loss more acutely. He threw his galleys to the floor. Dammit. Stop this. He repeated to himself the words he'd written to Eve when he left: *"You must do the thing you think you cannot do."* Eleanor Roosevelt had been right: an authentic introduction, he realized, was this thing. The answer to the mystery of love began not in Lorelei's thoughts but in his own soul.

Ruth, strangely, kept his spirits up. He no longer acted as if she were his cross to bear, someone he had to be nice to. He began to reveal himself to her, as she had to him. They'd even started to laugh in each other's company. She was too weak now to get up, even to read very much, so TV occupied most of her time.

One night when the six o'clock news was about to go on, Evan turned to Ruth to tell her what he knew she needed to hear. Ruth turned down the volume with the remote.

"I think I'm ready to be friends again," he said.

Ruth sighed. "As far as I'm concerned," she said, measuring her words slowly, "we are very, very good friends. In fact, you're my best friend."

"Well, then," Evan said formally. "We should celebrate." He went over to her lounge chair, leaned over, and gently gave her a chaste embrace. When it appeared she wasn't letting go, he started to make a joke about clinging ex-lovers but then noticed she was sobbing against his chest.

"Help me," she cried. "Help me."

Evan held her.

"I don't know myself anymore. I look in the mirror and I see…I don't know who that gray woman is. The only one I recognize is you. I'm dying and I'm scared, and all I can see is the void. I've long been an atheist, but now I've begun to wonder. Do you think there's more…?"

Evan eased Ruth back into her chaise so he could look at her directly. "Do I think there's a God? Is that what you're asking? Do I think there's more after we die?"

She thought for a moment. "I think I'm asking, do we have souls? A part of us that stays…beautiful? That stays, period?"

Evan wondered where to begin, how to present her with his deepest personal beliefs—beliefs he'd shared with no one. In the old days, she'd have brought him up short in any such conversation, even mocked him, as if his willingness to engage in such a discussion—of God, of an afterlife, of the soul—signaled a weakness. She'd have viewed such existential questions as yet another sign that he was too philosophical, unconventional, spiritual. Or she'd bring up serious subjects and then not listen to his opinion.

He remembered those times vividly, and so he hedged. He might now have quoted Goethe, who was certain he'd been on Earth "*a thousand times before,*" or Benjamin Franklin, who believed he would "*in some shape or other always exist,*" or Yeats, one of whose poems begins, "*Many times man lives and dies.*" But he decided not to dodge Ruth's question.

"I believe each of us does have a soul. I don't know what happens to it, where it goes. But I believe it lives on."

He felt the tension between his eyebrows ease.

She touched his cheek with her cool fingers, looked into his eyes, her expression compassionate. "Ah, Evan, dear one, it'll be okay. Really it will." Strange, her comforting him.

"It won't, and you know it."

"I know," she said. They both laughed—a loony, sobbing, rolling laughter that escalated the way it did when he and his friend Johnny were kids in church and the sermon was droning on and they would burst out uncontrollably after they caught each other's eye. "Don't," she gasped. "I'm too weak for this. It'll kill me."

But they couldn't stop.

40.

ON A SILVERY DAY IN LATE APRIL, Eve rustled around
in her closet for something to wear on her date with
Jeb that night. Frustrated at the chaos in her draw-
ers, bewildered by the dreary rags drooping from
wire hangers, she threw them in piles on her bed. A
few things would still be good, surely. Contemplating a lacy camisole she once loved, she wondered if
Jeb would speak of his love for her, as he had on that
long ago winter night. *Please, no, too soon.* She threw
the camisole in the discard pile.

They had dated several times since that night, and
he had been a model of reticence. Yet she knew he was
having trouble hiding his desire for something more
than the friendship she so cherished. She found herself edgily awaiting the moment when he'd return to
the subject.

Meanwhile her bed was piled high with a mass of
sorry frocks, woeful picked-over tag-sale items that remained at the end of the sale, when there's no choice
left but to give them away to last-minute stragglers. The
clothes held fond memories, but little else. She tried on
the long flowered skirts, khaki Capris, and sleeveless
white shirts then the denim cutoffs, striped boatneck

T-shirts, and shifts suitable only for summer and said, "Out."

She filled three plastic leaf bags for Goodwill, threw in some old lamps and coffeemakers gathering mold the basement, and felt a burden lift. She would borrow Jeb's pickup truck, far larger than her own, and be done with it in one haul. She looked at herself in the mirror, as if to prove that she existed. *Ye gods, woman. Get thee to a hairdresser!* Seeing her bedraggled self, she had to admit it had been a dismal four months.

She went downstairs to the kitchen to make breakfast: sausages, eggs, coffee. As she ate, she realized that the ache in her chest that for weeks felt like rotting apples had gone away. She could now think of Evan without it coming back. She was a little thin, a little drawn, a little shaggy, but at least her face no longer looked blotchy with anger and hurt. Her eyes were clear. She was sleeping again. She was eating more.

By this time next year, she'd be a bit plumper, and Evan Cameron's earnest promises of true love would be but a faint memory.

She didn't believe this.

Sun was pouring through the windows of her bedroom when she went back upstairs. Feeling at once sated and light, she wanted, suddenly, to dance. She donned old flesh-colored tights and a leotard from one of the discard piles and found a pair of unworn toe shoes with the ribbons sewn on. She wrapped her injured foot carefully before putting them on, then moved about the studio cautiously at first, testing her balance. She stretched at the barre. She inserted the CD of *Romeo and Juliet* that Jeb had given her, cut to the track of the balcony scene, and, tentatively at first, stepped gingerly across the floor as if preparing for the grand pas de deux. She lifted her strong arms with the precision she'd mastered as a girl and with a refinement she could have only as a woman, and rushed en pointe into the welcoming arms not of her lover but of her life.

41.

ONE BALMY SPRING MORNING FIVE MONTHS AFTER SHE
ARRIVED AT EVAN'S, possibly days away from the death
she kept resisting, Ruth became highly agitated. She
cried out to her nurse. Her voice was so feeble Marge
could barely hear her. But Ruth repeated her incoher-
ent message as though it were her last, drifting off in
midsentence, exhausted after each try. For the rest of
the day she stared vacantly at Marge or at Evan, accepting a chip of ice now and then. But she communicated
nothing.

"Can she understand us?" Evan asked Marge.

"Probably, yes."

When he wasn't looking in on Ruth, Evan immersed himself in the page proofs of the anthology.
There was a deadline, as usual, so this time the proofs
would go directly to the printer, where they would be
held until he finally finished the introduction. Publication was set for the week before Thanksgiving.

Actually, he had finished an introduction. A miracle in itself. But when he read it over, he ripped the
pages in half and dumped them. What he'd written
was depressing. Any careful reader would see behind
the façade of cheer he'd adopted to mimic Lorelei Layton's voice and feel his underlying gloom. What had

emerged was a pervasive picture of an anthologist who was lovesick.

That would be he.

If he couldn't convey love's depths, then he'd have to go back to the saccharine nonsense he'd originally written. He knew that overcoming his writer's block would mean unblocking whatever lay deep within him that had tied his tongue—and, he believed, driven Eve away. But what would such an excavation take? A crane?

"Mr. Cameron, come quickly!" Marge leaned through his doorway.

"What is it?"

"Ruth would like to speak with you," she said, and in a whisper added, "She's very upset."

Evan went immediately to Ruth's side.

She was having trouble speaking; each word sounded so forced, so difficult to form, that Evan had to lean in to hear the sound and then somehow divine the meaning.

"Find Eve," she whispered.

He had never mentioned Eve's name; he'd hid her from Ruth as though Eve, and his love for her, didn't exist. "What did you say?"

In a voice suddenly strong, she said, "Go find Eve. You must. Find her and be with her."

His heart stopped, and when it resumed it pounded so hard he had to lean against the wall for support. He was able to breathe, but his exhale sounded like a sob. "Eve won't be found," he said, sobbing. He wheeled around and stared at her, confused and terrified, like a child entering a haunted house. He moved close to her. "How do you know about her?"

Her eyes, ringed with darkness, could not meet his. She sat up on her own for the first time he could remember, buoyed by an energy that seemed foreign. In a monotone, she spoke without looking at him, "I read your letter to her."

"My letter to her?"

"Yes. A long time ago. Read it and tore it up."

"Tore it up? What letter?"

She paused, still sitting upright. "When I had just arrived here…and saw this…woman's name on the envelope, a woman I'd never heard of. I steamed it open."

She paused, struggling to breathe. Evan waited implacably for her to continue.

"I was so scared. You were in love with a stranger…I wondered whether you were going to marry her before…"

He trembled. "Before?"

"Before I died. I thought she would come here and find me and beg me to leave. Where would I go? I'd die alone."

He felt thrown into the eye of a tornado. At this instant, there was nothing left in his life but a black funnel cloud.

Moments passed before he could catch his breath. "You're telling me you stole my letter to Eve? And then you destroyed it?" He was conscious of a sound like a gunshot in his ears. "That letter meant everything to me," he managed, helplessly reconstructing its contents, written so long before, in his head. "It contained an…apology. A promise of a future—of my love." He was aware of his own tears. "You've gone all this time knowing I wouldn't hear from her, knowing I was suffering—and never said a thing?"

She fell back on the bed and turned toward the wall. "I…"

"I've been taking care of you! How could you live with this?"

She managed to roll over to face him. "I have more." Her voice was now ghostly, her words quavering.

Oh God.

"Eve called you. Here. Last winter."

It took a while to let this in. "Where was I?"

"Out." She gulped for air. "And I told her we were married."

Evan collapsed into a chair. This was treachery unknown to him. "She thinks you're my wife?" He said it with as much horror as disbelief. Beaten, he buried his face in his hands, knowing now that any flicker of hope, any remnant of possibility for any plans for the future, had come to an end as surely as Ruth's life was about to. Her plot was indeed a botched attempt at murder. All that failed was that he remained alive.

"Do you know how many days and nights I've struggled with the question of why she won't see me? What I had done to lose her?"

"Please," she said.

He waved his hands. "Please what?"

"Understand."

"Understand that my love life is over? I know that. You win."

"Understand not you, but me."

In her haunted eyes was longing, not fear of him nor shame for what she had done. She wasn't asking for pity; she was asking for something he at once realized he had never given, to her or to Eve. She was asking him to see her life, her waning life, as she saw it, to put himself in her place.

He couldn't. In what seemed like hours later but was just moments, he rose. He walked to the bed and put his hand gently on her tear-stained face.

"I'll try," he said, and left the room.

42.

RUTH HEARD EVAN'S RETREATING FOOTSTEPS AND THE
CLOSING OF HER DOOR, castigating herself for her blind-
ness. How could a man in the prime of life embarking
on exciting new love be asked to grasp the agony of a
woman about to die alone? How could he comprehend
the terror that engulfed her when she saw the letter,
another woman's name and address written so carefully on the envelope, on the elegant stationery Ruth had
once bought him? She had permitted herself this vi-
cious survival tactic knowing that her kind of selfishness would make no sense to him and never could—not
to the Evan she had loved. So why had she asked?

She was still sitting upright, still feeling strong, as
if momentarily infused with an otherworldly blast of
energy, when she called for Marge. "Get me a pen and
paper, will you, please? Third drawer of the dresser."

Marge objected, knowing Ruth's strength wouldn't
last. "No, you must rest. You mustn't sit up any longer.
Maybe later—okay?"

"No, now. It must be now."

Evan said he would try to understand. She would
help.

43.

EVAN'S HOME WAS NO LONGER A REFUGE. His discovery of Ruth's perfidy had left his body contracted, the bitterness making him ache. He called Scroopman in New York, asked for a meeting to discuss the introduction—clearly he was powerless to write about love in his present condition—and flew to Kennedy Airport the next day.

"Write about what Lorelei would want," his editor said yet again. "Put yourself in her head and go from there."

"Impossible. My head's different now. I don't see love the way she does."

"So go through her rejects file. Then figure out what love is to her. We're not interested in your views; we're interested in hers."

The man was remorseless. Still, the rejects file was a good idea, and Evan went to Norton's research department later that same afternoon. There, hundreds of files marked Rejected Entries, spanned two decades. He marveled once again that love letters—rather than, say, historical, biographical, or literary letters—had so consumed his compulsive predecessor, and, what's more, had elevated her to the world's most celebrated anthologist. Love, a subject so long relegated—like childcare—to the world of women, doesn't generally rank up there with politics or economics with the popular press.

Her rosy scribbles at the tops of the unused letters were jovial, poetic, often cranky and always unpredictable. Sometimes she'd say no to a letter but draw a little a flower beside her statement and add thoughts from some famous person or other. "*The post is the consolation of life*" was scribbled on one ardent suitor's letter dated March 12, 1973. Evan recognized the quote but couldn't place it. Today, it would be a word: "Sorry" with no period at the end. On another letter, written in 1984, Layton had scrawled the words of Francis Bacon: "*I forgot to say that one of the pleasures of reading old letters is the knowledge that they need no answer.*" Half the fun of living among these quirky files was coming across these comments.

The files that he needed to find were from the 1990s. He knew little about this decade, perhaps because so few of her letters from the period were included in the anthology. This he attributed to the internet, to cell phones, to Ms. Layton's waning interest in condensed modern letters, and to the fatigue that must have overcome her at this point in the project. The files for each year of the decade were thin, confirming his hunch.

He took out the first: "Rejects, 1990." On it she'd written, "*Let those who may complain that it was all on paper remember that only on paper has humanity yet achieved glory, beauty, truth, knowledge, virtue, and abiding love.*—George Bernard Shaw "

Evan shivered. The last time he'd read words of Shaw was last winter, in Eve's guest room. Lorelei Layton had scribbled "AMEN!" next to the quote in thick red marker, the ink so densely pigmented that it had bled through the file's cover onto the top few letters in the file, making them look bloodstained. The fantasy of blood on the letters thrilled Evan: all those failed lovers who had been, like himself, betrayed—lovers whose words were deemed too sodden or their thoughts too boring for public consumption. Blood mail. Bloody mail. Bloody awful mail.

He began leafing through letters from famous authors, movie stars, poets, musicians—the ones she rejected. Her "No!" or "Do not include" were scrawled on the top right-hand corner of each; "Dull" or "Windbag!" graced several. Evan read on, caught up now in the effort to decipher her reasoning. Some seemed discarded because they were more business letters than love letters; others because they didn't seem to have a clear recipient in mind, as if the writer were in torment but had no discernible tormenting lover.

One letter written with a calligraphic nib in a heavy hand jumped out as if the author had used neon ink: "My dearest Evisha," it began. Evan held his breath as he looked at the signature. It was dated January 10, 2001, and was from Vladimir Golyakovsky to Madame Eve Golyakovsky! A large red "NO!" was scrawled across the top right corner but with no word of explanation. It read:

> *My days have been long, and Moscow isn't what I remember. I know you wanted to come, and I am sad that I had to say no. You're correct, my dear: despite my defection, this is my home, and you have every right to see it—I've been wrong to keep putting you off. We'll come back here someday, I promise, perhaps when you retire and our lunches*

can be long and leisurely and the wine and fatigue won't interfere with your work.

More worrisome, though, is your feeling that I don't love you. I don't know how to reassure you, my dearest, except to say that I do! I feel today exactly the way I felt when I saw you, a mere ingenue, and knew you would one day be my wife.

I hope you are well and that your cold has gone away. You looked slightly weary when we parted. Do get plenty of sleep while I'm in Moscow.

I miss you with all my heart and look forward to our date on the 4th, when I get home. We'll see a Giselle who looks promising, although none will ever compare to yours.

Prashshai ^ Te,
Laddie

A perfectly nice, loving letter. What was the matter with it? Why the scarlet "NO!" scrawled across the file cover? What had Layton objected to? Was it that Laddie had admitted to denying Eve a trip to Russia, and thereby turned a "love letter" into an apology? Was it because he believed her life should be secondary to her work? Or because he was Russian and formal in his speech? But no, George Balanchine's equally formal letter to Maria Tallchief had been included in the collection, with the words of Iris Murdoch scrawled at the top in pink ink: "We can only learn to love by loving."

And how did Layton get this letter? Did Eve know it had been considered for the collection? Or that it had been rejected?

Evan was awash in the misunderstanding and misery these love letters caused their authors. In only a few months, his own life had been destroyed by them. *"The post is the consolation of life"* were the words emblazoned on that first file. Voltaire. "No, Monsieur Voltaire," Evan said out loud, "you got it all wrong with that word consolation. The post is the desolation of life."

He threw the file on the floor and walked out of the research department, not bothering with the lights. In the cab that took him back to his hotel, he remembered Eve's earliest words: Does a flower by Georgia O'Keeffe not speak? A face by Gauguin?

Oh, yes, Eve, they do. He'd gotten a crush on words, as if Puck had squirted him with the juice of a flower and the first thing he'd seen was a word. He'd betrayed the woman he loved with this dopey, infantile crush.

But he had another chance. If he couldn't have Eve, if he couldn't excavate his own deepest feelings, if he couldn't comprehend these love letters or determine Lorelei's reasons for rejecting them, at least he could begin his new project right away. This time it would be a project of his own, one that he would understand. It would be an anthology as brilliant in its own right as Layton's was. He would never again let his boss or anyone else stand in the way of what he wanted to do.

He would write his book on cars.

44.

Dear Ms. Golyakovsky,

You don't know me, but you know Evan Cameron. I hope for his sake you will hear me out.

I've done a terrible thing, and I told Evan just today. When I did it, nothing mattered to me except to get what I needed: a place to stay while I was dying—for I will die any day now. The only one in the world who would take me in was a man who was in love not with me, but with you.

I showed up at his doorstep asking for shelter. He transformed his office into a room for me, paid for new clothes, books, my food and drink.

On his desk was a letter to you tucked under a lamp with some bills. It was sealed. I steamed it open and read it, and became frantic. All I could think of was that, once you heard I wanted to stay with him, you'd insist that he send me away after the few days he had first offered me. But I had no place to go. So I ripped up the letter, and I told him I sent it out with the bills.

I pretended to be his wife in another desperate attempt to save myself.

Then I watched as Evan became more and more miserable waiting to hear from you, wondering why you didn't respond. I watched him race for the mail every afternoon, and still I said nothing.

May God forgive me this terrible cruelty.

If you can accept that it was I who poisoned your feelings for Evan, and remember how you felt about him six months ago, then you must do what I say.

Ruth stopped and fell back into her pillow, exhausted. Her pen dropped to the floor. Marge ran to her with ice water, and Ruth took it with both hands and struggled to put her mouth over the straw. The nurse held her head to the cup, as if she were an infant, and said in a low, motherly voice: "Don't write anymore, dear. Whatever you have to say, you've said it by now. Whoever reads this will have heard you."

"No, I must finish this." Ruth pulled herself forward. "Please write for me."

And so Marge, calculating that her patient hadn't much longer to live, took the pen, and Ruth dictated in a rasp a few sentences the nurse could barely understand.

Marge then put the letter down and tucked it under her charge's lamp—as Evan had months before—to search for the address of this woman, Eve Golyakovsky, in Vermont. Ruth remembered that the town was Dover or Grover, something like that, but she had to be sure. Marge would have to find the exact address, track it, and call to be sure that it was received. As her final act on Earth, Ruth could not risk another undelivered letter.

45.

Evan's treasured car, the white one that stayed mainly in a friend's garage in the Haight district, was a rare, fifty-six-year-old 356 Porsche. It was produced in Gmünd, Austria, right before the Model A came out and the Porsche plant moved, in 1950, to Stuttgart. Evan had lovingly removed the four-cylinder standard 1.1 liter engine it came with and inserted a 1.5 liter engine he took out of a wrecked '55 Speedster. He was far from being a professional mechanic, but he prided himself on being able to tinker.

Meanwhile, he found within him the introduction. He'd taken the rejects file home and knew he'd finally cracked the code that determined Lorelei's choices: it was the gift of handing over one's heart. Too many letters were more self-serving than loving; they lacked... the magic of love. That's where Lorelei's true genius lay—in determining who felt this magic. Evan's intro highlighted this genius.

He'd carefully pinpointed her finest qualities. "No other anthologist in the history of letters has been so fascinated with the men and women who wrote love letters," he said in the first paragraph. "She found their letters more moving than sonnets, poetry, music; her curiosity about written words passing between lovers was so great that each time a new letter came in that she deemed passionate enough, unselfconscious enough, intense and loving and expressive enough for inclusion in her collection, she'd be so excited that she'd delay the press date. She was known to have postponed publication in some cases as long as five years."

She was quite a woman. Of course Laddie's letter had flunked her test, Evan realized. So tame, so measured, so prosaic, so detached—as though written by a school guidance counselor. Here was a man who responded to his wife's pleas for reassurance of his love by essentially saying, "Silly girl!" No wonder Ms. Layton scribbled her no so boldly, angrily even, hoping no doubt to blot out forever such condescension, at least blot it out of her anthology. No, Lorelei Layton would never stand for such patronizing pats on the head!

Evan wondered whether Eve, at the time she received it, had the same response to Laddie's letter.

"To Lorelei Layton," Evan had written finally, "love was a passion so great that all other emotions were secondary. She was thrilled by the freedom of giving away one's heart. Giving away every beat."

Evan had only to edit the intro now—another day's work, two at the most—and this whole project would be done. As a reward, he'd take a break, get out of town. He didn't know where to, maybe to the high desert near Moab, where moonlit hikes in the Arches and Canyonlands National Parks made him more comfortable, possibly, than anywhere else on Earth. Or maybe just down the coast to Santa Cruz—anywhere, as long as it was far away from work. And from Ruth.

Another getaway possibility was going to Laguna Seca Raceway to check out the classic cars. He'd drive down in his own comfortable 911 Porsche—not the fragile 356, like last year, but his "new" 1968 baby, strong as a bull. He wasn't about to enter any competition. He'd just go to take the rally in and give the black beauty some badly needed exercise.

Yes, the Raceway. He turned off his computer, threw some clothes into a bag, informed his neighbor, Jennifer, that he was leaving, and took off.

The cars at the track were magnificent, like show dogs in the hands of fussy trainers, each competing for top honors in grooming and performance. One man, dressed in a white suit, used Q-tips to illustrate how clean his engine was. Evan drove his new model in the middle of the pack with the top down, relishing the twisting back roads of Monterey, inhaling the other cars' exhaust as if it were cologne. The wind cleared his head, and the rhythm of the machine beneath him reminded him of what contentment felt like. There was no past here, no pain.

The rally lasted all afternoon. Then, to Evan's regret, the drivers returned to the racetrack. He stepped from his car, a pilot disembarking after a dangerous mission, and realized this freedom was only a temporary reprieve. He'd soon have to go home.

This was new, this dread of home.

He started toward the hospitality tent, seeking Scotch and perhaps a discussion of, say, brake fluid, to take his mind off his woes. A blonde, lanky woman some ten yards away from him was standing next to a Porsche almost identical to his own 356 but painted pale yellow. She was staring into the open hood, hands on her hips. He approached cautiously, his own hands in his pockets, when she straightened and looked toward him.

He'd seen her before. He could swear to it. She was attractive, with Renoir cheeks and a full body, this time encased in jeans and a jacket. with PENNZOIL emblazoned on the back. His mind flew back to the David H. Koch Theater in New York. Was that where he'd seen her? The woman he'd nearly trampled in his rush to get to the lobby, to meet Eve?

"I'm afraid I'm in trouble," this Circe of the rally said. "Do you know anything about engines?" Her voice was husky, her accent sweetly French.

Does Mario Andretti know anything about driving? Evan's heart pumped like a piston, but he kept his voice neutral. "What's the trouble?"

"I'm not sure. I drove in the rally, but, as I was coming onto the grounds, the car started to buck like a frightened racehorse. I was able to get this far, but then it let out the most awful noise and just died. And now I can't start it again. The engine keeps looking at me as if I'd strangled it."

"Let me take a look," he said. "Could be as simple as a clogged fuel line."

Reading in its pumps and wires a language as explicit to him as a child's Beginning Reader book, he declared, "It's the gasket. You have a tool box?"

"In the trunk. I'll get it."

Her face had been close to his as he inspected the engine; now she moved away and he rued her departure. His sense of loss took him so by surprise that he was afraid he'd fall forward and get swallowed up by the engine.

He recalled the day he had left Eve—when she had banished him—and felt his face flush once again with shame he'd never had a chance to live down. In the few moments it took for her to return, however, he had righted himself and was able to concentrate on the mechanical task. It took him nearly an hour, but, when he finished, the engine was purring.

She had stayed by his side throughout, not so close as to be a distraction but interested and involved, handing him tools when he requested them, like a surgeon's aide. At last he stood and faced her. "That'll get you where you're going," he said, "but you should have someone check it out when you get home. Someone who knows something about Porsches."

She smiled. "I thought my mechanic already did. I had him do a complete tune-up before I left."

A pleasing thought struck him. "If you're in the Bay Area, I'll do it myself. I use a garage in San Francisco, and you can park it there."

He couldn't believe what he'd just said.

Her smile broadened. "Afraid not. My house isn't ten minutes from here. But, if you tell me your name, tell me about how you got to know Porsches so well, and accept my thanks, I'll take you there. We can order a pizza."

"Evan. Evan Cameron. But my interest in Porsches takes a long time to explain."

She laughed. "I've got time."

What was happening? "Let me make a guess," he said. "You like ballet."

The question evidently took her by surprise. "No. Not really."

"But last fall, around Thanksgiving, weren't you at the Koch Theater? Seeing *Romeo and Juliet*?"

She laughed. "Hardly. Last fall I was in Thailand. And I don't know you well enough to tell you what I was doing there."

Not the same woman at all, then.

"So. Pizza chez moi?" the woman asked.

"Sorry," he said. "Distracted. Sure."

"I was saying it isn't fair for me to know your name when you don't know mine. It's Karen. Karen Dessay."

She extended her hand and he took it, feeling its warmth and the heartiness of her handshake.

It was what he once knew, this way of easing into a date; it was once all right with him. He'd have to figure out some way to make it all right again. "So," he said. "Pizza. Can you add a beer?"

"Two."

"We'll pick up a six-pack. I'll want to hear about you, too." He felt better.

"Now you're talking long," she told him, and loped toward the front of her car, graceful and carefree. She tucked her hair under a hat and put on her sunglasses. She wiped a Chapstick across her lips and smiled at him. "Hate chapped lips," she said. "Come on. We'd better hurry."

Two long strides brought him up to her, and he touched her shoulder. "I'll follow you to your house." He might actually enjoy himself for the first time in months.

46.

EVE WRAPPED THE PINK PORCELAIN SALT AND PEPPER
SHAKERS—a salt ballerina with her pepper partner—
and carefully lay them in the Goodwill pile. Cleaning
her house of clutter was getting to be a thing with her,
and she stormed through her clothes closet and garage yet again, attacked the clutter in her bookshelves,
cabinets, kitchen, even the sugarhouse. She'd again
borrowed Jeb's truck for hauling, lending him hers in
exchange, and this morning filled it with old ballet
books, many signed by the authors. She'd give them to
the music school quickly—before the impulse passed.

Divesting herself of these things from her past
buoyed her, made her psyche feel more spacious. She
liked her new, spare, minimalist self. She made more
coffee and began looking through another pile of artifacts: pictures of famous ballet stars. Pavlova and
Nureyev, Makarova, Farrell. Her more recent favorites:
Peck, Mearns, Osipova. Buried inside them was a little
book with a cushioned plastic cover, "My Diary" written on it in light blue, girlish script. Eve had started it
when she was ten. As she began turning the pages, she
was touched by her own self-conscious handwriting
over the year or so that the entries covered, the script at
times upright and small, at other times large and slant-

ed and exaggerated—as if she'd been trying to figure out who she wanted to be by deciding on a graphic hand or a curlicued one. But what her thoughts had most often been about, she noticed, was her grandmother.

She'd been thinking about her grandmother over the past two days. That she was the kind of farm woman who rolled her own driveway, her own road, with wooden drums at a time when there were not yet plows. Played hostess for many "kitchen junkets," parties to which neighbors brought homemade cakes and the town fiddlers showed up to play their tunes. People came long distances then, even in the worst snowstorms. They'd dance the Portland Fancy or the Virginia Reel in Big Eve's frigid stone house, warm themselves up with frequent nips of hard cider from the jug, throw logs into the ever-burning fire.

Eve grew nostalgic as she read snippets of her childhood days. Big Eve, on cold days like today, put hot freestones in her granddaughter's boots to protect her tiny feet. And then, if Eve begged, rub in liniment, a greasy homemade brew of castor and birch oils, which she believed would keep Eve's bones healthy. Even today, with birch oil hard to find, Eve kept oil of wintergreen on hand—almost as good—to remind her of the comforting scent and of her grandmother's ritual.

Another memory was not so delicious. She recovered it in an entry she wrote when, at age twelve, she left home to train with Vladimir Golyakovsky, the man who would make her a star.

> *I'm scared. What will ballet school be like?*
> *Will there be kids there I'll like? Mr. G. is*
> *strict and scary. Grandma keeps telling me*
> *how good this is, but she's sad, I can tell.*

She knew why she'd been thinking about her grandmother. This time of year, at the beginning of summer, she always did. Big Eve had died in June—she'd kept going until sugaring was over and there wasn't much work to be done, then graciously passed away in her sleep. Eve had inherited her grandmother's passion for sugaring. She loved how the sap was gathered and put in a large tub on her grandfather's sled, how Granddad slathered his maple sugar on a hardboiled egg or a sour pickle.

Why do these memories make me so sad?

She read another.

> Grandma and Granddad fighting all day. I think it's about money. He wants to pay off the farm. Grandma says, who cares? He says he does. He wants them to stop working so hard. I think they're fighting because they have to pay for my dance lessons.

Haven't had the blues this bad since my grandmother died, Eve thought and stood up, trying to figure out what to do to get herself going. She'd tried everything—exercise, baking cookies, seeing movies—to get rid of this haunted awareness of loss. She was glad she had a date with Jeb tonight. She'd pay attention to him for a change, thank him again for all he'd done for her. She'd buy dinner, even though he'd protest.

Jeb—what would she do without him? She was able to relax with him now, to bask in the pleasure of being so cared for, so unambivalently loved—even if they weren't lovers. Jeb, selfless Jeb, wanted nothing from her that she wasn't able to give, nothing from her but... her. How could she not feel deeply toward him?

He seemed instinctively to understand her pain. Was it the loss of his wife long ago that made him so sensitive to her? Jeb seemed to know more than he actually knew about what happened between her and Evan, at least about what happened emotionally. Sometimes she felt that a well of sorrow lay within Jeb. When the two of them spent time together, she knew she could fall into her own abyss without being judged. Conspiring, she thought on these occasions. Breathing together. But over loss, not love. At these times, she wanted to ask him more about the wife who died but felt she'd be intruding—as he clearly felt about questioning her. Yet always he seemed to understand and even feel her pain, and sometimes she wished they could just ditch the hope of being lovers and simply speak openly as friends. But it would be the end of his interest in her, and she couldn't risk it.

She read what she'd written, age twelve:

> *I like the way Granddad is with Grandma. He listens to her. When I grow up, I want to be with a man like him. Grandma always acts funny around Granddad, like when he hugs her in the kitchen and whispers things. They seem to have a secret. They like to play with each other.*

She closed her diary, restless. She decided to go out, leave her memories alone for a while and wonder how a real farm woman like Big Eve would handle herself when she was depressed. She'd probably round up some Guernsey heifers and put them in the barn, drum up some warm pails of egg mash for them, and forget the silliness of the human condition. *I wish I had some cows to milk,* Eve thought, as if chores were the answer.

She'd go to the one place where she wouldn't be crowded by her possessions or her thoughts.

First, she'd have to tell Jeb where she'd be. He would arrive to pick her up for dinner at seven thirty. He'd sent fresh roses earlier in the afternoon—he always sent roses before their dinners together—and a note that said, "Can't wait." Had he sensed her heart was breaking? It was after six o'clock now. She needed a couple of hours by herself. So she dressed for dinner, threw on some lipstick, and tacked a note on her front door for Jeb.

She drove Jeb's pickup solemnly to the lot at the bottom of Burke Mountain, her private place, where she and Evan had been together just a few months before.

And there she sat.

Boy, did I need a little motherly love.

So I asked my mother, Venus—Goddess of Love, after all—how great love happens. What defines a love as great—that it's fiery? That it lasts? That it be life-altering while it lasts? That the lovers be celebrities or rich or...

"My darling boy," she said, stroking my wings tenderly. "I'm touched that you've come to me. I know you've been under tremendous stress. But what brings you to think about this question after all these eons? Could it be that your father instilled this idea of 'great' love into you?"

Yes, he had, I told her. And my career depended on it. And then it poured out: Eve and Evan were in a mess. They were not in touch. Within weeks, planet Earth would lose its most precious resource: me! I, Eros, was about to lose my loving hold on the universe.

"My dearest son. Listen to me. You've left a golden cloak of love around Earth that is immutable. Love operates there independent of your ongoing involvement. It is self-perpetuating."

I then told her about my deep feelings for the anthologist and the candymaker. My belief in their ability to surrender to love's magic.

She looked at me with all the kindness and wisdom within her, as though she were weighing whether to say more. Then she said, "You asked me a moment ago what great love is. This is your father's obsession, and it's absurd. Forget movie stars. Forget royalty. Forget whether love lasts an eternity or an afternoon! Forget whether it's experienced by gods or princes or accountants!

"What makes love great is the daily care and consideration lovers give each other," she went on. "The little ways, often unspoken, they choose to honor their beloveds and their own complexity; to empathize greatly with both.

"As I've always said: not all of us can do great things, but we can do small things with great love!"

"You've always said that, Mother? I don't remember those words."

"Well, they're actually Mother Teresa's, dear. She shared them with me some time ago, and I've lived by them ever since."

Do small things with great love. I like that. I like that a lot.

But if Eve and Evan can't achieve the small things—like getting back together—with great love, then I'm history. I imagine a heaven without me, and all I see is mist.

47.

KAREN WAS NO EVE. Nor were any of the women in his past, or, he now realized with horror, his present or future. For him, there was no one and would be no one besides Eve. She had made it impossible for him to consider alternatives. He knew this depressing truth within a second of entering Karen's spacious house—had known it all along.

Eve once asked him, "What are 'sleeping buddies?'" She wasn't being coy, using a euphemism; hooking up and hanging out weren't part of her past. She couldn't imagine them.

"It's what you do," he said, "when you don't have the real thing."

Like now.

But now that he had had the real thing, how could he go back?

He'd tried. Instead of beer, he'd made Karen one of his special margaritas while she went to change. When she returned, resplendent in jean shorts, pink shirt, long legs and cleavage, he was dazzled. She was incontestably attractive, and her lighthearted manner and dogged eagerness to please brought him back to his pre-Eve days. But this time, that willingness just exhausted him, and when they finished their drinks and pizza, his heart rebelled.

"I'd better get going," he said.

"So soon?"

She was standing with her back against the door as though to bar his exit. Candlelight from the dinner table shone in her eyes, and a smile caressed the corners of her mouth. A cell phone on the coffee table rang; she ignored it.

"Can I keep you a little longer?"

"Sorry, no."

He was behaving unfairly, he knew, as if she were his jailer.

Eve alone could rescue him.

No, he thought, *I have to rescue myself.* For, even if he never saw his beloved again, never touched her or heard her voice, he knew she had changed him fundamentally. He felt open now, vulnerable, redeemed. And Ruth, that traitor, had given him the exquisite gift of empathy. His life as he'd known it for nearly half a century was over. The solitude he once treasured, the anthologies in which he buried himself, the women he sought but couldn't put up with for more than a night or two—all these he now recognized as devices to keep from deeply knowing himself, from being known, and from giving the gift of his heart.

At that instant, he determined at last to chuck the introduction he had written for Lorelei Layton and to write the one he'd forsaken. The one that would express not just who she was but who he was. The one that she of the pink ink would have written a "YES!" next to. He would write of love, of its billion varieties, but of its singular breathless magic.

He would write, but first he would act. To let Eve go now without one final effort to get her back felt like a crime against himself and against the heavens.

He also knew this was crazy talk.

Still, as sure of his mission as an evangelist promising his flock the Hereafter, he knew he had to go back to her. Right now. Whatever her feelings for him. He wouldn't wait for Ruth to die. If this was heartless, he was nevertheless going where his heart was. He would leave straightaway. And he'd drive. He owned an extraordinary car; he'd enjoy it.

He lunged toward the door. Karen, wide-eyed, let him pass.

48.

HE WAS NEAR BOSTON, five hours away from Eve's house. He'd spent hours composing what he would say when he got there. He had to be precise, explain why he'd used others' words rather than his own—harder still, tell her of Ruth's treachery.

Having not quite broken the habit, he was haunted by these words of Anne Boleyn: "*My last and only request shall be that my self may only bear the burden of your Grace's displeasure.*"

He smiled grimly. *So close to my love's home town, and I can think only of execution....What ingenious defenses I have!*

He resolved that his words would come spontaneously. Eve would have to take his stammers for poetry. He could not turn back. She was an expert on body language. Surely she would see the depth of his feelings and—if she still loved him—she'd understand. *Damn! If only she'd received my original letter, none of this would have happened and she'd be eager to see me now.* For the rest of the trip, Evan listened to jazz—Dave Brubeck, Ahmad Jamal— trying to chill out his raging heart.

"*Oh continue to love me—never misjudge the most faithful heart of your beloved L...*" So had Ludwig van Beethoven written to his Immortal Beloved. And then:

Ever thine
ever mine
ever for each other.

Whoever the Immortal Beloved was—and no one would ever know for sure, however many theories abound—she had spurned him. The heartbroken composer never married.

Evan spent three nights in comfortable motels along the way. By the time he pulled up in Eve's driveway, it was six thirty on a Saturday night. Her truck wasn't there. He got out, shook what now felt like permanent cramps out of his legs, and walked toward her door. He was strangely calm, a soldier on D-Day.

He smelled the pine, the sweetness of Vermont air in the summertime. Memories—the good ones—of their Christmas together filled him.

He reached her door, his throat so tight he was afraid he could make no sound at all. If she would see him, if she would have him now, he would never let her go. He'd sell his place in San Francisco and stay here if she didn't want to move. He could edit, anthologize, write here as well as anywhere. He'd learn yoga. Learn skiing. Learn chain-sawing.

The door was shut. She'd told him she never closed it in nice weather, and this was nice weather. There—tacked on under the brass knocker in the shape of a lady's hand—a note on yellow paper in Eve's big, friendly scrawl:

J—

Had an errand to do. Meet you at the Inn at
8. Can't wait to see you. Order Champagne.

xx E.

Evan stopped breathing.

Jeb!

Damn! What were they celebrating? Why did she sign the note with little loving x marks? *Oh my God, I've been deluding myself! I'm too late.* Evan stood frozen at her doorstep, reading and rereading Eve's note, uncomprehending, as if it were written in Sanskrit.

She'd moved on.

It was now six forty-five. He had to go somewhere to think.

He got back into his car and drove out of Glover, racing south on Route 122 until he arrived at the spot they'd shared, the abandoned parking lot at the bottom of Burke Mountain. His thoughts slogged through his brain in nightmarish slow motion, like legs that refuse to budge in a dream chase. "No one else has come here with me but you. No one else even knows about it," she had told him.

Did she come here now with Jeb?

As Evan pulled into the old parking lot, darkness was settling on the mountain. The few remaining patches of snow on the shady side shimmered in shades of contrasting whiteness. The fog was thick now; he was all alone. No, over there: he saw one other vehicle, a grayish pickup truck, or maybe it was green—hard to tell at this hour with its lights on. Too foggy to see its driver. Evan turned his lights off so he could watch nightfall envelop the mountain, darken it as black as his mood. He was all alone in a forty-five-year-old 911, three thousand miles from home, and the woman he couldn't live without was about to meet her lover and drown in Champagne.

That note, Evan thought. "Can't wait to see you." That should have been for me.

49.

THE SITE BROUGHT EVE PEACE. The sun had disappeared behind the mountain, and fog covered the lot. Lulled by the quiet and the friendly dark, she thought of her saplings, her new evaporators, Luann, Vermont itself—a life that seemed to her as lovely as a hot bath in December. And maybe Jeb could be part of it.

A car pulled into the lot and stopped, as jarring as a wrong note blared in an orchestra. It was a foreign car, she knew that, but what kind? A sports car? Here? Yes, a Porsche! Evan loved Porsches, promised her a ride in his. Of course it could be any other make—she couldn't tell one from another—but this reminder of Evan made her let out a loud sob.

There was a man in the car. *What if...*

She shook off her fantasy. Stop it, Eve. Just stop it. But the trespasser had desecrated her sacred spot, and she started the truck's motor and drove out of the lot with a squeal of her tires, not knowing where to go but sure she could not stay by the mountain if it was no longer hers alone.

She drove into town, parked at the Old Cutter Inn, and got out. It was only seven fifteen, and she didn't want to wait for Jeb in the restaurant or in the lobby by herself. Her heartbreak would be too obvious to everyone.

The library. She could clean up her smeared eye makeup. She could browse, look for a long, steamy novel to befriend her this summer, maybe have a chat with Heidi, who'd made Burke Mountain Library on the Green so comfortable. Maybe she'd take out a book for Jeb. It occurred to her that she had no idea what Jeb reads. If he reads. It would be eight o'clock in no time.

The library was deserted. It was late for browsing, though sounds from the office at its rear told her that Heidi was still there, probably doing some paperwork before closing. Eve scanned the sections: Biography, Health, Fiction, and next to it, American History. Propelled by an invisible hand, she chose not Fiction but American History and stopped short before a series of anthologies, some half dozen of them. One, its dust jacket slightly torn, drew her hand to it, and she took it from the shelf.

The Civil War: Artifacts From an American Tragedy
By Evan Cameron

Evan! The enormous volume of essays and photographs felt hot in her hand, as if it were animated, electrified. A James M. McPherson quote, "*Indispensable and exceptional. The best collection we are likely to have in our time,*" graced the back of the jacket, along with other words that blurred before her suddenly wet eyes. She opened to the dedication:

For Ruth

Stark. Enigmatic as a Sphinx. Did he write it out of gratitude? Love? Its spareness heartened her, for even if it were filled with meaning, she was free to give it any interpretation she wanted. Which gave her the courage to turn to the back flap.

The book's heat was suddenly scalding, and she dropped it, her breath gone from her body. Then, too weak to stand, she sat down next to the book, carefully picked it up, and again looked at the flap.

In the black and white picture, Evan was standing in a clearing in the woods with his back against a tree. He held a book in a hand extended toward the reader, as if offering a bouquet of words. Not the usual author's photo, so literary and ponderous. Although he was unsmiling, it was a perfect likeness. Open, kind, a little tough, as if he were teasing someone, holding flowers behind his back while holding back that smile. She remembered the expression from the first time they made love—here, in his eyes, was the same delight he had shown her then. *Just try me. You'll like me. Because God knows, woman, I sure like you.* The picture must have been taken at least two years ago, she realized, when the book was published. He looked the same—so magnificently masculine—but older, she thought, than he had when they were together. She studied it lovingly, crazily, and was filled with a longing so intense she wanted to scream her need to the sky.

What a hypocrite she was! How could she have denied the truth to herself for a second? Or even tried? To think of Jeb replacing Evan, to imagine that he could take Evan's place. Who was she kidding? Evan had betrayed her, lied to her, disappeared when he said he would be with her always. Yet she knew that the love they'd shared was too deep to dismiss: it was nonnegotiable, indelible, forever. They had fallen in love. Even if she never saw him again she would never stop loving him. It was all over, the self-delusion: it was Evan or nobody.

So much for carefully bringing the lovers to-gether at the foot of the mountain. Although, separated only by their vehicles, they're as blind to each other as if they were still on separate coasts.

Evan drives to Vermont on his own initiative but then, even when I try to make life easy for him, he lets Eve slip away on a date with Jeb. How dumb can one anthologizer get?

Yes, yes. It was I who led Eve from Fiction to American History in the library. The photograph of Evan, I believed, would remind her that Jeb was history. A wink here, a prod there, as I told you—in this case a nudge so subtle that I can claim ignorance if Jove catches on.

The cars, I admit, were heavy-handed. I'd still call it "doing small things with great love," though, not intervening.

And not enough. My deadline is approaching. I'm scared.

50.

THE PICKUP TRUCK, Evan noted dimly, put its high beams on and drove past him out of the parking lot. The fog in his brain cleared at the same moment the mountain sky returned to a rich inky black. He would go to the Old Cutter Inn and walk into the same restaurant at which Eve and he had eaten just months before. She would see him and remember it's him she loves.

He waited until he was sure the two Vermonters would be together—the note had said eight o'clock—and walked into the Inn at eight fifteen. He sat for a moment in a rocking chair near the sleigh table, then moved over to the couch in front of the fire. No Eve. He went to the bar, ordered a beer. From this vantage point, he could survey the restaurant as a patron, without looking like some drifter. He walked around the bar, then into the restaurant. Still no Eve. Just two old men swapping stories and a teenage couple holding hands. He looked inside the men's room for Jeb. Empty. Waited in front of the ladies' room. No Eve. They were not in the restaurant, which left one possibility: they were upstairs together.

Evan felt himself flush, as though it were Jeb who had caught him naked with Eve, as though the shame were his. He managed two sips of beer, then noticed a couple way over to the right of the bar behind a giant oak post—obviously the Inn's most private table. It was made up as if for an intimate party: Champagne glasses, a single red rose in a cobalt-blue glass vase.

The big man was happy, wearing a jacket and tie and a Nick Nolte smile on a craggy, weather-beaten face. It was Jeb, dressed up, though minus the beard. Pouring something for the woman he was with, for the waiter, too—obviously Champagne—leaning over, trying to kiss her. But the woman didn't look like Eve. All Evan could see of the woman from his seat at the bar was a ponytail, the wisps of hair at her temples the color of a roan. And the weirdest sensation pulsed through him—a refusal to know what he knew. It could only be Eve, yet he would not let it be. Please, God, make her someone else.

The waiter was smiling. He knew the patrons he was serving. Now the big man was holding the woman's face in his hands, leaning over, whispering something to her. She put her hands over his. Was she about to kiss him?

Evan was transfixed; he couldn't stop watching them, until the woman with the russet ponytail stood up, and it was of course Eve, taking Jeb's hands in hers. She had such a serious, reverent expression on her face that Evan, aghast, took a step backward, lumbering and bewildered as a bear in a trap. He tried to take one more look at the happy couple in the corner but felt a wave of nausea course through him when he realized he would never hold that dear face in his hands again.

Why not go up to them now, even though it would horrify all three of them? Why not be a man, make her choose between them, take the chance? What else had he come all this way for?

Are you crazy? She's made her choice! Her words came back to him verbatim: "Do not ever call, write, or try to see me again. If you do, you will get no response."

That hadn't been merely anger speaking. She had a life without him now, had for months, only he'd been too caught up with his pathetic macho lover's fantasy—and with Ruth—to recognize it. He'd needed to believe she loved him, or he'd never have made it across the country. If he went up to them now, he might jeopardize Eve's chance to be loved by a man who clearly had no problem speaking his heart, no ridiculous life circumstances to hurt her, no mistakes to plague her. A man who hadn't been waylaid, consumed by others' love letters. He resented Ruth for coming between him and Eve, railed at her for her cruel selfishness. He would not subject his beloved to the same torment, would not force his own drama on the man to whom she was right now speaking so intimately. He would not ruin Eve's life.

He paid his bill and, eyes staring fixedly ahead, walked out of the Inn as resolutely as he had walked in. The prospect of a drive back home in his beloved car, if Eve wasn't next to him, felt compelling, life-saving. It would mark the beginning of the rest of his life alone.

51.

I SAW HIM. *I know I saw him.*

Eve was reeling after the evening's agonizing ordeal. She had run out in the middle of Jeb's avowals of love, distraught after seeing what must have been a mirage but had looked as real to her as his father's ghost had looked to Hamlet. They all must have thought she was insane, chasing after that stranger leaving the bar.

She'd left Jeb and his Champagne and his plans. She'd run out to the parking area, crying, "Evan, come back, it's me!" until Jeb came after her and asked, "What's going on?"

Still she persisted in her chase, paying no attention to Jeb or to what little reason remained. Seeing no Evan, only the back of a black sports car peeling out onto the main road, she tried in vain to see whether it bore a California license plate—all the while suspecting that the man in the bar could not have been Evan, the sports car not his.

She stood still, finally, listening to the diminishing roar of the Porsche engine as it tore its way up the county road.

She knelt at the side of the road, drained. Her fine logic from a few hours before and its impulsive, unwitting cruelty to Jeb, shamed her.

She dreaded the explaining she'd have to do to Jeb and thought of bolting, like the wild animal she'd just become. She hadn't lost her sanity like this since she'd thrown her black toe shoes from her final *Swan Lake* performance into Laddie's coffin, in a spasm of desire to make him take her life as a dancer with him.

Well, now she would be free of Evan, too. And of Jeb.

She turned to face Jeb, still shaking. "I've made a terrible mistake. I wanted to love you because you deserved to have anyone you choose, and you chose me..."

"I know it. I know."

"And because I do love you. You're the finest man I know. I thought enough time had passed...and that I was ready. That's why I wrote the note on the door."

Jeb touched her cheek. "You thought you should be ready," he said softly. "And you thought you should love me."

Eve looked him in the eye. "It's a dirty trick. On me, too."

He turned away from her. "We'll talk more another time—okay?" he said.

Driving home in her own truck, she went over the night's events again. They got muddier in her mind, not clearer. Who was the man in the car at the foot of the mountain, if not Evan? Nobody ever shows up there. And why were we the only two people in the lot? At the time, she'd had the fleeting conviction that the driver was Evan. She also had felt, oddly, as if she were being guided to that spot, led there by a decision not completely her own. But then why wasn't she guided further? Brought face-to-face with the man in the car? All reason told her this whole line of thinking was ludicrous.

It was a puzzle. If by some miracle Evan had come to town, he would not be trailing her incognito. He'd

have gone straight to her house and presented himself. That was his way; he was that formal. And he'd surely have called first. He'd have...

What am I thinking? He'd have done none of it. I told him not to call. I told him never to show up. If ever I've been cruel— cruel enough to turn someone into calcified stone—it was with that note I sent him. Face it: the man was not in Glover tonight but in his flat in San Francisco, collecting others' love letters and eating dinner with his possessive little wife.

Oh, stop, she thought. *What you should be worrying about is your life without Evan, not with him.* As a wave of fear surged through her, she recalled her grandmother's words when Eve had flubbed an important audition. "You're a big girl now, dear. Nothing can make you unhappy unless you let it."

Oh Grandma, how wrong you are.

→

Jeb sat in his truck and stared motionless into the night. He had lost her even before the battle began. He felt hollow, and he imagined himself collapsing over the steering wheel like a scarecrow loosed from its pole. He sat for a long time. There would be no Eve in his future, so the present was colorless. *Should I move away?* he wondered for the first time ever. *Other parts of Vermont are just as beautiful.*

A couple left the restaurant and walked hand-in-hand toward their car. Anita Lawrence, he realized, and her husband, Malcolm. Both in their eighties. He'd been to their golden anniversary party two years before. Good folk. He smiled, remembering the time their collie got caught in a culvert and he'd had to crawl in to rescue it. The void began to fill. He saw Al and Mamie

Cooper—he'd helped them rebuild their barn after that awful fire. And Mark Hamilton, whom he'd rushed to the hospital when Bill cracked up his car on Route 18. And the Ryans, the Greenes, the Lochridges, and the Perrys. Dozens of people, all vivid in the parking lot as though they were really there, all joined now to remind him of his stature, to give him solace, to pay back his acts of comradeship with their love.

No, he would not leave West Glover. The blackest night of his life couldn't darken this little corner of the state he loved. It was his home.

52.

It's true what they say about funeral homes, Evan thought as he went through the dispiriting task of negotiating how best to dispose of Ruth's remains. This one was peopled with squat men with matte black hair that appeared coated with mascara. Evan forced himself to look at the tiny, restrained man who unctuously approached him—Peter Lorre in *The Maltese Falcon*—nervous fingers combing a few lifeless jet strands forward along his scalp.

"Age of the deceased?" His whiny voice managed to make the question seem prurient, as if he hoped she might have been too young to die.

"That was her business," Evan said.

The man, his terrible little mustache black too and dull as tar, pursed his lips.

"Proof of her death, then, sir?" He said the sir sarcastically.

"Proof? Look at my face." Evan was amazed at the troll's bad taste, thought he had some humanitarian gene missing. What did this man need other than the body and a check to cover the funeral?

Seems he needed a document. A death certificate. In multiples, so there could be no question about it, so no one in the hierarchy of funeral handlers could doubt it. Evan had them with him.

How do you guys do this all day? Evan wondered but refrained from verbally assaulting a man who, after all, was only doing his job.

His fury was intensified by more questions, all posed with almost agonizing hushed politeness—a furtive aggression suggesting that the answers to the questions were dirty, unspeakable.

"Where will the deceased be buried? Or will she be cremated? And if so, would you like us to provide the urn?"

Evan choked out a "no" to the cremation and the urn.

And then came the infamous question, the one he was waiting for, the one that lit up the sallow man's eyes. "What sort of coffin did you have in mind?" His nervous, ingratiating smile and his quiet, solicitous voice confirmed for Evan that the goal of this nasty interview was, of course, money. Did the troglodyte realize that choosing the ideal container into which to fit the finicky Ruth was not about marble versus plywood?

He would take no shortcuts, make no assumptions about Ruth's desires. He'd promised her he'd honor her good taste when, as she groped for forgiveness, he'd said goodbye.

53.

EVAN PEELED HIS LINEN SHIRTSLEEVES OFF HIS DRENCHED ARMS. It was June 24, the day of the funeral, and black clouds, behind a burning sun, promised rain. A stickiness as thick as floor wax accompanied temperatures in the mid-nineties up and down the Northeast coast. Residents of towns along the Long Island Sound from Mystic down to Rowayton, limp as sautéed spinach, had stayed indoors for half the month. Even at the beach, horseshoe crabs and jellyfish filled the shoreline at low tide, their remains littering the sand in numbers that baffled marine experts. Storms were longer than they had ever been before.

"Who could live in this molasses?" moaned John Greene, head of the Walnut Hill Cemetery in Weston, Connecticut, where Ruth was being buried that afternoon thanks to Claire. She'd provided Ruth with a plot near her home, where she'd asked to be buried.

"The question is not who could live, but who'd show up," Claire replied tartly. She was nervous enough about the proceedings, which were already starting. She was also aware that there might not be a crowd. She had alerted these far-flung relatives and friends to the news of Ruth's death and paid for the notices in the *Weston News* and the *San Francisco Examiner*. She had arranged for a limousine service to deliver guests to the cemetery and return them after the service to nearby airports in New York and Connecticut. "I'm happy to pay for all this," Claire added. "I'd like my friend to be honored."

John Greene comforted her with two words: "They'll show."

Guests had begun fanning themselves with the program. Claire had designed it simply enough. It said "Remembering Ruth" on the front under a pen-and-ink drawing of a calla lily. There was no poem of consolation inside, no prose promising salvation or delight in the hereafter, only the names of the speakers, Evan Cameron and Claire Barrett. Embarrassed at having fallen in love with others' gorgeous words of love, Evan refused to attach to her burial anyone's famous words. Only the words of the living would do, spoken by the authors themselves.

He'd spent days thinking about love, this man who months before had thought it exclusively a province of the gods, or at least of men who wrote like gods. It had come to him suddenly, the number of fantasies mortals attached to the word. So many shoulds came with the question "What is love?" Lorelei Layton thought love should be a torrent of emotion, as though nothing but a constant bloodletting counted as a real connection between lovers. And Ruth: she'd thought love wasn't an emotion at all but a template lovers should fit into. Evan's father had believed love should be devotion. He himself had once thought love was pure and should be offered with no conditions attached.

And Eve—how she wanted a moving, fluid, love! She'd begged Laddie to unfreeze their ice sculpture of a marriage—which is what he thought love should be.

Why had he then always refused her, wanting instead "to have and to hold" her, to keep their union as idealized and programmed as a choreographed pas de deux? Was it fear of his own inability to connect? If so, then perhaps the love she'd now found with Jeb promised to be closer to what she'd long craved. Maybe she now felt it was a friendship, warm and close, rather than a collaboration. And who's to say their love wasn't passionate? Hell, it could set off missiles, for all Evan knew.

No matter now. The ceremony would start with Evan then Claire and be as stark and unsentimental as Ruth had been in her last days. He looked around. An elderly woman leafed through the bible on her lap, the edges of its black leather cover rust-colored and frayed with age, its well-used gold-tipped pages as green as tarnished brass. Three little kids up front, grandchildren of a friend of Ruth's, were turning their programs into airplanes, setting them free and onto the heads of sweltering adults. Two teenagers— other grandchildren, perhaps—were handing out cups of lemonade to the group, who, collectively, had begun coughing less from thirst than from boredom. The tent itself, erected to protect attendees from a blistering sun, looked droopy. If it didn't rain any second, they'd all melt down like the Wicked Witch of the West.

He was smarting still from what Ruth had done. Finding empathy was one thing, but full forgiveness was doubtful. Right to the end, she begged him to understand why she'd acted as she had, claiming that in her battle for life she had regrettably made him a casualty. Not regrettably enough, though. He understood all but the ruining-his-chances-for-happiness part. He was a man, he reminded himself, not a saint.

So humanity and sorrow competed in his heart as the clouds fattened but wouldn't let go of their bloat. He glared at the feeble notes he'd prepared. His own words now looked meaningless.

He'd actually worn a tie in this heat, the same one he wore the previous November, when he first saw Eve at the ballet.

Eve. He could still see her as she was at the ballet—not her exact features but the light that seemed to envelop her. Who was it who told him that on the stage some actors had to have spotlights, while a precious one or two magical ones, the real stars of each era, could light up the house without them? Was it Scroopman? In any case, Eve was to other women what stars were to other actors; she carried her magic within her.

Once he had been in her light.

When fifteen seats had filled, Evan stood up and took his place at the jerry-built podium, adjusted the rickety microphone, wiped his forehead with his handkerchief. A sudden memory of Proust's words came to him. "*People do not die for us immediately, but remain bathed in a sort of aura of life which bears no relation to true immortality but through which they continue to occupy our thoughts in the same way as when they were alive.*" The last sentence struck Evan as perfect: "*It is as though they were traveling abroad.*"

In the spirit of Ruth as this traveler, Evan began.

"Hello. I'm Evan Cameron. I'm here to honor the memory of Ruth Anne Gottman.

"Ruth was not easy." He didn't say it to get a laugh, but it did, which emboldened him. "She was uncompromising. She often said she only had two speeds: full speed and off. She could have total relationships or none. Our friendship made me a stronger, clearer person and a better man. For when at last I found the woman to whom I wanted to give my all, I felt equipped to give it."

Evan took a breath to deliver his closing words—and looked out into the eyes of the crowd. At its fringes, he saw Claire beaming up at him with her teary approval, city-proper in her pale gray suit. To the right of her sat a woman with russet hair in a peach dress with a straw hat pulled down over her eyes, eclipsing the sun still peeking through ties in the tent so that she appeared ablaze. Who was that woman? Inexplicably, his heart quickened, as it always did, foolishly, maddeningly, when a woman with Eve's coloring appeared. His eye was drawn to a young girl two rows behind her, in a halter top, shading herself with an umbrella. He didn't know who she was, either. Not relatives—Claire said she had none—so strangers. There would be no miracle.

His eyes burned as though he had been gazing directly into the sun. He introduced Claire, who walked up to the podium, back straight, still serene and cool as a princess, all signs of nervousness gone.

"I want to read you the words Ruth wrote for this occasion and asked me to deliver."

A hush, as the guests paid close attention.

Claire opened the envelope, as though about to announce an Academy Award. "I haven't seen this yet," she said, smoothing it out on the podium. She put on her glasses and began to read:

My friends:

In these last days, I've been thinking about love. It was always on my mind, but I had fun-

ny ideas about it. Sadly for me, those ideas kept me from keeping it.

You see, I left the one man I ever loved.

Worse, I did something unspeakable that hurt him.

Evan, can you ever forgive me?

There was a gasp in the audience; they knew, after all, who this "Evan" was, since he had introduced himself. Evan was horrified. The funeral, Ruth, her treachery, the heat, her apology...would she now haunt him from her grave?

Claire finished the ceremony with her own sentiments about her friend. A breeze gently brushed the guests' foreheads, their arms. The brunette put away her umbrella. The woman in the peach dress stood up, smoothed her skirt, and got ready to leave. The children had become quiet.

The irony was as overbearing as the heat. Ruth's words, channeled through Claire, hardly cheered him. They only highlighted his loss. He gathered his notes, stuck them in his manila envelope, managed an embarrassed goodbye to Claire and to Ruth's friends, and looked around for the airport limo. There it was, on the hill. He ran toward it. He wanted to go home.

You've seen me panicked, even despairing. But now, with one day left before my demise, I'm terrified. And paranoid. I feel as though Evan and Eve, like Jove, want me to fail. Jove wants to save on my heavenly 401K plan, which amounts to you-can't-imagine after all these eons, so I get that. But the other two? They're willing to sabotage their love to end my career? To try Tinder for connection? Really? I shouldn't take it personally, but it smarts.

It takes a Cosmos. But just take a look at it. Down there, a world of anger, hopelessness and misunderstanding separate my two would-be great lovers, from sea to shining sea. Up here, Jove thinks I'm done for. Venus thinks I've done all that I can, big and small— short of defying my father's command, which she warns against passionately, gravely. And no job offers have come in, not a one. Bleak.

Time is up. For them and for me. What I see on my calendar for the coming year is me, reassigned to nothingness.

And no more bountiful seedlings of great love to plant and nurture on Earth ever again.

54.

Evan's neighbor was on her way out as he entered his apartment.

"Wow, hi," she said. "I just put a bunch of packages on your desk. And I watered your plants. That little one, the fern? Don't think it's going to make it."

"I'll be home for a while now—you won't have to be my mailperson anymore," Evan said. "And hey, I'll get another plant. I hate ferns anyway."

She looked at him, he knew, like any twenty-two-year-old who has just discovered a person who hates any living thing.

"Whatever. Bye!"

Already Evan was steaming. If John Scroopman thought he was going to divert his attention again with an onslaught of "urgent" new projects, he was seriously deluded. No amount of money could persuade him. There was one project and one project only that was urgent for Evan now: the vintage car book. Other manuscripts could go to hell. He'd send them all back without opening them.

A FedEx package just dropped at his front door, the size of a pizza box, was no doubt yet another Scroopman missile. How did the FedEx guy get there between the time Jennifer left the apartment and now, just moments after? His editor was on the warpath; he wouldn't upset himself by looking at it till he settled in. He closed the front door, put his manila envelope on the hall table, hung his jacket in the closet, and ignored the packages piled on his desk. He took a long shower, scrubbed off the heat of the East Coast, the stale air and radiation of the airplane, the cloying emotions of the funeral. Then he unpacked his travel kit, changed razor blades, and shaved. Put on khaki shorts and a blue Laguna Seca T-shirt. Although still late afternoon, with the time change it felt like the black, dreary hours of early dawn.

He'd go down to the wharf for a walk and then dinner. He checked his messages; there were none. He glanced through his mail: nothing interesting. He looked at TV listings in the paper, saw Top Hat was on at eleven, decided he'd watch it. Yes: Fred and Ginger, then *Motor World* and a double shot of single malt. Then a Henning Mankell thriller to put him—he hoped—to sleep.

Hungry, he grabbed his wallet and left his apartment, tripping over the FedEx package still lying unwelcome on the welcome mat outside his door. He picked it up to put it inside, noted that it was stamped on top "Keep Upright," and irritably checked the hazy blue ink for John Scroopman's cramped, hurried signature. Instead he saw the postmark, "Glover, Vermont," and the return address, in large script letters: "Christmas Eve Candies."

He stared at the three words for a long time, wondering if he was hallucinating. Was fatigue driving him insane? He looked away from it, then looked back. The letters still spelled out Christmas Eve Candies and were probably written, he now realized, in Eve's own hand. Evan's hands shook. He was breathing so hard he thought he might be having a heart attack.

He raced inside to the kitchen, stiffly holding the package upright as directed, as carefully as if it were a pot of soup just off the stove, and opened it, pulling out a pale yellow box with a clear cellophane covering and a yellow bow. Adrenaline shot through him, making him tremble more now, or shiver, he couldn't tell which. Inside the box were neat rows of maple candies sitting in tiny yellow paper baskets. Eve's maple sugar candies. Not little hearts or men or leaves, though, but cars: even rows of bite-sized candies in the shape of cars. Perfectly shaped Porsche 911 Cabriolet Turbot convertibles. Precisely like the one they had viewed at the Manhattan Porsche dealership the previous fall, their elegant sloping hoods as delicious as in real life. Evan's hands were still shaking, his heart still beating dangerously. A coronary wasn't yet out of the question.

He found himself wondering whether she'd realized that the candy box was the same pale yellow as the car they'd looked at, a question that seemed just irrelevant enough to focus on and calm his pulse.

Wait, there was a note inside. He pulled it out.

Evan,

Be my good angel. Come back and I'll never let you go again.

—Eve

Evan read the words over and over as if they were written in code. Maybe in fact it was a code. *Be My Good Angel* was, after all, the name of Lorelei Layton's love-letter anthology. The phrase itself was written by George Bernard Shaw to his beloved Ellen Terry.

Now Evan's head was spinning faster than his heart was pumping. Eve sent him a love letter in someone else's words!

But why? Had she forgiven him for his Cyrano antics? Oh God, let it be true! He steadied himself enough to find the phone. He fumbled the earpiece only once and dialed her number. She'd changed the message. "Hi, you've reached Eve. I'll be away until June thirtieth. Please leave a message and I'll get back to you when I return."

He left the shortest message he could think of: "It's Evan. Call me!" and hung up. He stood looking down at his feet wondering if there was anything else to do. Famished now, all tremors gone, still clutching the letter, he ran out the door for that dinner.

"I thought you'd never come out," said a low voice behind him.

He whirled around and there was Eve, perched on the wrought-iron bench at the entrance to his building. For a moment he just looked at her, a vision of Eden in a white T-shirt and jean skirt, her shining russet hair bobbed and tucked behind her ears. He opened his arms. She stood and fell into them.

"Oh Eve, my Eve."

Evan hugged her tight until he was sure she actually was Eve, then held her at arms' length as if to confirm yet again that it was she, then clasped her to him once more. They kissed until she gasped. He didn't dare let go.

Tears streamed down both their faces.

"How did you get here?" he managed finally, still holding her with one arm, the other reaching for his handkerchief. "What are you doing here?"

"It's a long story...which I'll tell if you'll let me breathe."

He released her, but only slightly, and dabbed at her tears. Never again would his defenses prevent him from speaking or showing his heart. Never again would he stand there opposite her, helpless, not touching her, not holding her, the way he had those many months ago. He was done feeling threatened, done walking away. He would claim her now; he would give her no more of a chance to wriggle away than he gave himself. This time they would work it out.

"C'mon, let's drive." He pointed up Leavenworth Street to his car. "I need to move."

She took a deep breath. "Okay."

He pulled her to his side as they walked up the hill, stroked her hair as she nestled her head into his shoulder.

"Don't cry, my darling," he said gently. "Everything's going to be okay now."

"I think you said that once before."

Once inside the car, he fastened his seat belt, then hers.

"So," she said, "this is the old car with no airbags?"

"I like to think of it as an antique. But yes, no airbags."

"You won't kill us?"

"Not if you say what I want to hear."

She sniffled as he gunned the motor and sped up to the Presidio. "I had to come to say some things in person." She was looking at him and touched the nape of his neck gently, almost cautiously, as though unsure whether she had the right anymore. "I want you to know that I think taking care of Ruth as you did was the kindest, most selfless thing I can imagine. Letting her into your life was so brave, particularly after I'd been such a possessive jerk."

"Wait. How did you know about Ruth if my letter never got to you?"

"In a minute." She began talking faster. "Where are we going?"

"Across the Golden Gate Bridge. Up to Mill Valley, or maybe to Stinson Beach. Sonoma, maybe. Canada. Go on."

"All I knew about love was that it was supposed to be in the service of something—dancing, skiing, farming. I kept talking about breathing together—even when I first met you— but then choked our love. Our heavenly love."

"Shhh," he said. "Breathe." He would just have to let her tell him how she knew about Ruth at her own pace.

"I was so afraid of ever being controlled again I let the one man who wasn't trying to control me get away. No, worse: I banished him." She was sobbing now.

He was driving too fast.

"I'm not afraid anymore," she added. "Except of crashes."

He slowed down. "Sorry, it's just that I've waited so long for this. For you to be here."

They said nothing for the length of the bridge and for miles beyond it.

55.

FINALLY, EVAN PULLED OFF THE HIGHWAY. The exit said
Sebastopol. They drove another ten or fifteen minutes, and then he stopped the car and came around to
help Eve out. She'd stopped crying somewhere around
Sonoma, but her eyes were blackened with dried tears
and mascara, so he dampened a corner of his handkerchief with bottled water and gently rubbed them clean.
When she looked up at him, she saw not a happy man
but an agonized one.

"You okay?" she asked tenderly, taking his hand.
"All you've been doing is cleaning me up."

"Eve, listen, if your feelings are still what they were
last February—and I remember your words vividly—
just tell me now. I swear I will never press you again."
He came dangerously close to saying, "One word from
you will silence me on the subject forever" but mercifully stopped himself.

Not fast enough to ward off a knowing look. "You
sound remarkably like a certain Mr. Darcy," Eve said,
then bit her lip. "I'm sorry. Go ahead. I'm listening."

If ever a man's face held the stress of the past months,
Eve thought miserably, Evan's did. Thinner now, the lines
around his mouth and eyes were etched more deeply, as
though he'd been too long on the slopes and rivers with-

out protection. In her eagerness to talk, she had failed to notice the physical effects of her months-long withdrawal from him. This, she thought miserably, was her worst sin. Not just letting him go, but not fighting for what she knew she had, for what she'd always wanted. She'd left him looking...ill. She had a momentary desire to cover him with a protective, soothing balm.

They walked side by side along a narrow, flower-filled path off Bodega Highway. She stopped, looked around, saw no one, and reached up and kissed him. He returned her kiss harshly. Yes, he seemed to say, you made a mess of me.

I know, I know. She stroked his ravaged face. *Maybe,* she thought, *maybe this fatigue isn't all because of me. Maybe it's because of Ruth, too. All that caregiving...* Eve struggled to find the words to apologize for hurting him so badly. "I'm sorry," was all she could manage, looking at him with every defense gone. And then she saw that he, too, was trying to speak. She suspected he was struggling, even more than she was, to find his voice, captive for so long in a world of famous lovers' verse.

"I thought my deception had ruined my chances with you," he began hoarsely.

"You were correct."

He winced. "But using others' words as I did was worse than mere deceit. I'd finally found the feelings I'd always wanted to have, feelings I'd only fantasized about and now had and then proceeded to disguise them, disguise myself."

"Hush. I know."

"Are you ever going to let me speak?"

"I guess, if you must, but see, I have something to show you!" She was crying and reaching into her skirt pocket. He wiped her eyes again.

"I'm not finished," he said. His face had lost all color. "When we left each other at Christmas, I left my soul behind, not just my heart. I knew I would be a sick, soulless man forever, unless we could be together. When it became clear that we would not, I was resigned to feeling adrift for the rest of my life. My great love, the love of my life, was gone."

"You don't have to explain."

But it was clear that he did have to. "I have more to say." He smiled wickedly. Express his feelings? Why, there's nothing to it.

"See, I've been told all my adult life that the reason I'm not married is that I have problems with closeness. I'd heard this 'intimacy problems' diagnosis from so many people for so many years that I'd come to a point of just nodding in agreement, like, 'Yeah, you're right; I'm a relationship flunky.'

"But Eve, I never believed it. And the moment I saw you, I had my proof. I wanted you desperately—and not just because you're luminous—and well, you've got those great legs. Every day we've been apart I've known that I can love you in a way that makes us both happy."

She was moved, but she was still Eve. "Sounds good. But what if it turns out we don't get along?"

He considered this. "We'll just have to conspire to hammer it out. Because we're never separating again."

She reached into the back pocket of her skirt yet again and this time handed him the letter Ruth had written her. "Read it."

He read the letter. And then he read it again.

"So you do understand everything!" he said.

"I do!"

They stood still facing each other as Evan seemed to be trying to calculate when and where and how everything happened.

"I'll faint if I have to stay still and answer more questions," she said. She reached for his hand. "So could you at least tell me what you thought of my candy molds? Good job with the Porsche shape, no?"

"Really good." He pulled her head to his chest and held her there until their breathing was in sync. Only then did they begin walking back to the car.

She looked up at him once they reached it. "Where do we go now?"

They stopped short. A bird—a huge, bright gold bird the size of a balloon creature in the Macy's Thanksgiving Day parade—landed atop the Porsche and calmly looked their way. "The eagle has landed," Evan managed to whisper, both to alert her to a bird on his car and to not scare it away. They studied the otherworldly creature, with its rich, sun-kissed gold feathers reaching all the way down to its toes and circling in a fluffy necklace around its neck. It sat there looking strikingly sentient, unfazed, like a movie star.

"Look at her eyes," Eve whispered. "They're the color of my finest grade A amber syrup. She's completely adorable!"

The eagle seemed to be focusing a merry gaze on both of them, looking back and forth, and opening and shutting her beak as if announcing something wonderfully exciting. Her eyes blazed; she seemed infused with joy. Why was she so happy? What news did she so want to share? They were self-centered enough in their own happiness to believe her ecstasy had something to do with them. Was it possible, Eve wondered aloud, that the eagle knew that they'd come back together? And cared?

Before they could move closer to her, or even smile back at her—really before they could blink—she'd flown away. All they saw was a dizzying flash of light piercing the gathering darkness of the evening sky. If it weren't for a single tawny, lustrous feather left floating on the hood of the car, surrounded by shining specks of gold—eagle dander?—they would have had to conclude that her presence had been an imagining, a lover's hallucination, or just a dream as ephemeral as stardust.

"THE GOD OF LOVE HAS TENURE!"

This time the gossip after Jove's morning briefing was ecstatic. All the heavens were abuzz. Harps harmonized gloriously across the skies. Every god and goddess was congratulating me at once! It was celestial bedlam!

When Jove called me in, he was not wearing his helmet. (When he is, there's no question as to whether he's in a good mood. He's not.) Lightning bolt in hand, winged scepter by his side, he began.

"I like those two! Sort of Fred and Ginger. Except he's no Fred."

"True, sir. Eve was the dancer."

"Yes, yes. I know that." Lulu, Jove's eagle, squawked merrily as Jove opened the file. "Now let's see: You promised me you could orchestrate a great love, did you not? Great as Burton and Taylor, Beatrice and Benedick, as I recall?"

"I did, sir."

"And have you orchestrated a great love, my son?"

"I have not, sir."

Thunder pelted the sky. Lulu flew over onto my lap and ducked, burying her beak under her arm.

"No, you say?" Jove sat back then, put his feet up on his desk. He didn't seem shocked.

It was going to hurt me, this confession. "It's not that their love won't be a great one, sir. I suspect it will.

Love has transformed them both dramatically. And I have no doubt that it will last. It's just that I was incidental, sir. What I did was merely orchestrate an infatuation. I've been so busy sparking infatuations all these millions of years that I'd begun to believe I was sparking great love. I wasn't."

"Go on, my son."

This was the first time in centuries my father called me "my son." So I went on. "Recently, I'd looked around and come to wonder if human love was infatuation—just skin deep, a hook-up, a momentary madness. And I thought that since I could kindle it, I could make it last. These modern women and men, wired up and broadcasting photographs of themselves in their short-lived liaisons all over cyberspace to prove they have love in them, were incapable of depth, I thought. Only I could spark magic that would last. Oh, sir, I feel so foolish."

Jove looked at me—I don't know how to put it—kindly. "And now what do you believe?"

I took a deep breath, as that darling dancer would have suggested. "That perhaps I don't deserve my title. That human love is alive and well and can thrive without me. That I had as little to do with Evan and Eve's ultimate happiness as I had to do with your love for Venus. That they did the work of creating a great love—and I, hamstrung, merely hovered over them and hoped."

"Hamstrung, eh?" Jove rolled the word over on his tongue as though he'd bitten into a sour celestial apple. Moments later he asked, as thoughtfully as I've ever heard him frame a question, "How would you have handled you, if you'd been me?"

"Handled it, you mean?"

"Handled you. How would you have handled a son boasting the elevated title of God of Love? And the mortals-worshipping title of Eros? A most powerful god who'd come to believe he was so indispensable to humans that they couldn't even feel love, let alone experience its depths without him?"

I was stunned. Is that what he thought?

"Come, come, my boy. You're acting like that tongue-tied anthologist."

"You mean, all this...was a test?"

"I don't like that word, test. Sounds so petty—so ungodly. I was simply getting nervous. Any God of Love that governs today's universe has to be an adult, not a mischievous cherub. He has to have arrows made of something sturdier than steel, darts with more than stardust on them. He has to have humility as well as ingenuity. Arrogance will not do! He has to believe that human love is as varied, as problematic, as poignant and triumphant and true as your love for Psyche—who, may I remind you, was also mortal."

And waiting to see me, I realized. I thought of my wife, my glorious wife. I thought of our daughter, our Pleasure.

"So," I said with a whine even I could hear, "this was about making Cupid grow up. Is that it?"

"Don't be bitter, my boy."

I thought about all he'd said. At one time I'd have hated him for it. But I felt something else. Something deeper, more tender even. Gratitude maybe.

He moved his lightning bolt. The whole visible sky and untold galaxies lit up, dazzling universes flashing one great smile at me. "And now, perhaps we ought to celebrate that job security of yours."

I looked at this god I so loved to hate, and my heart swelled. "I'd like that, sir."

"And don't call me sir anymore, Eros. You're all grown up now." He sounded almost wistful. Lulu did a little dance around Jove's helmet. And yes, of course, she was weeping.

I felt renewed, with purpose again, and with so much more to do.

—End—

Acknowledgments

We are so grateful to Joni Evans, who first fell in love with the book, and to Lou Aronica, who loved it enough to publish it.

About the Authors

Dalma Heyn is the author of *The Erotic Silence of the American Wife; Marriage Shock: The Transformation of Women into Wives*; and *Drama Kings: The Men Who Drive Strong Women Crazy*. Her books have been published in thirty-four countries and became bestsellers in the U.S. and abroad.

Richard Marek, who has edited and published works by such authors as James Baldwin, Robert Ludlum, Peter Straub, and Thomas Harris, is the author of the novel *Works of Genius*, which was named one of the ten best books of the year by the *Los Angeles Times*.